She hoped the darkness hid her expression…

Maria stared up at his strong profile, fair in the starlight, as he smiled down at her.

"You think it really doesn't matter that I'm not a true grandson of the estate?" he asked.

"How could it matter when there are such strong family bonds?" Maria answered simply.

"I like that," Struan said. "And I like this." His arm came around her and he swung her toward him. She thought of Romayne before his lips found hers— then the delight of the moment and her quickened heartbeat put every other thought aside.

But reality intruded after a while, and Maria felt sure this was his way of paying Romayne back. She said, mock-severely, "Time we went back. For someone sworn to dodge the matchmakers' wiles, you play with fire, Struan Mandeville!"

The Tender Leaves

by

ESSIE SUMMERS

Harlequin Books

TORONTO • LONDON • LOS ANGELES • AMSTERDAM
SYDNEY • HAMBURG • PARIS • STOCKHOLM • ATHENS • TOKYO

Original hardcover edition published in 1980
by Mills & Boon Limited

ISBN 0-373-02453-3

Harlequin edition published January 1982

CHAPTER ONE

MARIA paused in her packing, her eyes dreamy. When Mrs Jensen had asked her to accompany her back to New Zealand, she could have had no idea that Maria had recognised it for a minor miracle. Coincidences were always happening, of course, but she had a feeling this had been meant to happen, and happen with perfect timing just one week after she had found that picture of what surely must be her unknown father's boyhood home ... her renegade, worthless father.

Just imagine ... if they hadn't lived next door to Willow-field, a guest-house in Osterley, she'd never have met Alberta Jensen, that redoubtable-at-first-sight figure, but who had proved to have a heart of gold. Anyway, in her years of training and in this last year of private nursing, Maria had met many like Alberta and had liked them for their forthright natures, free of humbug, and sincere.

Maria's married stepsister approved of Maria accepting this chance of a trip, and of being able to stay on in New Zealand for three months. 'It'll be like a holiday for you and a paid one. You deserve it after the way you nursed Mother. With Johnny in hospital most of the time, and living so far away, there was so little I could do, and with Rod's baby due just before that, their hands were tied too. You go off and enjoy it to the full. That sea voyage sounds heaven to me, much more of a relaxation than travelling by air. We're thrilled for you.'

Maria didn't mention the picture. Shona would have been less happy about the trip if she'd known her young stepsister was going to try to trace her real father's family. So would Rod. They'd have been terrified the members of that family might have been tarred with the same brush.

Maria had never wanted to know anything about her father. Colin Willoughby, her stepfather, had been all any father could have been, never treating her any differently from his own son and daughter. He had given her his own name, too.

When Maria had been old enough she had asked her mother why this had been done. Her mother had told her the truth then, about her own father. 'I didn't want him to have any part in you, or to be able to trace you, ever. I looked to the years ahead when, if he grew old and lonely, he might need a daughter to look after him. Then he might have found you and ruined your life just as he ruined mine—at least ruined it for a while, till I met Colin. Rufe was so unprincipled and unstable, I didn't dare risk you coming under his influence as a child. At the time of the divorce he was in Australia and I'd come back to England. I moved shortly after that, leaving no address.'

Maria had laughed. 'He'd have had a hard job trying to trace us, Mother, with a name like Smith!'

Jane Willoughby had laughed too. 'I thought of that, but I wanted to put it beyond possibility. Of course he never knew of my second marriage. I've been so fortunate. All that early misery was worth it, for the happiness I've had with Colin. He opened a door on a new life for me and perhaps I did for him too, for he was so sad and lonely when he lost Rod and Shona's mother. He deserves every bit of joy we've had in each other, and most of all for the kind of father he's been to you. Always remember my experience, Maria, in your lowest moments, that when one door closes, another opens. Not right away, perhaps, but some day. It's trite but true.'

That had been said so long ago, but now Maria had proved it. She went across to the old chest where, under the paper lining, she had found the letter and picture. Since then she'd wanted to find out more. Not about her father, but about his family. He had now become a voice from her past, a voice symbolised in the black of his handwriting, in a few well-expressed phrases of regret. Perhaps the sentiments expressed were hollow, as scoundrels often had a wayward charm, but she was glad she'd read them. It must have been when her mother had had him traced to have divorce papers served on him. Not all the letter was there.

Perhaps her mother hadn't cared to keep whatever had been said in the earlier pages, but the remnant had said:

'It's the only thing to do, of course, divorce me. You need to be free of the mistake you made in your green and salad days. I've been a drifter all my life, Janey. I brought great sorrow to the best of parents. That's why I never talked of them—I couldn't bear to. I'm better out of their lives and yours—and better out of my daughter's life. Odd to think one has a child one has never seen, hadn't even known existed. I wish you'd told me what you'd called her, but never mind. I wonder if I might have become a better man had I known about her. I doubt it. Old habits die hard. I'll wish you well, and hope that some day when you're free you'll meet up with the sort of man you ought to have married. That's all. It sounds hypocritical from me, but you gave me some rare moments of happiness, for which many thanks ... so just God bless you both,

Rufe.'

There had been one more thing in the folder, a picture roughly torn from some pictorial magazine. A hillside sheltered a gracious old home, surrounded by English trees and some Maria couldn't recognise, much more exotic-looking.

The trees almost hid the outbuildings, but the whole place had a prosperous air. It was a wooden house, probably painted white, with green windowsills, but this picture was old and just in black-and-white. There were two towers and it was roofed with what looked like terra-cotta tiles. Dark pines massed behind the house and all manner of vines and creepers hung from its eaves. In the meadow in front of the house, sloping downhill, grazed sheep and cattle.

Across the patch of sky above the pines the same writing as in the letter, only more faded, had scrawled:

'I remember, I remember the house where I was born.
The little window where the sun came peeping in at morn;

He never came a wink too soon, nor brought too long
    a day;
But now I often wish the night had borne my breath
    away.'

The poignancy of that verse of Thomas Hood's had got
to Maria. Was she reading too much into the fact that it
was scrawled across *this* picture? Was it the house in
which her father had been born? She knew he was a New
Zealander and that she had been born there. Day by day the
desire to find out if she had any living kin of her very own
had niggled at her, a longing to go out to that country on
the rim of the world, and to find that house.

To her New Zealand had always looked just a tiny
squiggle on the globe against the huge land mass of
Australia. On looking up more details, she was discour-
aged to find the squiggle was, after all, bigger in area than
England and Scotland. She found comfort in knowing it
was much less dense in population. At the foot of the picture where the caption had been torn off was a fraction of
print that read: '. . . es Bay, New Zealand.' A larger scale
map set her back. How could one find a bay in the myriad
inlets of an island country of the South Pacific, a bay
whose full name you did not know? Supposing she found a
bay ending in those letters, or even several bays, her only
hope would be if they were small enough to have very few
farms on their shores. But now she could try.

Maria and Shona and Rod had been in and out of the
guesthouse since childhood, regarding it as their chief
source of income in high-school days, washing dishes,
making beds, mowing lawns. Mrs Jensen had been there
two months, sightseeing round London and the South of
England. Earlier she had spent some time in Hampshire
where she had a great-nephew from New Zealand on a
study-course on an English farm. Maria had met Struan
Mandeville when he had come up to London to visit his
great-aunt and take her to see his favourite places in the
city. Mrs Jensen had asked Maria on one such excursion,
but she had had to refuse as she was busy with lawyers
that day, concerning her mother's estate, but she had found

the big New Zealander rather fun when she had shared a
meal with them at the guesthouse. You could see there
was a strong bond between the aunt and great-nephew.

'What good pals you are,' Maria had exclaimed, at a
moment when he'd scored a point in bantering with his
aunt.

Straun had grinned. 'We are, but nevertheless, I wouldn't
have dreamed that when I developed appendicitis over
here she'd up and fly across the world to be at my bedside. It gave me quite a shock. I thought I must be at
death's door when she walked in. I could have died of
fright!'

Alberta Jensen made a face at him. 'You're exaggerating
things. I'd been thinking of taking another trip over here
and hearing you were in hospital, your grandmother and I
decided I might as well make it right away to make sure
you had a proper convalescence.'

'And so you did, my revered great-aunt!' He turned to
Maria. 'This gave her a wonderful excuse to rent a cottage
... the epitome of rural England's charm to most New
Zealanders is a cottage with a thatched roof. It was in one
of the villages of the New Forest. I was pampered within
an inch of my life—not that I didn't lap it up! Then we
took a tour of the north-west counties. I returned to work
and she came up here to the outskirts of what she calls the
pearl of all cities ... and rightly so.'

Maria liked their love for London. It made her look at
London with new eyes, trying to imagine what it must be
like at first impact to people from thirteen thousand miles
away. But she hadn't had time to accompany them on their
jaunts.

She took the folder with that intriguing house picture in
it and put it at the bottom of one of the cases she would be
taking to New Zealand. She folded some summer wear and
put on top of it. She heard the gate click and looked out
to see Struan Mandeville come striding up the path. He
looked like a man in a hurry.

As she brought him into the room she realised it wasn't
haste, it was temper. His abrupt: 'Are you alone? I want
to see you,' both surprised and dismayed her.

He wouldn't sit down but turned to face her, arms folded across his broad chest. 'I'd like to know what's behind this business of you accompanying my aunt all the way home!'

Maria blinked, said, 'Didn't your aunt tell you? She's not sensitive about her condition, is she? It's because of her diabetes.'

He made a gesture of brushing that aside. 'I mean the real reason. She doesn't need anyone for that, not my redoubtable, self-sufficient Aunt Alberta. She's being bland and wide-eyed. I know the signs. Aunt is usually forthright and blunt, so the moment she becomes guileful, we know.'

Maria was still too astonished to be indignant. She said in a bewildered tone, 'But what *could* be behind it? *I* can't think of anything. It could be you don't know enough about diabetes to judge. Mrs Jensen told me she'd developed it only a year ago, and you've been here longer than that, I believe. I nursed a man in hospital once who thought it was just a case of an injection of insulin once a day and you were back to normal. We had to get him used to the idea that you have to be stabilised ... adjusted to a new way of life ... understand what a fine balance there is between intake of food and output of energy, in relation to the dosage of insulin. It's quite a science, in fact. There's also the matter of regularity in meals ... one postponed too long means there isn't enough carbohydrate in the system to balance the insulin, which is a very powerful drug, and the patient can suffer insulin shock which is a lot more serious than having over-much sugar in the system, and can be very tricky with air travel.'

'Why particularly air travel? I wish you could have seen her when she turned up at my bedside after her flight from Auckland to Heathrow. She was as chipper as could be.'

A slight edge crept into Maria's tone. 'You aren't in possession of the facts. Naturally, she spared you the details. She turned up at your bedside exactly a week after landing. She flaked out at the airport and was taken into a nursing-home for a few days to re-stabilise her. It came on her so suddenly she hadn't time to get out her glucose tablets. I daresay the hoo-ha of getting through Customs had suddenly told on her. Long distance air travel needs to be carefully timetabled and diabetics are very unwise to come straight through. She ought to have had a few days at Los Angeles and she'd have been fine.

'You cross the International Date Line, remember, so even if you use one watch on one wrist at New Zealand time, and one on the other at English time, the difference in mealtimes can still upset the works. She gave herself her shot exactly twenty-four hours after the one she'd had in New Zealand, at her usual time, pre-breakfast, that is. But unfortunately, by the airline schedule, they weren't serving breakfast right after that big dosage but settling down for slumber, so she had too long before a substantial meal. The airline would have served her something had they known, but she hadn't told them. Consequently it caught up with her and she collapsed. Does that answer your question, Mr Mandeville?'

He looked very setback and as annoyed as most people are when their anger isn't justified. He recovered, said, 'That still doesn't explain my aunt's lack of candour.'

'Lack of candour? But she told you it was because of her condition she was taking a nurse-companion with her. Doesn't that add up to frankness?'

'It may seem to, but it doesn't explain the bland look my aunt gets on when she's up to something. There must be a reason behind this. So I'd like to know. I thought you might have told me what it is.' He paused, added, 'Unless you've reasons of your own for not telling me.'

Maria felt a faint prickling at the nape of her neck and recognised it for rising temper. Watch it, Maria, it won't do for two of you to lose your cool.

She said chillingly, 'I find this conversation extraordinary. How could I possibly tell you if your aunt has anything else in mind save asking a trained nurse to accompany her on a sea voyage back to her home? If she hadn't known me she'd have advertised for someone, I expect.'

He clutched at his hair, said, 'It's so out of character. She's always been so independent.'

'A lot of people are independent when they're in their

full health and strength. As a nurse I've seen this happen
time and time again—of late, in private nursing, even more.
You see a big business tycoon, with a gentle wife. He's made
all the decisions, put as much energy into organising their
holidays as into running his business, then all of a sudden,
wham! A coronary. He has two major surprises ahead of
him. One, that he finds he isn't indispensable in his business
world; two, that the wife he'd always thought dependent
upon him is most unexpectedly capable, and copes not
only with some of the business problems but has a core of
steel within her that makes her adept at dealing with a
frustrated and often petulant husband. Sometimes it adds
up to greater happiness for both. So perhaps this condition
of your aunt's has made her more reliant on other people.
Does that take a little of the heat and suspicion out of you,
Mr Mandeville?'

Perhaps it was unfortunate that she added the last sentence. He was fair to ruddy and so the colour showed
immediately on his high cheekbones. 'I still think there's
something. I agree ... in fact I bow to your superior knowledge ... you sound exactly like a Sister Tutor addressing a
class of raw recruits ... that she may be less independent
than of old, but it would have been more in keeping in
spite of the upset she had, for her to mutter that she'd
jolly well show us all she could manage the trip back or
she'd find herself being fussed over for the rest of her life!'

In spite of herself, Maria recognised this as very likely,
but after all it *hadn't* taken Mrs Jensen that way, had it?
She looked reflective. She'd been a little surprised at the
time of asking that Mrs Jensen had seemed so tense in her
persuasions. She'd seemed astonishingly relieved when
Maria, after a night's consideration, had said she would
accompany her to New Zealand. But what could—she
looked up to see a piercing regard in the blue eyes above
hers.

He said sharply, 'Are you sure you know nothing? You
and Alberta haven't hatched anything up? You yourself
have no ulterior motive in wanting to go to New Zealand?'

It was an unfortunate choice of words. Maria felt her

cheeks flush. Her tone had a bite to it. 'Mr Mandeville, watch what you're saying! You sound suspicious and ... and ridiculous. What on earth could——'

He made an impatient gesture. 'Ulterior doesn't necessarily mean I suspect you of wrongdoing. It's a very much abused word. It means something remote, beyond what is said or seems to be on the surface.'

She cast her eyes up. 'Oh, save me from the purists! I'd never have suspected you of being so pedantic. I thought you were just an open, out-of-doors New Zealand type ... a farmer at that. Look, your aunt would be horrified at the tone you're taking, at your imaginings. What interest could I possibly have in going to New Zealand except to accompany a woman with a medical problem?'

At that very moment she remembered the clipping in the bottom of the suitcase at her very feet and her gaze flickered.

He said instantly, 'I don't know. But there's something—perhaps not suspicious, but something neither you nor Aunt Alberta want me to know. . . . Oh, I get it. No wonder you look embarrassed. No wonder you blushed. All right, I understand. I ought to. Aunt Alberta has tried it on before. You needn't be embarrassed. I can easily handle that.'

Maria's hazel-green eyes were wide with astonishment. 'I haven't the faintest idea what you're talking about. But now *I'm* asking *you*! What *is* going on?'

Now he looked self-conscious. Not that she was sorry about that—he deserved to. The silence between them was awkward.

Finally, she tapped her foot impatiently. 'Come on, I haven't got all day! You began this and seem to have solved what's bothering you. Out with it. I've a right to know. If not, I'll march straight in to Mrs Jensen and demand she tell me.'

A restraining hand flashed out, grabbed her wrist. 'No, don't do that. Perhaps my aunt does need you on board ship.'

'I can't see what she'd pay my passage for if she didn't. But carry on ... what other motive could she possibly have? I intend to get to the bottom of this. I don't want to be involved in anything less than above board. Tell me, Mr Mandeville!'

He said, unexpectedly, 'Aren't you being stupid ... calling me Mr Mandeville? Aunt introduced us by our first names. You've suddenly gone all mid-Victorian. I find it ridiculous to start being so formal just because you're mad at me.'

'I'm glad you realise I'm mad—very mad at you. And you've put yourself in this silly position. I give you two seconds to tell me what you thought we were up to. And take your hand off me!'

His mouth tightened. 'All right. You won't like it and I don't suppose you'll admit it. I can give it to you in one word ... matchmaking!'

Maria got such a shock she stepped backwards, then reeled as the back of her knees came into contact with a coffee-table. She regained her balance, exclaimed, '*Matchmaking!* I couldn't be more astonished if you thought I was conspiring with your aunt to blow up the New Zealand House of Parliament! Oh! You mean *you!* But you can't. You won't even be in New Zealand. D'you mean you've a brother or something over there, whom your aunt wants to see married? But that's——'

'I'm going back home. Not as soon as you, but fairly soon. Aunt told me, with a great deal of satisfaction, that you'll be staying with her at least three months, and she added that who knew, you might fall in love with the place and stay.'

Maria said, between her teeth, 'With the *place*. A very natural remark from Mrs Jensen, who loves her homeland so much. Mr Mandeville, all this time I've been trying to hold on to my temper, but not now. You must be the vainest man I've ever met—and I can't think why! You aren't the tall, dark handsome man of the average girl's dreams. No, you're broad, stocky, and you've got sandy lashes! If your aunt *has* anything like this in mind, I can only think she must despair of ever marrying you off. What I'd like to do right now is storm in and tell Mrs Jensen I won't take the position, but I'm damned if I'll allow an insufferable creature like you to rob me of the chance of a voyage like this. But believe me, the moment I hear you're nearing New Zealand, I'll book my own air flight back here! Be good to your aunt and stay in England long enough to give me at least a month with her there to get her well stabilised again if by any chance she gets at all upset by the trip back—though with shipboard time just getting altered half an hour a day, it's not likely,' she added.

'Take yourself off now, but before you go I want you to remember that when your aunt invited me to go out sightseeing round London with you both, I turned it down. All I did was share a meal with you at the guesthouse, a guesthouse I've run in and out of since I was about twelve!'

To her immense chagrin he burst into a great guffaw of laughter, holding his sides. 'I just wish Aunt Alberta could have heard you—especially your description of me. She'd have laughed her head off!'

Maria was nonplussed. 'You must be the most extraordinary family. I don't know what to make of you. Why would she?'

'She's got a bee in her bonnet about me just now. I can read her like a book. She's trying to save me from the clutches, as she would put it, of someone she actively dislikes. So I was suspicious. But you've convinced me. If you'd been in it with my aunt, you'd have come out sightseeing with us. She's cooked it up herself. I apologise.'

'Well, how good of you,' snapped Maria. 'You apologise, so that makes it all right. *Apologise!* You ought to *grovel.* I don't think I've been so angry for years. But for your aunt's sake, I won't give it another thought. You're probably wrong about her. People of your colouring are apt to leap madly to the wrong conclusions. But'—she had an inspiration—'if I dimly suspect your aunt *is* harbouring matchmaking ideas in the little time we have left here, I'll tell her that by the time I come back to England I shall probably be engaged to my stepbrother's wife's brother!'

What a volatile man this Struan Mandeville must be. He immediately looked most interested. 'I say, how intriguing. What a quaint relationship! If you had children, and your stepbrother had, what relation would they be to each other? There must be a name for it, surely.'

'I haven't the faintest idea,' said Maria, unwilling to laugh, not at the tangled relationship, but because he'd accepted as truth the attachment she'd invented on the spur of the moment. Well, it might serve to bolster up her declaration of disinterest in him. She added, 'And if she does put you into the position of having to tell her that, you might add: "Besides, she probably wouldn't marry me if I was as rich as Croesus and with diamonds on all my fingers and toes." Because that's exactly how I feel.'

It was decidedly disconcerting. The wretched man seemed to be enjoying this verbal sparring. His chuckle was actually infectious. 'I can see I'm going to have to grovel, really grovel. I shall abase myself. I'll add to the riches and the diamonds that you have a distinct aversion for men with sandy lashes. I take it that the lucky fellow you've set your heart on is as black as the ace of spades? Still, you're pretty dark yourself ... except for a glint of chestnut. I think contrasts are better, for the next generation, otherwise the family looks tend to get monotonous.'

'I think,' said Maria faintly, 'you're quite, quite mad! If all New Zealand men are as mad as you, I'll stick to Englishmen!' Then laughter bubbled up in her and she sank down on a handy chair till she got over it.

'You're a damned good sport,' said Struan Mandeville. 'I thought I'd really blotted my copybook and if you'd blown the gaff to Aunt Alberta, she'd have torn my liver out. Now that we understand each other so well, and I've nothing to fear from Aunt's usual stratagems and plots, how about coming up to London with us for a dinner and a theatre? Aunt can't get enough of them.'

'Never in your life. I've plans of my own for tonight. My stepbrother's been in London all day, and he's calling for me on his way home and taking me off to High Wycombe for dinner with the family.'

Struan cocked a sandy brow at her. 'Including his wife's brother.'

'Including his wife's brother,' Maria agreed, with truth in actual fact, if not in the implication she was in love with the aforesaid relation. 'So scram. I've very little time left.'

'See you tomorrow, then,' he had the nerve to say, and added, 'But never a word to my revered great-aunt.' He departed whistling.

The tune registered. She flashed after him. He turned, one brow raised. Maria said, mock-severely, 'I forbid that song.'

He looked blank. She explained, 'It could give your aunt more ideas ... it's "Whistle and I'll come to ye, my lad." That's definitely out as far as I'm concerned!'

Struan chuckled and went on his way, but Maria was very thoughtful as she returned to the house. She was sure he'd got the message. That as far as she was concerned, not even a matchmaker with the cunning of the serpent would prevail against her determination to remain unmoved in any way by this vain, cocksure New Zealander. Because she had meant what she said; as soon as she heard he was on his way home, she would terminate her visit to the land of her birth.

The memory of her own reason for accepting Mrs Jensen's offer flashed back on her. But what if the time therefore was too short for her to trace that household where her own kin might be? A desolate feeling swept over her, akin to that experienced the day of her mother's funeral. She loved Shona and Rod, they'd been as close as a true sister and brother might have been, but it was still a fact that now she had no one left in the world related to her by blood, except a rascally father who didn't as much as know her given name, and somewhere, probably, uncles and aunts and cousins. The grandparents, no doubt, would have died long since.

Well, if she did have to curtail her stay with Mrs Jensen, it didn't necessarily mean that she would have to leave New Zealand. If she found out that bay, she could then concentrate on looking for that house. Pity that Mrs Jensen and her relations lived at the Esk Valley, near Napier, in the North Island. Mother and her husband had lived in Dunedin. Later, when Rufus had disappeared, Jane had lived on there with her baby. 'Then I was tied to the city,'

she had said. 'It's a lovely university town beside the sea,
but I no longer had transport for escaping from city streets
to the mountains and lakes of Central Otago. Your father
loved both the sea and the mountains.'

He'd loved the sea. The caption had mentioned a bay.
Her mother had met her father in Christchurch—that much
she knew. That probably pointed to his being a South
Islander. But what a coastline to examine on a map! The
whole of the West Coast of that island was a narrow strip
backed by great alpine ranges; the fretted outline of the
Marlborough Sounds had a myriad inlets and curving bays;
the Kaikoura Coast on the east had mountains sweeping
down to the sea. Maria's heart sank, then lifted, and her
chin with it. She *wouldn't* be dismayed. This trip, with all
expenses paid, had been dropped into her lap. She would
regard it as a springboard.

Struan Mandeville seemed a man insensitive to set-downs.
He came in the next morning with his aunt, full of confidence. He carried an armful of large photographs. 'I wondered what Aunt was up to when I was commanded to
bring up all my photos. I had these with me, to demon-
strate talks I've given on our type of farming, at various
agricultural and stock meetings here. She thinks you should
see the sort of place you're going to.'

He began flicking them over. 'Heronshaw is so named
for the rare white heron, and the blue herons that fish in
our lagoon. We have a sort of table-land where the Kotuku
River comes down from a spring in the hills above us, and
widens out into a sort of swampy pool. It attracts the water-
birds and we've had it declared a sanctuary. We don't want
duck-shooters there in May. We get pied oyster-catchers,
stilts, all manner of waders. Grandfather is a great bird-
watcher. This lagoon spills over to cascade down a mini-
ature cliff and flows on to join the Esk River. The Kotuku
is only a stream at most times, but in heavy rain it's a
torrent.'

Aunt Alberta said anxiously, 'Don't make it sound so
dramatic, Struan. It's mild and gentle country compared
with some of the big mountain sheep stations in New

Zealand. We can be into town in less than half an hour.'

Maria saw Struan give his aunt a shrewd look. 'Fright-ened I'll scare her off, Aunt? You must admit it's not exactly like some of these closely-settled English farms. Better she should know.'

Maria said, with a distinct chill in her voice, 'Last year, in the depths of winter, I was nursing in a household much more remote than anything you'll show me, I'm pretty sure. Your aunt has talked of a semi-tropical paradise ... of orange and grapefruit trees, palms and vineyards. This was a Welsh farm I was on, and a very isolated one.'

He had a glint in his eye that mocked her. 'Haven't you heard what a land of contrasts New Zealand is? Look....' he put a large aerial view in front of her.

Heronshaw lay exposed to the view of the camera, nestled into the folds and valleys of green hills that over to the west were rimmed by range upon range of snow-covered mountains with between them and the homestead, foot-hills apparently covered with dense native forest they seemed to call bush.

'It's still hard to find planes that crash in the area at the back of us, even if below are the citrus orchards, the apricots and nectarines, the vineyards and great paddocks of sweet corn grown for the canning factories.

'Those ranges are the Kaiwekas, the Kaimanawas, and not for nothing does Kaimanawa mean the heart-eater. Be-yond them is Taupo, where in the ditches, when thermal activity is at its peak, you can see steam rising, yet at the far end of Lake Taupo, the largest lake in New Zealand, are the snow-covered shoulders and ski-slopes of Mount Ruapehu.'

Maria looked unimpressed. 'Am I supposed to shiver with apprehension?' She put a finger on the lower right-hand corner of the photograph. 'What's that, Struan? It looks a fairly wide road to me, or is it an illusion and just a farm track?'

His lips twitched. 'Touché! It's the main highway from Taupo to Napier, five minutes downhill from Heronshaw.'

She said wickedly, 'On this Welsh farm you couldn't even see a road. We were up a farm track a mile and a half from even a third-rate road, and when we had snow, even a week later we had to sled up all our supplies from there. Are you ever cut off like that, Struan?'

His grin was good-natured. 'You win ... hands down! One shouldn't have preconceived ideas. I guess it's because I've only known you here ... at Osterley, ten miles from Piccadilly.'

'Oh, well,' said Aunt Alberta complacently, 'you'll know her a lot better than that before too long.'

Struan Mandeville's quick glance at Maria said as plainly as could be: 'What did I tell you?'

Alberta continued, 'I've told Johanna and Athol that Maria will fit beautifully into life at Heronshaw. I can just imagine Athol taking her off bird-watching. She's a bird-watcher herself, Struan, did you know?'

'No, I didn't. That *will* be bully for Grandfather. Better pack your Wellingtons, Maria. There are quite a lot of things I have yet to find out about her, Aunt. Our Miss Willoughby is something of a mystery to me.'

Alberta looked surprised, even, Maria thought, a little uneasy. Why? Maria decided she was being fanciful. Then Alberta said, 'In what way?'

His voice had a meaning drawl in it. 'Oh, just that few girls would take off for an unknown country at a moment's notice, or nearly. I wondered why.'

Alberta's tone was sharp. 'It's *not* unknown to her. She was born there. She can't remember it, of course, but I imagine anyone would leap at the chance to see the country of one's birth.'

Maria blinked. 'I didn't think I'd mentioned it. I was less than a year old when Mother brought me back to her own land.'

'Mrs McGuire mentioned it as soon as I came to stay here—natural enough when she knew I was a New Zealander. She said: "Oh, the girl next door was born there but has lived most of her life here."'

'Where were you born?' Struan asked.

'Dunedin, a long way from Eskdale. But I'll visit down there when I've finished my month or two at Heronshaw.'

'Month or two? But I've planned for you to stay at least three months!'

Maria laughed lightly, 'Well, I'll just play it by ear. I'll stay as long as I think you need me.' Her glance flickered to Struan. He knew what she meant. When he came home, she would take off for Dunedin.

He said, easily enough, 'Good idea to see all of New Zealand while you've got the chance. There are some very good tours.'

She shook her head. 'No, I'd hire a car and explore in leisurely fashion. Mother left me some money and asked me to take a long holiday with it. Though I think she had Europe in mind.'

Aunt Alberta went off at a tangent. 'Have you ever been to Salzburg?'

Maria nodded. 'It's one of my favourite places, but why Salzburg in particular?'

'Because of *The Sound of Music*, and you being called Maria. It's so fitting.'

Struan laughed. 'My aunt has a sort of phobia about names. No wonder she fell for you! Maria has always been a favourite of hers.'

Alberta nodded. 'Had I had a daughter I'd have named her that.' The beaky face gentled and she looked a little pensive.

Struan lightened the moment, said, 'She can't stand fancy names. I once had a girl friend called Fleurette and she disliked her before she even met her ... my nice open-minded aunt! The next one was nicknamed Bonnie ...'

Alberta struck in, 'And the third, heaven help me, was Winsome. That couldn't have been more of a misnomer. That girl was about as winsome as a boa-constrictor! If she'd been a pretty, gentle girl it wouldn't have mattered.' She burst out laughing at the look on Maria's face. 'Don't worry about Struan's feelings, he's used to me.'

Struan said severely, 'But Miss Willoughby isn't, Aunt. I'd better warn her you're a fire-eater and much, much too blunt.'

'Well, I never did hold with people pussyfooting round trying to be all things to all people and pretending to like

their son's girl-friends when if they'd brought them up to
respect their parents' opinions, they'd be more likely to take
notice of them. But not to worry, Maria, I don't mind
people being just as blunt back to me.'

Maria said coolly, 'That's unusual. Blunt people don't
take kindly as a rule to a matching bluntness. We'll deal
very well together if you let me speak my mind too. I don't
like havering. I'm very much a yes-no person, though
I'm——' she paused.

Struan, a gleam in his eye, said, 'Though you're what?'

She knew she was committed to finish that. 'Though I'm
careful not to hurt people's feelings.'

His blue eyes gleamed with mischief. 'Aunt, you're about
to be put in your place! I can see Maria will deal famously
with you. She thinks you hurt my feelings by criticising
my girl-friends and gave me lots of complexes ... including one that makes me resistant to people with misguided
matchmaking instincts.'

Maria made an impatient gesture. 'I did not! You don't
look in the least as if you need anyone to fly to your defence. I meant this girl Winsome. Maybe that made her
aggressive, being called that. I knew a girl whose mother
called her Angel all the time, instead of Angela. It made
her spit sparks. Angela in itself is a beautiful name.'

Struan chuckled. 'I think you have something there. Winsome changed her name to Winifred—legally. And you're
right. If I'd really fallen in love with the boa-constrictor, it
wouldn't have mattered a hoot what Aunt Alberta thought
of her name or her nature. But Win was rather fun. We
merely partnered each other round. Anyway, here's a photo
of the homestead. These chaps who do aerial photographs
made a small fortune in our district among the big property
owners. Ours got into a photographic book of the province.'

Maria said in as calm a tone as she could manage: 'Did
these photographers go all over New Zealand? And were
books made in each province?'

'Yes. Not all were selected for inclusion, of course, but
certainly the older ones were, as examples of early and
later Colonial style buildings—mostly wood, with a few
exceptions.'

'Are they still obtainable, these books? I'm rather interested in architecture.'

'Are you?' His voice held surprise.

She nodded, said, 'Yes, my stepbrother's wife's brother is an architect. I tend to get caught up in other people's enthusiasms.'

'And especially his,' suggested Struan, with meaning.

'Especially his,' agreed Maria equably, and added, 'So this is Heronshaw. How very beautiful!'

This was a different style of house altogether from that black-and-white picture in the bottom of her case. Whereas her father's home had a long central verandah with conical tower rooms at each end, and was roofed with tiles, this house was L-shaped, with what was almost a courtyard in front, with a fountain, much more modern, and with wide landscape windows instead of old-fashioned sash ones. No dark pines shadowed the back of the house, and this one seemed to be in pearly stone, brick-sized lozenges, with a rough surface, and had an almost black roof, probably of some composition—decramastic, Struan informed her.

But that mention of books of photographs of homesteads of every province had heartened her. A much better chance of identifying a building than seeking for a homestead belonging to people named Smith!

CHAPTER TWO

TIME flew. Struan Mandeville went back to Hampshire in a day or two, and Shona came up from Somerset and Rod's wife, Merle, from High Wycombe, and the two of them whisked Maria off on what she thought were shopping orgies, and after making her spend more than she'd ever spent in her life in one go on clothes, added some glamour items of their own buying.

'This,' they informed her, 'is what families are for. The house lease is bringing all of us a bit extra, so for once this is going to be spent on you.' Maria vowed they were bossy-boots, that it was no great shakes being the youngest of the family, but was touched to the heart by their generosity and pleasure in doing this.

Struan Mandeville came up again for two or three days to see to his aunt's packing, which turned out to be a tussle of wills between the two of them, with him determined to reduce what she was taking home to reasonable proportions and with Alberta equally determined to distribute souvenirs to half the inhabitants of Eskdale, as well as the family, which seemed considerable.

Maria heaved a sigh. 'You two are certainly alike in temperament! It's like the mountain and Mahomet. Struan, I think this looks like needing a mediator, and unhappily that means me!'

He grinned, 'So you'd like to bang Mahomet's head and the top of the mountain together ... but what would that solve? You'll never get this stuff to Southampton, even if you take a taxi from here.'

'What I need is the wisdom of Solomon and the patience of Job,' Maria declared. An idea struck her, and she looked away so he shouldn't see the calculating gleam in her eye. 'Oh, I've had an idea. As you're so obviously adept at travelling light, you'll have space to spare in *your* luggage. Mrs Jensen, if you could decide what you won't need till Struan gets home ... your winter woollies for instance, we could leave them for him to bring.'

He looked at her sourly. 'It's not wisdom and patience you've got, it's the cunning of the serpent, my girl. That settles it, as you knew it would. You know I'm travelling by air. I'll get this crammed in if it kills me.'

Alberta chuckled. 'I do enjoy this. Gives me a real family feeling. Much much better than that light dialogue Romayne and you indulge in, Straun. I wonder if you realise how much that sort of talk isn't you.'

Oh dear! She was putting her foot in it again. Struan didn't seem put out, however. 'It's light and amusing. Leave that poor girl alone, Aunt.'

'It would soon pall if you had to put up with it for a lifetime.'

Maria decided Alberta must be checked. She said in a firm tone, 'Don't try to sell *me* to Struan, Mrs Jensen. It just won't wash. Struan decided long ago that matchmaking lay behind your desire to get me to Heronshaw, but I soon reassured him he need have no worries on that score.'

'Why?' demanded Alberta.

'Because she loves another,' said Struan flippantly. 'And even if she didn't, she doesn't like vain New Zealanders with sandy eyelashes ... she likes the traditional type, tall, dark, handsome. Sorry about that, Aunt. But take her just the same for your own comfort on the voyage. She says she's going to book a return flight the moment she hears I'm coming back to New Zealand. You over-reached yourself this time, old girl.'

Surprisingly Alberta didn't deny it. Struan was surprised too. 'What's the matter? You must be out of form. Or——' his eyes narrowed, '*is* there another reason behind it all? Though what——'

Alberta did look bland then. 'Exactly. What other reason could I have except for company, or matchmaking? And I would like to get on with this. Oh, answer that phone, would you?'

It was Rod. 'I thought I'd find you next door, Maria. Look, Johnny and Shona are having a trip to London, bringing their estate car. They'll go back via Southampton, and take your luggage. I'll bring my car. Merle would like to see you off too, and she can leave the baby with her sister there. How about that?'

It solved everything and stopped the arguing. Maria made a sweeping gesture towards the piles of Alberta's undisciplined shopping on her bed, 'Now, if I can get all this, and that, into a *Not wanted on voyage* trunk, and the Willoughby family undertakes to get it to the ship's side, will it set your mind at rest, Struan?'

He surveyed her flushed face. 'I thought Aunt Alberta had gone off her rocker when she decided on a sea voyage and a companion, but I'll say this for her, she certainly picked a good 'un, and when I see all this I realise that the guff about finding air travel not so hot for diabetics was a lot of codswallop ... it was only in order to get all this stuff home. I nearly brought Romayne up to help you pack, but——'

'But you wisely decided I'd not fancy that. How astute of you! When is Romayne going back to New Zealand?'

'Shortly before I leave. In fact we might wangle it yet so we travel together.' He looked wickedly at his aunt who, surprisingly, refused to bite.

When Maria retired that night, she felt very glad that his aunt's matchmaking plans had been brought into the open and effectively scotched. She had felt much more natural with Struan since.

The good ship *Marora* lay at its moorings at Southampton, as gleamingly silvery as the gauzy-winged flying-fish she was named for. Maria felt a stirring at her heart as she looked up at her, passengers already on board lining the rails, others still boarding her, burdened with too much luggage, probably gifts pressed on them at the last moment by well-meaning friends. Some were sad because they were leaving the land of their birth; others jubilant because they were returning home after long months or years in exile.

Sea-birds wheeled above her, wings glinting against the cobalt sky of the glorious day Hampshire had put on to farewell them. It *was* romantic to travel by sea, a glamour no plane ever possessed because on board even one of the big jumbo jets, lives touched so briefly, but here, in the month it would take to sail across the Atlantic, through the Panama Canal, and through the romantic South Seas to Auckland, new friendships could be forged that might change the whole course of some lives. Love could blossom, illness break out, life itself begin, or end. Maria said so, leaving off the last thought.

A voice broke in, Struan Mandeville's. He'd been back in Hampshire for some days and promised to come to the wharf. 'Very right and proper, dear Miss Willoughby. It's the true setting for a romantic serial, glamour, glamour all the way. Almost you persuade me to cancel my air flight and join you on the way.'

Alberta took him seriously. 'Dear boy, why don't you? I've never really approved of all this rushing from one

hemisphere to another. We weren't meant to flip at ridiculous speeds from one season to another ... from one temperature to another. We're meant to accustom ourselves
slowly. Everyone's tired after packing up, so going by ship
you can have a glorious holiday in sun-drenched tropical
seas before unpacking and plunging into the maelstrom of
work again.'

Struan laughed, shaking his head. 'Grandfather would
just about murder you, Aunt Alberta ... he prides himself
on the fact that though Heronshaw is efficiently run, it's
not a rat-race. Maelstrom indeed! Can't be done anyway.
I've those lectures to attend and two papers to give. Well,
let's get you on board. I expect that shipping clerk got you
extra boarding passes for your guests? Of course he did.
For an old warhorse you sure can charm the birds off the
trees, Aunt Alberta!'

Maria was delighted to find she had a separate cabin, a
small one off Alberta's, and their own bathroom. Alberta's
was a spacious one, so they'd have no feeling of being
cooped up.

They embarked on a tour of the ship, and the ones who
were staying home confessed to itchy feet. Struan looked
at his watch. 'I must go off for a moment. Romayne wanted
to bid you *bon voyage*, Aunt. I got a ticket for her ...
shouldn't be long. At least she has one of the virtues you
admire, Aunt, punctuality!' He disappeared.

'I could ha' well done without that gesture,' said Alberta
sourly. 'And take that look off your face, Maria, I won't
hurt her feelings, I'm civilised enough to conform and be
polite, but I'd like to know what that mad dog of a Struan
thinks he's playing at.'

Rod suddenly burst out laughing. 'Mrs Jensen, at first I
had all sorts of big-brotherly feelings about my sister going
off to the ends of the earth, but not now. You're so re-
freshingly honest that Maria can't possibly come to any
harm while she's under your wing.'

Maria looked appalled. 'Rod! Your little sister is twenty-
five and a nursing Sister and I'm supposed to be taking
Mrs Jensen under *my* wing. That was the whole idea.'

Rod twinkled. 'I think you'll just be a couple of friends.'

'Why, I think so,' said the redoubtable Alberta, 'because we are two of a kind. You've got sense, young man, and know friendship doesn't find a difference in age, a big difference, any barrier. Maria will fit beautifully into life at Heronshaw. I knew that as soon as I found out what a lovely relationship exists between the members of your family ... you may be steps, but you're all kindred spirits if not kin to each other.' She looked up. 'Heaven help me, here's that shilpit creature and me hoping for once she'd slip up and be unpunctual ... the less time I spend in her presence, the better it is for potential ulcers.'

Fortunately she'd dropped her voice to just above a whisper, but sheer guilt made the rest of the party almost too effusive towards Romayne. Anyway, Maria liked what she saw. How could anyone describe this girl as shilpit? ... No washed-out negative personality here. She was tall, elegant, with a beautiful skin and features cut with cameo-like clarity.

Maria said, 'Taking off like this to the other side of the world is such an adventure for me I'm glad to meet another New Zealander who's returning home soon. I hope it won't be long till we meet again, Miss Averell.'

'It won't be. By now I'm dying to get home. My relations here didn't want me to hurry back. They kept thinking of something else I ought to do or see, family celebrations and so on, shows, plays, pageants, the lot, but two years is a long time to be away from home. I'm guessing you won't be away from England as long as that?'

'It's indefinite,' Maria told her. 'I'll see Mrs Jensen well settled in and then I'll take off and see all of New Zealand I can, especially the South Island, before coming home.'

'The South Island? Any particular reason ... relatives perhaps?'

'No, none at all. Just that I happened to be born there—and spent my first six months of life in Dunedin. One is always curious about the place where one first saw the light of day.' She encountered a strange look from Alberta, who turned away very quickly.

Romayne nodded. 'Well, our sheep station isn't too far from Heronshaw ... inland a little, near Rissington, so

I'm bound to see something of you. Make it Romayne, will you?'

Very pleasantly said. Why was Alberta so anti? Could it be that despite wishing her nephew to be married, she was possessive, didn't think any girl good enough?

Surprisingly Alberta said, 'Glad you turned up, Romayne ... would you do me a favour?'

Romayne looked astounded but recovered quickly, and said, 'Sure. Something you want me to bring home for you?'

'No, something I want you to take away for me. Oh, not yet, but when the "all ashore" sounds, I'd like you to take Struan away ... go and have dinner together, and don't, for the love of Pete, wait on the quayside. There's nothing more traumatic than waving farewell from the ship's side. Would you?'

Maria saw Struan nod assent to Romayne, who said immediately, 'I couldn't agree more. It takes such an age. In that respect I'd rather travel by air, the getaway is so much quicker. Ships take such an age to pull out into the stream and the farewell songs can be so poignant—oh, not for us, who'll meet again so soon, but for those who are emigrating.'

Maria felt she was going to like Romayne. Pity Alberta didn't. But what real man would let his aunt dictate his choice of a wife, or girl-friend? Struan had swept them all round to point out a hovercraft going across the water to the Isle of Wight.

The 'all ashore' sounded; Maria's relations kissed her goodbye and left hastily in Struan's and Romayne's wake. 'Well, thank goodness that's over,' said Alberta. 'Let's find out a few things for ourselves while the rest hold streamers and call out meaningless nothings across a few inches of water, longing for the ship to sail. I'm glad we got the first sitting for dinner—suits my diet better.'

Through their porthole Maria saw their party making their way across the wharf. The only one who turned was Struan Mandeville. The late afternoon sun glinted on his strikingly fair hair, paling the tawny tints. Even from here you could see the intense blue of his eyes. Pure

Scandinavian, she'd think. Memory flooded back on her, puzzling her. Why had she said that scathing thing about his light eyelashes? It was most attractive. He sketched an affectionate gesture of goodbye, as if he'd thought they might be still watching him.

Romayne swung round too, then swiftly, as if jerked like a puppet on a string, she swung back, clutched Struan, and to Maria's astonishment, buried her head against his shoulder. How extraordinary! She'd seemed so cool, so collected. Struan's hand came up to her back, patted it. It lasted for only a moment. Romayne seemed to recover herself, and drew away. Maria, fascinated, saw them continue on their way, Struan now holding her hand, then they were engulfed by a crowd of latecomers surging on to the wharf. Maria was assailed by what she felt was an inexplicable sensation of anticlimax, even of loneliness. How absurd ... she had four weeks and more of shipboard life ahead of her, in which to meet and mingle with scores of interesting people. But why did she suddenly feel she didn't want the ship to sail?

At last the ship parted the links that held her to the land. Just a few inches of water at first, but symbolic of a separate world even if for long enough they would be still in sight of land, that lovely south coastline and the Isle of Wight.

Alberta said briskly, 'There, that's our things put away —come on up on deck, child, now that those sickening farewells are over and we can get on with the voyage. We'll take stock of our travelling companions as we go. No doubt some will be pains in the neck, and some a joy to meet, but we'll go canny at first. A mistake to get too involved too soon.' But she was certainly pleased to see one of them.

He was at the rail, but swung round at the sound of Alberta's voice. 'Alberta, how good to see you! I thought that voice was familiar. I didn't even know you weren't in New Zealand.'

Alberta drew Maria forward, introduced her merely as a young friend travelling back with her. This was Donal

McFie of Wellington, but whenever his work brought him to Napier, he stayed with Alberta. This time it had brought him to London, but instead of flying back to save time, as usual, he was taking his leave so he could have a sea trip.

He'd be about Struan's age, Maria decided. She liked the way his eyes had lit up when he saw Alberta. Some wouldn't bother with a woman her age. He said immediately, 'Which sitting for dinner are you having? Good, so am I. I prefer the earlier one. Look, I'll buzz off and see if they can possibly get me at your table. Dinner companions are always such an unknown quantity.'

Alberta chuckled, 'And better the devil you know than the devil you don't, eh?'

He added considerably to the pleasure of the voyage for Maria in an unemotional way, partnering her in deck games, dancing with her some evenings.

She felt that the trip across the Atlantic towards to the Panama Canal and the Pacific Ocean divided her life and her world in two. When this lovely gleaming white ship forged over the Equator in that other sea, anything could lie ahead of her. Perhaps her life would turn full circle, if she could find out a little about her father, see where he grew up, even find mitigating circumstances for his footloose irresponsible life.

Sometimes in the privacy of her cabin Maria took that picture out and wondered. Had he really felt he wished the night had borne his breath away, or was it weak self-pity, not genuine remorse?

She had no desire to meet him, a man who had deserted his girl-wife, who had been a lonely immigrant. But she would love to find that house with the towers, perched on the hill. In her heart she called them the towers of Camelot. Her own forebears might have gone from it long since but surely some essence would remain there of their lives?

They struck it rough passing the Azores, but to her delight Maria proved as good a sailor as Alberta. How humiliating it would have been had the patient (if Alberta could have been termed that) had to turn nurse! But then the seas calmed and the carefree serenity of shipboard life became a reality, with dawns of sheer delight, framed in a porthole like a picture in a locket, and sunsets of unbelievable splendour viewed nightly from the teak rails.

Even in this age of modern communication, a ship was a world of its own with a thousand or more people living within the compass of one vessel, no one able to leave, no one from the other world entering. Alberta was already much less stiff in her joints, benefiting from Maria's expert massage. She injected her own insulin, using an automatic injector, so Maria's duties were light. Much better, in that regard, for a diabetic to be independent.

Alberta thought Maria spent far too much time with her, except for the games with Donal. 'It's not natural for you to sit reading with me for such long stretches.'

Maria laughed. 'It's such heaven to have the time, and this ship's library is excellent. They cater for such a terrific variety of tastes. I'm schooling myself to sample most of them. I'm rather given to re-reading old favourites. I was always a loner as a child, Alberta.' (She'd dropped into Donal's affectionate use of the Christian name.) 'That is, till Mother married again and brought me the companionship of the grandest family one could have wished for. But I've never been one for crowds and in the main prefer having just one person around to talk to. Oh, goodness, that sounds somewhat selfish.'

Alberta wouldn't have that. 'No, you're good at mixing when you have to, but you have a quality of companionship that augurs well for marriage when you meet the person you'd want to spend the rest of your life with. The ones who need the constant stimulation of parties and fresh faces are the ones who get fed up with married life. Oh, perhaps that's too sweeping. Some people like crowds when they're young and are surprised to find their tastes changing, but in general this is true.'

Alberta's conversation certainly did run on marriage a lot. At times it made Maria uneasy, especially as Struan seemed to occur in the talk so soon after that. She guessed that to Alberta, Struan was the son she'd never had. She hoped that things wouldn't be made too uncomfortable for her if Struan arrived back in New Zealand fairly soon. She had a feeling that once Romayne left England, he wouldn't be long following.

Maria was familiar by hearsay with the family at Heronshaw now. It was a large estate, climbing up from the valley, over a hill, and down the other side, and had three houses on it plus some shearers' quarters. Alberta lived in one house called Amber Knoll. 'A sort of dower house,' she said, twinkling, 'if we had such things in New Zealand. In short, the house the old folk at the homestead retire into, when the young ones take over. In this case, however, the dower house skipped a generation. When Athol, my brother, and Johanna his wife retire, their granddaughter and her husband will take on. Though they'll stay in their own house, a fairly new one, built in ranch style, in cedar, with white facings. It's on Hibiscus Hill. All three houses get views of the sea from the Mahia Peninsula to Cape Kidnappers. I was a schoolteacher and married one, so Gregory and I moved all over New Zealand, both islands. When retirement came, Johanna said why not take the Dower House. So we altered it so it can be in two wings when we get Struan married off and settled in Heronshaw. It's a house for a family, and as it turned out, is rather too big for Johanna and Athol now.'

Get Struan married off. Was it an obsession with Alberta, and perhaps with Johanna too? But they didn't like Romayne. Maria must walk carefully. However, that needn't concern her for weeks. Not in this floating island paradise.

Alberta continued. 'Judith and Ramsay have two children so far, but there'll be four before Christmas—she's expecting twins. She's a twin herself, of course. And she's delighted. She always wanted four, and says this saves her a whole nine months! Christabel, her younger child, is six, and Timothy's eight, so it's time the other two popped along. Judith is a born mother, enjoys her children tremendously. Of course Johanna is the same type, ought to have had half a dozen herself, instead of just one. Johanna seems so young for a great-grandmother, but then she was married at twenty and a grandmother at forty.'

Goodness, the son must have married before he was of

age. If there was a tradition of early marriages in the family no wonder they wanted to marry Struan off, a bachelor of thirty. Not for the first time Maria wondered where the twins' parents were. Perhaps their father hadn't wanted to continue farming the estate. He might have been nudged into early matrimony too, to get him settled down at Heronshaw. That was always a mistake. Children should be allowed to follow their own bent. She wouldn't ask, any interest in this family would only encourage Alberta. The family were probably going to find Struan would be married before long, despite their opposition to Romayne.

The sea breezes grew warmer every day as they entered the more temperate latitudes and inevitably the passengers began to look forward to going ashore at Cristobal. The stay there would be brief, then they would move forward in convoy through the Panama Canal, but it would be exciting to explore a foreign town even for a short while.

On the tenth day out they could see Puerto Rico lying as a smudge on the port side and to the starboard was Haiti. The temperature was eighty-two and they were three thousand six hundred miles from their port of embarkation.

All day excitement simmered as they neared land, with land birds flying about them, and twilight finally dropping very suddenly, one moment a purple-grey blur, the next velvety darkness blotched with golden short lights. Cristobal.

Formalities were at a minimum. They were merely warned to keep to the main streets, not to wander back among the docks, but to go straight ahead. Maria and Alberta and Donal were in a party, and much as they loved shipboard life, were looking forward to having terra firma beneath their feet once more.

Huge trucks were already unloading, the ship was refuelling, great crates of vegetables were coming aboard, piles of fruit, and the soft balmy air seemed to caress their skins. Maria wore a filmy apricot dress, sleeveless, with a scooped-out neckline piped in white, a gold metallic necklace bought at the ship's shop about her tanned throat. Her hair, brushed back from her temples for coolness, gleamed

in burnished light in the powerful floodlighting the loaders
were working by.

She put a hand under Alberta's elbow for the step from
the gangway, while Donal assisted another woman not so
young, and then in turn Maria felt her elbow taken from
the other side. Some kindly new passenger waiting to come
on, no doubt, or an official. She looked up to give a word
of thanks, and gasped.

She saw a pair of big shoulders clad in tussore, a broad
strong face, fair to tawny hair, the bluest of eyes and brist-
ling sandy brows. 'Struan Mandeville! How on earth did
you get here?'

He grinned, well pleased with their astonishment.
'Mainly by air. I had the chance of joining a sheep-meat conference in the States on behalf of Federated Farmers, was
smitten with the idea of a shortish sea-voyage and was lucky
enough to get a berth. How's that for a surprise? I've been
on and checked in, saw people were already leaving the
ship and didn't dare risk trying to find you on board, and
took up my post here. Good grief, am I seeing things?
Donal McFie! ... how are you, Donal?'

He was introduced briefly to the rest of the party, for
no one wanted to miss anything possible to see in the time,
because next morning they were joining the convoy of
ships at the crack of dawn.

Suddenly for Maria this whole trip took on a new
dimension. She felt as if she had come alive, stopped dreaming. Alberta too seemed on top of the world. Maria noticed
that with misgiving.

Exotic palms flanked the streets, with some fine buildings gleaming whitely. 'This is just like a film set,' said
someone, 'especially with the policeman in those comic
opera-type uniforms at every corner.'

Struan said in Maria's ear, 'Nothing comic about it ...
they mean business. Notice they're in pairs? Different
uniforms too, in each pair. At a guess I'd say military and
civil police, the flaps of their holsters are open at the ready;
they wouldn't hesitate to use those guns. They've one at
each hip and a truncheon swinging from each hand. Were

the passengers briefed on not straying from well-lit streets or going into questionable dives?'

'Yes, we were. Pity these shops aren't open, that'd keep some of them out of trouble, lost in the fascination of shopping, though if these prices are American dollars, they aren't bargains.'

There were wine shops open, some entertainment, but it was soon exhausted and they came back to the ship ahead of the others because Struan and Donal were as eager as the two women to be up at dawn and not to miss one moment of the passage through the Canal.

How fascinating it was to travel through these man-made cuts and lakes, to look at these pointed islands and realise that once they were mountains, that rivers had girdled their bases and trees and birds had found their own paradise on the slopes and glens that now lay fathoms deep beneath them. It was a miracle of engineering, a triumphant battle against the scourges of nature, an end to the terrifying voyages around Cape Horn, yet you had the sense of jungle kingdoms violated.

They spent the day in wonder as they dipped down, or rose through the locks, or steamed across the great lakes. The rails were crowded all day. It had magic in it, certainly, for Maria, in the journey with ships in front of them and ships behind them, but there was even more enchantment for her when finally, at night, they slipped into the Pacific Ocean. How strange to think that this sea that lapped the west coast of the Americas also lapped the east coast of New Zealand where the sun first woke the world.

Struan said whimsically, 'We like to think that as we're on what's called the Sunrise Coast it gives a special something to the grapes of our vineyards, and therefore to our wine, that it holds the sparkle of the sunshine in a sort of pristine tang that's given to no other. Rather cheeky of us, perhaps. And fanciful.'

Maria disagreed. 'Why not? I like parochial enthusiasm —and fancies. If Keats could get all fanciful and long for "a beaker full of the warm South" ... what was it? ... Um, "tasting of Flora and the country green", why shouldn't you feel your wines have the tang of the sunrise?'

He turned from his contemplation of the cobalt sea to look at her. 'Maria, that's delightful. Isn't that in the poem that speaks of "beaded bubbles winking at the brim"? No wonder Aunt Alberta loves you!'

She felt her cheeks warm. 'You mean because she's so fond of poetry?'

'Yes, and because you read it to her. She told me. She values that quiet half-hour in the cabin, after dinner.'

'It's a shared pleasure. I miss my stepfather for that. We did a lot of reading aloud in our family.'

'Then you'll fit in well at Heronshaw. Gran and Grand-father are crackerjacks at reading aloud. They must have spent hours reading to Judith and me when we were chil-dren, even as pre-schoolers.'

Maria reflected that there must have been a time when the twins' parents had lived at Heronshaw.

Struan said, 'That dress is ideal for a sea voyage. It's both blue and green. How clever of you to choose it.'

Maria glanced down at it. 'My stepsister bought it for me. Shona has wonderful taste. She was a textile designer before she was married, and still does a little. This is one of hers. They called it Sea Rapture. Donal made the same re-mark as you about it. He's interested in colours, does a bit of painting in his spare time, he tells me.'

She saw the sandy brows come down. He said abruptly, 'I noticed he spends a lot of time with you ... is he en-amoured?'

Maria burst out laughing. 'You sound like something out of a Regency novel, Struan! No, not in the least.' She looked mischievous. 'To be quite candid, on the way across the Atlantic we formed an alliance ... to protect each other.'

'Protect each other—from what?'

'From the effects of moonlight on the boat-deck. Corny, isn't it? But when you get cooped up on a ship with loads of unattached people it seems inevitable. Donal rescued me one night in the glamorous Caribbean from ... I'll go all Regency too and say from the importunities of a lonely and amorous ship's officer. I'd had one of my spasms of

wanting to be alone and ought to have had more sense than
to wander quite so far away from everyone else, just to be
able to think without someone buttonholing me for conversation. Some of these chaps think a woman travelling
without male escort must be as man-hungry as they're
woman-hungry. I was quickly disabusing his mind of that
idea when Donal stepped in and clinched it. Then——'

She paused. Struan prompted her, his blue eyes very
intent. 'Then ...?'

'Then he suggested he was having a spot of similar
bother himself. I might act as a smoke-screen for him. He
didn't want to get emotionally involved with anyone on
board a ship and he'd had a bit of trouble, so how about it?'

Struan's lip curled. 'How bolstering for his ego ... being
sought after.'

Maria was shocked. 'Struan! Donal isn't in the least vain,
if that's what you mean. He'd never have hinted at such a
thing if he hadn't had to rescue me. Perhaps you think I'm
boasting about a conquest too?'

His voice was rough. 'Of course I don't. But be careful
with that same fellow. It was a good line as far as you were
concerned ... putting it on that basis. Very cunning. That
way he could have the undoubted pleasure of your company, even dally a little, without running the risk of you
taking him seriously.'

Flakes of anger stained her cheeks. 'Struan Mandeville!
What an extraordinary thing to say! In a woman that
would be termed cattiness! That puts me in the class of a
good-time girl, not for serious or lasting relationships.
Thank you very much!'

To her consternation and chagrin he burst out laughing. 'Oh, rot, I meant nothing of the kind. The wonder is
you haven't been snapped up long ago. You've got just
about everything—looks, figure, and a sort of clear-eyed
honest way of looking at life. You goose, I merely resented
his attitude on your behalf. I promised your stepbrother
that when I got to New Zealand I'd look after you. He said
I'd better see your penchant for helping lame dogs didn't
get you into any trouble, so I didn't like the idea of Donal

McFie using you. He has some rather tough ideas about women and their motives. I know.'

Maria was mollified, said, 'Well, look at it squarely, the aid was mutual. I've been around a bit and wasn't likely to take him seriously. I think it was chivalrous of him to let me know his reasons, that he had no intentions towards me. Oh, dear, isn't this a stilted sort of dialogue? I think you must be fair, Struan, there *are* two or three predatory females on board and I've quite admired the way he's not let it go to his head. For all that film-star look he's a canny Scot at heart, and so, I suppose, are you. Mandeville sounds a Norman name, but Struan is surely Scottish. Was your mother a Scot?'

She glanced up at him, from her contemplation of the bow-wave parting the waters into creamy froth, and was surprised to see a strange look cross his face. It passed and his face was expressionless looking down on her. Only his voice betrayed some inner disturbance. 'I've no idea. She might have been anything from a Scot to a Scandinavian lass from Dannevirke or Norsewood. My sandy looks needn't necessarily mean Scots ancestry at all.'

Maria was completely bewildered. 'What can you mean? Your father would know your mother's ancestry even if she died young—I've realised your grandmother must have brought you and Judith up. You live with your paternal grandfather because your name is Mandeville, so——'

'So it means we were adopted. Johanna and Athol were adoptive grandparents. And better people never breathed. It's unusual, but they were still only in their early forties. I've no idea of the stock whence I sprung.'

He stood very still waiting for her to comment.

She said slowly, 'Whereas I—as far as my father is concerned—know only too well. He was a rotter—a seaman, who promised to settle down on land when he married my young mother, but the call of the sea, or else an inability to take responsibility, was too strong for him. Not for me, because he didn't even know I was coming. He was dishonest, weak, charming, I believe . . . so perhaps not knowing anything might be a good thing. At least it leaves you your imagination. And your mother must have loved you very dearly to have given you such a fine name. Struan Theodore. I made quite a study of names when I was doing maternity. We were always being asked. Theodore means the gift of God. I suppose you knew that?'

'I didn't really. I thought of it as rather old-fashioned. I'd rather have had an ordinary name for the second one, when I was a kid, like James or William or David. Struan, of course, simply means a stream. But you mean——?'

'I mean whatever your mother's story was, and it could have been a sad one, she still thought of you as God-given —which is the divine right of any child ... given to the world. The world would be a lot poorer for many a child who couldn't name its father ... or be acknowledged by him if he did know. Just think, what would the world be like without Leonardo da Vinci's *Last Supper*—and he was born outside wedlock. If *he* hadn't been able to rise above the circumstances of his birth—or if he'd never been born—that heritage in inborn skill and genius would have been lost for ever.'

She stopped and self-consciousness flooded her cheeks warmly. Struan laughed, put a finger out, flicked the cheek nearest him. 'O wise young judge,' he said teasingly yet tenderly. 'A Portia come to judgement. Sorry I sounded touchy. I have the most wonderful grandparents any child could wish for, and had an idyllic childhood, brought up on Heronshaw with all that land and sea and the most caring concern. But just sometimes when people ask me "What part of Britain did your forebears come from?" it gets me on the raw. And, Maria, you may have had a father of whom you couldn't be proud, but generations of more steadfast folk must have triumphed over *his* genes, because you'd never have fooled my aunt otherwise. Anyway, Donal isn't going to whisk you away at Tahiti. I've an idea he thinks I can escort my aunt and he can have you to himself on his trip round the island. He wants to see the Gauguin museum.'

'Then he has another think coming. I want to go out in a glass-bottomed boat over the coral reef and see that fascinating underworld of the sea. No time for both, so

I'm opting for that, whoever else is going where.'

'Then that's three of us for the coral. Anyway, come on down to Aunt's cabin. I unearthed that big map of our area last night and dropped it in on her bed. That gives us room to spread it out.'

Alberta was looking at it when they arrived in. Struan said, 'I want to show Maria where the nearest hot springs are ... up on the coast road going north, Morere Springs, a lovely place with bush walks and lovely gardens and a cold swimming pool and a hot mineral one side by side. See?'

But she wasn't looking at his pointing finger, she was staring at the name she'd seen blazoned in big black print across the whole province. She'd heard it *said* many a time by these people, but had never seen it *spelt*.

Now she said, as if the words were forced out of her. 'It's spelt with an "e". An "e" ... I thought it would be spelt Hawks Bay. Not with an "e" in it. Hawkes Bay.'

They both gazed at her, puzzled. What was so strange about that? Struan said rather lamely, 'Well, it was named after Admiral Hawke, and not the bird. But what's—I say, Maria, are you all right?'

She had lost all her colour. He grasped her two hands, said, 'Sit down for a moment. It's this heat, and the cabin's stuffy despite the air-conditioning. I'll get you a drink of water.'

Maria went along with him that it must have been the heat and allowed him to take her up on deck to a cool corner, shaded by awnings yet well exposed to the breeze, in a few moments.

Alberta let them go alone. She had a frown between her brows. It hadn't been the heat. But she couldn't for the life of her think why the 'e' in Hawkes Bay had excited the girl. Did she know anything?

That night Maria lay awake a long time thinking. Oh, she might yet find two or three bays ending in those letters. She'd never thought of a whole district being called a Bay. She'd never find one homestead in all that area, surely. It was as large as several counties rolled into one, if she

judged it by England. Then her heart lifted. If Providence
or coincidence or whatever it was had brought her to that
very part of New Zealand where she should begin her
search, she'd never give up till she found some trace of her
forebears.

CHAPTER THREE

ALBERTA seemed very amused at the situation. She took
what could be construed as a mischievous delight in having
all three of them about her. 'You're outnumbered, Donal,
I'm afraid, three to one in favour of the coral and the fish
... you'll have to brood on Gauguin all by yourself, though
for sure there are plenty of damsels willing—even eager—
to accompany an unattached male.'

Donal was unperturbed. 'How cruel you are, Mrs
Jensen! You ought to have murmured gracefully, "My
nephew shall escort me and you shall have Maria with you
to enhance the subtle attractions of this island demi-
paradise still further." '

Maria burst out laughing. 'It must be the result of so
many Georgette Heyers in the ship's library, but everyone
I know seems to be speaking from the pages of a period
novel. Besides, I'm not going just to escort Alberta. I want
to see the coral for myself. I may not come this way again.'

Donal drifted off and Maria was surprised to hear
Struan mutter, 'Do him good not to get all his own way at
times.'

Alberta grinned smugly, and Maria could have smacked
her. She thought this faint air of enmity that occasionally
showed between the two men had nothing to do with her.

When Struan had gone Alberta remarked, 'Not quite
such close friends as they were once. That'll show Struan.'

Maria didn't know how to answer that. She left it with-
out comment. Alberta continued, almost musing to herself,
'Struan would like to think Donal's judgment is at fault.
But it isn't. He's just got more discrimination.'

Maria wrinkled her brow. What on earth...?

Alberta laughed. 'You're dying to ask why, but you won't, so I'll tell you. Because Donal holds Romayne in even more dislike than I do.'

Maria said, 'Oh, there's Denise Goddard ... I wanted to ask her something,' and she took off along the deck in pursuit.

The afternoon in Tahiti was a dream realised. They were off the gangway at one-thirty, into heat that seemed tangible, like a canopy of burning air bearing down on them. They wasted no time on the stalls selling coral and bead trinkets on the wharf, but hurried across to get into the shade of the glass-bottomed boat awaiting them, decked with long stalks of red ginger blossom. They watched fascinated as they skimmed over the reef and cruised about as the pilot left the boat to his second in command, and dived down to sit on a formation of coral, and instantly scores, even hundreds of fish, brightly coloured and fantastically shaped, swam towards him open-mouthed.

Across the scintillating waters, too bright to look upon for too long at a stretch, dreamed the little town, its gaily painted roof and mission steeples set among pale green foaming verdure, that clothed its hills from summits to shoreline. All manner of craft skimmed about, in a sort of idyllic dreamy South Sea picture, lapped in luxurious heat, set in the ocean blueness like a jewel afloat on one of Spencer's faery seas. Morea, the island used for Bali Hai in *South Pacific*, dreamed on the water, wrapped in little mists that clung lovingly.

They came back to the ship to shower and to change because their clothes were sticking to them after their hour in the shops.

They arranged to meet again in the Hawaiian Lounge in the cocktail hour. Struan came towards them, debonair, refreshed, in tussore trousers, silk shirt, blue spotted cravat. Maria was conscious of a new pleasure in the looks of a man. Conscious too of a tribute to her own dressing, in his eyes as they roved over her.

She had on a cotton dance frock figured in pale green

with a plain white inset bodice and lining to the redingote-style skirt. Little cape sleeves made it cool and comfortable. She had caught back her shoulder-length hair whose chestnut lights were bleached a little now with long days at sea, and had tied the turned-under ends with a gauzy length of pale green. She wore mother-of-pearl earrings at her tiny ears and the shell beads Struan had bought her at the ship's side were twisted twice round her creamy throat and fell in a knot on the tight bodice. In this light her eyes were more green than hazel. Perhaps it was right that this competition for her company did something for her ego. She felt serene, confident.

Then Struan said to the pair of them, 'Oh, here's Donal coming now. He's so tall you can see him over everyone's heads.'

The clustering, talking crowds parted a little and they could see Donal was ushering someone ahead of him, a girl, also tall, who moved with fluid grace, whose dress looked simplicity itself, but costly simplicity. It was the colour of an oyster shell, faintly flushed, as she moved, with shot-silk pink, and her black hair, parted in the middle, had a pearl bandeau across it. There were pearl bubbles at her ears. She looked cool, delightfully groomed.

'Good heavens!' muttered Struan. 'Now how in the devil did *she* get here? And with Donal already! It beats cockfighting. I thought she was going back by air.'

Romayne!

Something leapt in Maria's heart for a joyous moment. He wasn't pleased to see Romayne on board. She hardly had time to analyse her reactions, because the next moment the elegant pair were upon them.

Donal said, rather ill at ease, Maria thought, 'Look what I found waiting on board when I got back from my trip round the island.'

Romayne said clearly, every word dropping with splintering force into the quiet pool of Maria's day-long happiness, 'Oh, but it's no surprise to Struan really, Donal. He begged me to move heaven and earth to get on board this ship ... even if Papeete was my last hope. At least we've ten days or so left before landfall.'

Perhaps Maria only imagined the succeeding silence lasted longer than it should have done. She wouldn't look at Struan. Why in the world should he have pretended it was such a surprise, if he'd asked her to make the effort? Surely no man his age need fear a great-aunt's disapproval so much?

Oddly, it was Alberta who broke the silence, saving the situation. 'Well, you've picked the best part of the trip. The Atlantic is rarely the better in a seaworthy fashion, though it treated us well this time.'

Struan, recovering, leaned forward and kissed Romayne lightly on the cheek she proffered. 'When I joined her at Cristobal I heard there was a full complement aboard, so I thought you'd missed out. Otherwise I'd have enquired and arrived back early. This is delightful, Romayne. I can't believe my incredible luck.'

His incredible luck! Maria would have given something to know what Alberta was thinking, and if later she might say something sharp to her secretive nephew? But what odds? It mustn't matter to Maria Willoughby. But just imagine. He'd been scathing about the way she and Donal had protected themselves from the importunities of shipboard life.

She turned a little, laying a hand on Donal's arm. 'I was just waiting till you appeared, to go in search of something long and cool. Denise and Jo are over there, shall we join them? Alberta, Jo has saved up some questions for you ... I met him when I went for my mail.'

Donal looked relieved, she thought. He had probably been wondering how he could leave this newly reunited pair to themselves without being too obvious about it. As she turned, with Donal, she caught a look that passed between Romayne and Struan. An odd look, and on his side, not a glad one. Why?

The sense of strain and air of slight deception stayed with them. They weren't a kindred group any more. Fortunately, Romayne couldn't be accommodated at their table. At Cristobal Struan had been fitted into theirs as, with

Denise and Jo, they had been five and it was a table for six.

Alberta said, under cover of chat at the bar, 'Mind, Maria, don't get all carried away and offer to let Romayne sit at your table in your stead. You're my companion and I need you.'

Maria's dimple appeared and her eyes flashed mischief. 'Do you now, Alberta Jensen? For what, might I ask?'

There was an answering gleam from the shrewd grey eyes. 'For moral support, not as a physical crutch. What game she and Struan are playing I know not, but I'll further no schemes of theirs.'

Schemes? Then Alberta hadn't missed that first bid of Struan's to pretend he'd not known Romayne might appear at Papeete, a bid that had been wiped next moment by Romayne giving it away.

Alberta wasn't one to let things go unremarked upon, but Maria wished she'd waited till she had Struan to herself. The chance came all too soon when Donal called Romayne away to be introduced to someone only too eager to get acquainted with so beautiful a newcomer.

Alberta said drily, 'And now perhaps you'll tell me, Struan, why you made out Romayne turning up was a complete surprise to you? She scuttled you the next moment, didn't she? What was there to be so secretive about? Just because I don't favour you getting involved with her it doesn't mean she can't please herself about how she travels home.'

Maria wished herself at the other end of the ship. She must think of an excuse to vanish. Struan said impatiently, 'Oh, Aunt, I think you took me up wrongly. It could be I'd known she was going to try to join us somewhere but didn't mention it because you go off half-cocked at the very sound of her name and why bother when it was so uncertain? It's not her fault she's her mother's daughter and she's not tarred with the same brush really. Once we got past Balboa and she hadn't let me know, I could have thought she wasn't going to make it so wondered how the devil she'd wangled it. *That* was the surprise.'

'Was it? I could have sworn you tried to convey a differ-

ent impression altogether, at first, but let it go. But it's
absurd to say she's not like her mother. She's exactly like
her—history repeated itself, even if she didn't leave it as
long as her mother and jilt her man on the very eve of
the wedding.'

Struan turned to Maria and said softly, 'There's something you ought to know. Or you may put your foot in it.
The man Romayne was engaged to was Donal's young
brother. And there were extenuating circumstances. But
Donal's still sore about it. There are two sides to every
story. Romanye hasn't come out of it unscarred. Better by
far to admit she'd made a mistake than to carry on and perhaps end up as another statistic on the broken marriage
records. I'm going to ask you both to treat this thing as if
none of us knew anything about it. We've got nearly a
fortnight to go, cooped up together on this ship, so let's
make it as pleasant as possible. Maria, you could help. I'd
much rather Romayne hadn't said anything, but I couldn't
have let her down in front of Donal. He and I were very
good friends. I don't want any coolness between us now.
You could make it a foursome if——'

The dryness still rasped Alberta's voice. 'You want
Maria to cover up for you. You wouldn't like Donal McFie
to think she ditched his young brother for you. It could
look like that, both of you in England, both of you returning at the same time. *Did* Romayne ditch Alastair for
you? I never suspected it at the time. *Did* she?'

'Oh, hell!' said Struan Mandeville between his teeth,
keeping his voice low despite its intensity. 'It's bad enough
without you thinking that. She did *not*. She's made a con-
fidante of me. I just met up with her again in Britain. You
know he comes up to Hawkes Bay sometimes, though most
of the time he's in Wellington. I meet him on that sheep-
meat committee I go to down there—I've always stayed
overnight at his mother's place and it could make it
darned awkward to have feeling between the families. I
thought——' he looked at Maria again with a raised brow.

His aunt guffawed—no other word for it. 'Struan, it's
just as well we're in the middle of a seething crowd, or for
sure you'd get your ears boxed! What girl wants to be used

as a smoke-screen? A fine compliment!'

He said savagely, 'You're putting words in my mouth. Yet I suppose I am using her as a smoke-screen. How about it, Maria? You're a good sport ... you agreed with Donal to protect each other from the amorous intentions of other males and females on the boat-deck ... how about some protection for me? Does that appeal to your sporting instincts, or did you fancy it only with Donal?'

Maria kept her colour down by a tremendous effort. He'd never know the fury that was threatening to consume her. She smiled coolly. 'It sounds to me as if *Donal* is more than ever in need of protection. It's a great pity Romayne ever came on this cruise. I can't expect *you* to feel that, of course, but I admire Donal for feeling so deeply for his young brother that he still resents him having been left in the lurch. Yes, I agree it *was* better than risking an unhappy marriage, but it's a great pity for Donal that she turned up here. And now he feels it's going to spoil a long friendship for him. So yes, I'll do it, *for his sake*. I'm not in the least offended. I don't need to be seeing *my* feelings are not involved. Okay, I'll play up to you.'

She expected Alberta to be scathing, so was distinctly surprised when she said, 'Cheers ... the first sensible thing I've heard. Watch it ... Donal and Romayne are approaching.'

Alberta was nothing if not thorough. She said to Romayne, 'I think the latter half of this voyage is going to be much more pleasant than the earlier weeks. How much nicer to be in a group of old friends than among a lot of strangers. It was so dull for Maria, crossing the Atlantic knowing Struan couldn't join us.'

A strange look crossed Romayne's face. Was it dismay? Maria had the sense of being caught up into something against her will. Lives could get so tangled, misunderstandings created. It had her puzzled anyway. First he'd seemed genuinely surprised, then he had played up to Romayne in possibly chivalrous fashion, then later he must have regretted this lest it threaten the friendship between him and Donal. But there'd been a sense of strain there even before

Romayne arrived. Maria gave it up. But she wouldn't see a kindly brother like Donal hurt any more by this pair. Deeper than that into her feelings she would not probe, wouldn't analyse why it hurt her so much to find Struan Mandeville less than above board. But she'd play it along.

Oh, how glad she'd be to get to Auckland, then to Hawkes Bay. After all, the real reason why she'd accepted this trip was because it could give her the chance of finding her father's old home. It could be in the Hawkes Bay Province, but also it might happen that when she finally got hold of a very detailed map of New Zealand, she might find other bays that ended as had that torn-off caption under its picture. You never knew, if she did find that home and her relations, they might have had word of him. There still might be a chance that he might have made good, made amends to them, if never to his ex-wife and daughter who, for him, hadn't even a name. A forlorn hope, yet hope was an irresistible emotion in most people's lives. She could live with hope till her search was ended.

She managed to disguise her feelings very well. None was so gay as she in the delightful dancing that followed the Tahitian dinner. Surprisingly Alberta Jensen was a very good dancer, and apart from Donal and Struan who knew it and took her up, she didn't lack partners among the older men aboard. And it *was* fun being part of a young foursome. The music was dreamy, the setting idyllic, the ship sailed serenely on, almost drifting on a dark, gentle sea that reflected the golden stars above. What was it about the tropics that made them shine more golden than silver?

Presently the moon made a pale track across the sable waters, and Maria found herself being steered away, most adroitly, from the big dance-floor to the deck, by Donal.

He found them a secluded seat, sat in silence for a few moments, then said, 'Maria, would you give me some honest answers to something that's been bothering me ever since I stepped on board and ran into Romayne? What's it all about? And where do you fit into the picture?'

Her heart thudded unpleasantly. What could she answer? Would she blunder and make things worse for everyone?

'I don't really know Romayne very much at all,' she told him. 'You've realised I'm really a paid companion to Alberta. She was staying in a guesthouse next to us. I'd just lost my mother and hadn't taken up a hospital post again, or continued with case-nursing, and I've always had a yen to see New Zealand because I was born there and spent the first few months of my life in Dunedin. So Alberta suggested I accompany her ... she had a diabetic upset flying out ... and spend three months with her at Amber Knoll.'

'Did she suggest it, or did Struan?'

Maria decided to sound a little coy, hesitated, said, 'Well, I forget whose idea it was in the first place.'

She could hear the smile in Donal's voice. 'I expect Struan did ... I don't blame him. Maria, we got into the way of protecting each other, let me say just this to you. Don't let Romayne Averell put any doubts of Struan into your mind. I think—in fact I'm almost sure—Struan didn't know she was coming on board, but he's a chivalrous sort of guy and didn't like to slap her down when he said that. I think she did it deliberately to make mischief between you. She's a man-eater—it runs in the family. If she suggested coming aboard when he said he wasn't going back by air after all, I think he probably found this conference in the States a godsend. He probably thought she hadn't a show of getting on, especially when he knew he was getting the last available berth from Cristobal. In vulgar terms, I think she's trying to get her hooks into Struan and he's far too good a chap for her, so just don't let her make mischief. She practically ruined one man's life, or would have if he'd not had it in him to make a comeback. I'll take Romayne's mind off Struan for a bit.'

At that moment Donal turned his head, said, 'Ah, here they come. I think Struan's getting a bit uneasy about the length of time we've been missing. Maybe he doesn't trust you in the moonlight on the blue Pacific. Leave it to me.'

Struan said, 'Ah, it's cooler out here. Were you finding it too hot and energetic, Maria?'

Donal said, 'She was, but I could dance all night, I love the heat. So do you, Romayne, being used to Hawkes Bay summers ... let's go and dance the night hours away.' He whirled her round and Maria and Struan were left looking at each other.

He said sarcastically, 'Well, I must say you're doing a great job of co-operation ... dallying on the boat-deck in the moonlight with Donal wasn't precisely what I had in mind. You're supposed to be giving Donal McFie the idea that you and I are falling for each other, remember?'

Maria turned her back on that moon and looked up at him, leaning over the back of the seat, glowering. She lifted her chin, said scornfully, 'Struan, you've got your wires crossed. I've just done a very good job for you and Romayne. Donal brought me out here not to dally but to ask me what the situation was, and where I came into the picture. And even though deception isn't in my line, I allowed him to think it was possibly more your idea than Alberta's that I spend three months at Amber Knoll. I was so convincing he even warned me I was not to let Romayne make mischief between us. So I'm helping preserve your friendship, and if I can do any better than that, tell me and I'll improve my tactics!'

He said, 'You beauty! I grovel.' He looked down on her and she thought his look was almost tender (Don't be silly, Maria, it's merely approving), then he gave a quick look behind. A couple were approaching. He came round, slid an arm about her shoulders as he sat down, she looked up startled, saw his mouth quirk up at the corners, and heard him say, 'I'll improve the shining hour myself. Here they come ... this should make them retreat....' His mouth came down on hers. Maria had a moment of wild wishing that this was for real. He held her too close for her to struggle and she dared not anyway. Once you embarked on a deception like this you were committed. She told herself she was doing this for Donal's sake and stayed in the circle of his arms.

He lifted his head about two inches and said in a laughing whisper, 'Have they beaten a discreet retreat?'

She said, her breath warm against his lips, on a fragment of sound, 'I don't know ... I can't see ... you're so much taller than I am, idiot!'

His laugh was low. 'Then don't move.' He brushed his lips lightly over hers this time, moved them to the line of her chin, then put his face against hers, just holding her.

Maria told herself despisingly that this then was what was supposed to be evanescent, the enchantment of moonlight in a floating irresponsible world, an artificial one. Something that was born of gossamer clouds and starlight, tropical breezes, sex appeal ... in an existence where no tasks filled your day, no duties kept you from making a fool of yourself.

She turned her face a little and was embarrassed to find her lips brushing against his. He said, 'Oh, very nice, Maria, you're a good little sport.'

She choked. 'A good sport! ... I was trying to whisper to you that I don't think anyone's there now, and I'm practically sure it wasn't Donal and Romayne. Why should they come back so soon? So you needn't carry on with this nonsense.' That made her feel a whole heap better.

He looked at her with mock anger. She could see the teasing light in those dark blue eyes between the bleached lashes. 'Nonsense? How can you spoil a moment like that? I found it enchanting and thought you might have too! Come on, now, didn't you get something out of it?'

She said drily, 'If I hadn't known what was behind it, I might have done, but I'm not a girl of eighteen, you know, ready to believe all men say. I'm twenty-five—and quite well balanced.'

He laughed in the most maddening fashion. 'I believe you hold it against me that I once thought you were going along with my aunt's never-ending matchmaking. Well, I suppose any girl would resent that. I was a duffer. Why didn't you—right now—utter angrily that I ought to remember you and your stepbrother's wife's brother have an attachment?'

She was struck dumb. She'd forgotten about that.

He said, 'Why don't you answer me, Maria? Shall I tell you why? ... Because that attachment simply doesn't exist. Come clean, it doesn't, does it?'

'How did you know?'

He chuckled. 'Because when we were seeing you off at Southampton, Merle and Rod asked me to call on them some time if I was over their way. I did, and it so happened Merle's brother was there too, *with his wife*. I realised you'd been having me on.'

She said defensively, 'I wouldn't have if you hadn't assumed it yourself. I just said what I'd tell Alberta if she tried any matchmaking with us, and you took me seriously. I thought it a good idea to let you go on thinking it.'

'Why?'

'Because no girl likes to think a man might get the idea she was chasing him. It was sheerly a defence mechanism that made me glad you'd got that idea.'

'So was it also defence mechanism that made you call this very enjoyable episode nonsense?'

Maria went to stand up. 'This is nonsense too ... talking like this.' But she hadn't a hope of freeing herself. She put a hand against his chest. That too was unavailing. She couldn't move him further away. She said crossly, like a child, 'Struan, if you kiss me again I'll—I'll——'

'You'll what? Scream? Oh, think what a scandal that would cause!'

'No, I wouldn't scream ... I'll bite you!'

His laughter was irresistible, bubbling up within him. 'Oh, Maria, you'll be the death of me! Besides....' his mouth came down on hers, effectively drowning out any more protests. When he lifted his head she said, 'Besides *what*?'

'I don't need to finish that. It was besides, I wouldn't let you, and I didn't, did I? What man would let a girl stop him kissing her?'

'A chivalrous man,' she said bitterly.

He disregarded that, said, 'Anyway, wouldn't you rather be here than on that hot dance floor?'

She looked up at him, 'Yes, if we could just sit and talk, Struan Mandeville.'

'I could think of better things to do, but I'll settle for less if that's what you really want. There are things I'd like to ask.'

She drew back a little, why she didn't know. Except that the knowledge that she might have a family in the Hawkes Bay Province made her a little guilty. Then she said sturdily, 'Such as?'

'Such as asking if you've ever been in love ... seriously?'

She laughed, relaxing. 'Yes. I was fourteen. Is there anything more serious than calf-love? He was my music-teacher and all of thirty-three. I was sure he adored me, was waiting for me to grow up. Quite suddenly he married the sports mistress at my high school. I was blighted for two whole terms.'

He laughed. 'Oh, Maria, you're so unexpected! But since then ... how many others have fluttered your pulses? Come on, don't tell me you've had no other fancies?'

'They stayed at that, the pulse-fluttering. It's a different thing from finding the one you'd like to spend the rest of your life with. And when you get to twenty-five you're more discriminating. It's so fatally easy to make a mistake.'

His arm about her shoulders tightened a little. 'You mean that because your mother had an unhappy first marriage, it has made you a little wary?'

'Perhaps. It does, doesn't it? It made me wary when I was nineteen. I saw every charmer as unstable as my father —quite unjustly, perhaps. Mother was just nineteen when she married my father.'

'But you haven't stayed disbelieving about love? About the real thing?'

'No, you see life in the raw in big hospitals, and in private cases, and you meet up with the idyllic side of life too, so I don't think I've any hang-ups.'

The moon, that had gone behind a bar of cloud, suddenly freed itself and shone right across them so that looking up she could see it glinting silver on those strawy brows and lashes. He seemed very intent.

'I rather like that idea. I'd never thought there could be an idyllic side to hospital life.'

'There is,' she assured him. 'Sheer devotion sometimes. Devotion that's tried and tested. There's a line of Stephen Phillips' that I like tremendously, he calls it :

' "Beautiful friendship, tried by sun and wind, durable from the daily dust of life."

'In hospital I once saw a man and woman taking fare-well of each other after fifty years of wedded life. I'm not so silly as to think it had been half a century of bliss—how cloying that would be—but it was so *real*, that fare-well. I had the oddest sensation that I actually envied that woman who was slipping out of life. I even thought that if it was given to all to have so perfect a moment, who could be afraid of death?'

She was silent, remembering. Then Struan said, 'Yes?'

'They were quite ordinary people, but articulate. He'd been an engine-driver, she'd been in a factory. They'd never had much money, but she said none of the highlights of life had cheated her. We'd had her in for months, and we enjoyed hearing her talk. They'd had a week-long honeymoon in a little stone cottage on the Isle of Mull. Getting to know each other in a new way, she said, and loving every memory of that week, even though they'd had to draw water from a well and cook on an open fire. She'd had three children, each one loved and wanted. It had always been a struggle financially, but they now owned their own house and managed comfortably on the pension. "And when I'm gone," she said, "the children are all near enough to see to their father. One of them will call in on him every day."

'She told us she'd carried red roses at her wedding, tied in a knot with white heather and a bow of tartan ribbon. She'd had a white dress and veil but couldn't abide every-thing white. As she put it, "I aye liked a splash of colour." Her Alex was sitting by her the night she died. Jessie was weak, but her mind was clear. I'd come in silently with something to moisten her lips, but I paused, unseen, in the doorway. He put his hand in his pocket and drew some-thing out, took her hand, opened it, and closed it over what we found later was a bit of red tartan ribbon and some dried heather. We left it there. I heard him say, "I thought you'd like to take this with you, lass, into that other world."

'I managed to melt away backwards without a rustle and by sheer will-power stayed dry-eyed. Because shortly afterwards he came in search of me to say she'd gone.'

There was a silence between those two people on the boat-deck. Then Struan's thumb moved over the back of Maria's hand. Odd how comforting such a fleeting touch could be.

He said slowly, 'Yes, an idyll isn't only composed of the ingredients we usually associate with that word ... moonlight and roses; sunlit meadows and daffodils under the trees at Heronshaw ... and *young* love.'

She didn't know how much longer they sat there, but presently Donal and Romayne came by, looking for them. Romayne's idea, Maria was sure. Romayne said, 'That sumptuous supper is on. Pity to miss it, you two. That is, if you've done murmuring sweet nothings in each other's ears.'

They came to their feet, laughing. 'What was that laugh supposed to mean?' asked Romayne, but she asked it nicely.

Struan said, 'Because we've been talking of death. Death in hospital wards, as seen by Maria. Sounds a grisly subject for a tropical night under a tropical moon, but somehow it wasn't.'

'No subject is incongruous handled properly,' said Donal.

Then Romayne said a strange thing. 'That's something I don't know about, handling subjects the right way, at the right time, to suit the right mood.'

Suddenly Struan seemed sorry for her. He gave a little laugh, said, 'We're getting in too deep for this time of night and my inner man is protesting. Lead me to that supper, Donal!'

Two dances after supper and they were all ready for bed, even Alberta, who was a stop-up. Romayne's single cabin was only four along from theirs. Maria was into her dressing-gown when she noticed her evening bag and remembered Romayne had asked her to put her filmy pink evening scarf into it. The night had been so still she'd not needed to tie anything on her hair, on deck. Romayne wouldn't be in bed yet. She slipped along, lifted her hand to tap lightly on her door, then arrested the movement.

A faint sound of sobbing was coming from inside. Maria felt appalled. All her training urged her to proffer help whenever need manifested itself, but you dared not intrude on this.

What could it be? She stole back, said goodnight to Alberta, went into the inner cabin, and stayed awake a long time.

Had this meeting with Donal McFie roused in Romayne regrets for the way she had treated his young brother, or even stirred up longings for the clock to be turned back and that engagement not broken? Or was she so in love with Struan Mandeville that even knowing Struan was turning his attentions to Maria to stop Donal from thinking his friend had been the cause of that rupture upset the girl when they had spent so long together on that deserted deck?

Maria felt a great distaste for the whole thing sweep over her, and something else too . . . the knowledge that in her heart she wished it hadn't been a stupid masquerade, but true!

At last she drifted off to sleep, lulled by the surging on of the great liner, her last thought that she would be glad when the day of landfall and the everyday business of living would be upon them.

CHAPTER FOUR

ROMAYNE seemed so bright next morning, Maria was inclined to think she'd imagined the sobbing. But even if it was for real, it could have been nothing more than a nostalgic mood of the moment.

The faint air of strain between the two men had vanished and day by day across the Pacific, Donal seemed to treat Romayne with more respect. He listened to her opinions, even seemed to be drawing her out, introduced deeper topics, resulting from the news bulletins they listened to each day in their newspaperless world of marine isolation.

She said so to Struan as they sunbathed by the pool days later, watching Romayne and Donal engaged in a game of water polo with some others.

Struan nodded. 'He thought she was a lightweight who didn't care tuppence that his young brother was hurt. She did seem like that at the time, living on the surface. Her mother brought her up to a butterfly existence, of course, but with Romayne it's only a veneer. She's more like her father than most people suspect. You've put the final touches on, Maria.'

She turned an astonished face to his. '*I* have? But how?'

'That first night on the boat-deck. We told Romayne and Donal we'd been talking about death, and Donal said no subject was incongruous handled properly. Romayne admitted to an inadequate feeling, and I saw Donal look at her for the very first time with respect. It was as if he suddenly realised there was more to her. It might be just a step from that to give her credit for courage in breaking that engagement. That would make it easier all round.'

'For whom?'

'For us all.'

'Yes, I suppose so. Oh, do you mean that if he thought she'd acted from the best of motives, it might not make for strain between you and Donal?'

'Partly that. I thought it was most unfortunate that because she didn't want Donal to think she'd come on board because of him, she gave him the impression that she'd done it to be near me. It only served to make him think she was never without some man in tow.'

'Struan ... is it possible she came on board because of *him*?' she asked.

'That *is* why. When we were leaving the ship's side at Southampton, we looked back and she got the most awful shock to see Donal standing at the rail. I don't think he saw her. She was upset. She'd heard he was in England, and had hoped she might meet him, and perhaps make a better impression on him—that he mightn't see her only as the girl who broke her engagement to his brother, mighty near the wedding. He was to be Alastair's best man and was so concerned about his brother that he had a showdown with Romayne, really let fly at her. She told me she didn't like the picture of herself he presented to her and would have welcomed an opportunity to wipe it from his mind. I expect he said things in his anger he shouldn't have done. We all do when we lose our cool.'

Maria said, 'Why is it so important to her ... to display another image to him? If Alastair is out of her life what can it matter?'

'Can't you guess? Haven't you rumbled it?' Their glances met and held. 'I don't want to say too much at this stage, Maria. It's a delicate situation. Donal would resent anything happening too soon. We'll keep playing it as a foursome—makes it easier.'

She managed to agree, then said lightly, 'I think that group at the rail have spotted some more dolphins. Want to go to see?'

He shook his head lazily. 'Nope. The sun's too warm and that little breeze too delightful to move. Besides, the view right in my line of vision beats any dolphin display hollow.' His audacious eye roved over the coral bikini concealing very little of her honey-tan skin. 'Though I think you should move over here a little. It would be a pity to get burnt.' His arm came out to draw her a little more into the shade. Her cheek was against his shoulder. It felt right, natural, and disturbing. What a pity there had to be these undercurrents!

She closed her eyes against the dazzle of the sun. He could mean only one thing. They didn't want Romayne flaunting another romance too soon, another conquest. Especially awkward in the confines of a ship. Back in New Zealand Donal lived two hundred miles from Heronshaw. Romayne's father's estate was only about ten miles away. But no matter when they came out into the open it was bound to make a coolness between Donal and Struan.

Romayne and Donal came up, dripping wet, and dropped on to their towels spread on the deck. Presently Donal padded off, came back with long cool drinks. Faintly from the Fijian Lounge came sounds of soft music. This was the

pre-lunch music hour. Maria wished they'd not been playing just that . . . it was wistful, haunting. 'Why did you make
me love you . . . only to say goodbye?'

Because that was what it added up to. She might just as
well be honest. In spite of herself she loved Struan, and
when her three months at Heronshaw were over, she
would move out of his life and in time when Donal's young
brother had got over his heartbreak, Struan would be
able to court Romayne without Donal resenting it quite so
much.

Just as they drained their glasses, a steward appeared at
Donal's elbow and proffered a radio-telegram on a tray.
They all sat up, concerned, which was natural on board
ship, when news was relayed like this.

He paused after he'd read it, looking down on it, which
did nothing for them, then he said with a dry inflection in
his voice, 'Relax, everyone. It's not bad news, it's from
my brother. Listen: "Don't delay in Auckland. Wedding
is advanced a week. I won't have anyone but you for best
man, so fly down. See you soon, Alastair." He looked up,
directly into Romayne's eyes, startlingly blue against that
black straight hair, said, 'How about that?'

Her cheeks had lost all colour, her lips were parted. She
looked eager as she said, 'Alastair? He's met someone else?
Oh, how glad I am, how glad!'

Donal's brows were down, his lips a thin line. 'Glad for
who? For Alastair? For yourself? Glad you need no
longer suffer remorse? This leaves you free to play the
field again, doesn't it, and know no guilt?' He uttered a
short laugh. It had no mirth in it. 'Not that you need feel
that way. It was the best thing you ever did . . . for my
brother. Jeannie is a girl of a different calibre.'

Maria and Struan seemed unable to move or speak.
Romayne uttered a small stricken sound, instantly sup-
pressed. Then they saw her pull herself together. Strangely,
it was Donal who looked suddenly as if he didn't quite
know where to go from there.

Romayne said, 'I don't expect you to believe it, but my
gladness *was* for Alastair. I know as well as you do that
I wasn't the one for him. Not that I'm hypocrite enough to

pretend it was for his sake I broke it off. I'll tell you the truth now, Donal. I broke it off because I realised I loved someone else. These things do happen. I wasn't prepared to marry Alastair and cheat him. I knew that this man, in all probability, would never look my way, so I wasn't weighing up chances. I just knew I couldn't go through with that marriage.

'But you've never credited me with any decent feelings at all. Though the last few days I was beginning to think you might. Foolish me! I even thought that some day your parents might forgive me. I loved your parents. But now I just want you to be out of my sight and mind. Enjoy yourself with Struan and Maria. I can amuse myself for the few days left remaining. Thank heaven I'm not at your table. Don't you three quarrel over this,' she added. 'I don't want to be blamed for breaking up any other relationship. Goodbye.'

At that Struan managed to heave himself out of his deck-chair and made a lunge at her, grasping her elbow in a hold that couldn't be broken. 'Oh, no, Romayne. *You* won't be blamed—*Donal* will. Maria, let's get going ... with Romayne. You'd better take a long hard look at yourself, Donal. Decide if you like what you see. You've carried bitterness too far, and anyway, no third person ever knows all that causes a couple to split up. Get going, girls.'

As in a dream he propelled them along. 'Go down to Romayne's cabin, and let's try to pull ourselves together.'

Down there they were at a loss, not knowing what to say or do next. Finally Maria said, 'Look, I'll go along to my cabin and get dressed. I'll leave you two to it.'

Romayne put out a hand and restrained her, her voice most surprisingly calm. 'No, don't, Maria. That was rather —horrible—but quite forgivable. He's very fond of Alastair. He's got something out of his system. He'd resented my ditching his brother very much, and it lasted longer than I'd dreamed it would, otherwise he'd have told me before this that Alastair was engaged and soon to be married. He didn't want me to stop feeling remorse. In a way, it's good to meet up with a brother so concerned.' She looked reflective, added:

'It's a strange thing, but it's done something for me too. I looked on Donal as so upright and honourable, so ethical. But he's stooped to being vindictive and now I can see he's just like us all, capable of mean actions and thoughts. Most of the time he's strong enough to resist them, but when he cools off maybe he'll think less hardly of me because he's slipped in his own esteem. Only I'm sorry it's made a rift between you and Donal, Struan. I can only hope it will come right in time.'

Struan shrugged. 'At the moment I'm past caring. I can think only of you. You were magnificent—not petty at all. And you didn't resort to tears. I really would have liked to bawl Donal out, but there were too many people too near. Most of them were too intent on the larking in the pool to notice, though. But I didn't need to do a thing. *You* were dignified and very cool. Well, I guess we've just got to carry on.'

'I'm sorry it'll make the last few days so uncomfortable,' said Romayne. 'Maria, this should have been the trip of a lifetime for you, not all snarled up with a situation like this. I ought never to have come aboard.'

Maria put out a hand. 'Romayne, we've got to take life as it comes. I admired you too. I'm glad you live in Hawkes Bay, even though you're a few miles away. I feel—perhaps particularly because of what happened this morning—that we've made strides in our friendship. New Zealand is very much an unknown quantity to me. Even the spot where I was born is hundreds of miles away and in another island. It'll be nice to have someone I know and like, within reach.'

Struan gave her a grateful look. 'Now I'm going to put Aunt Alberta in the picture. Romayne, I'll have to tell her exactly what was said. Do you mind?'

'No, she's been surprisingly nice to me the last few days.'

'That's because she's got to know you as you really are, not just as Lottie Averell's daughter, following in her mother's footsteps. You can't fool Aunt Alberta. She was bound to come to like you. I'll go to find her. Meanwhile, you girls get dressed.'

Maria's thoughts were chaotic. This could speed up the

relationship between Struan and Romayne. They wouldn't need to walk warily now there was a definite rift between the two men. She dressed and went back to Romayne's cabin, and as she opened the door she saw Alberta and Struan coming.

Alberta didn't seem in the least embarrassed. She said, 'Well, gal, you had guts, I'll say that for you. It's not easy to take a remark like that. It may have cleared the air, of course, and if Alastair's getting married, by the time Donal's been best man to him and seen them settled down, he'll probably feel he made a deal of fuss about nothing. And while we're on the subject, I'm sorry I sat in judgment on you myself. I was sure it was just a case of history repeating itself. That's not tactful either. No gal likes to hear her mother called down, but I don't know how to make amends without mentioning it. I daresay she was just young and foolish. So you're very welcome any time at Amber Knoll. This other thing will die. Right . . . there's the lunch gong. Come along, all of you.'

Maria was somewhat ashamed of her own thoughts. Romayne had been through a gruelling experience, yet she couldn't help envying her. It had cleared the way for her to become a frequent visitor to Struan's home and it was evident that Struan now put Romayne's peace of mind before his friendship with Donal, which was as it should be. But it left Maria out in the cold.

They plunged into shipboard activities with feverish enthusiasm, determined Romayne should have no time to mope. Not that she appeared in much danger of that. They saw Donal in the company of other people, mostly. That very day of the showdown, he'd come to Struan, said curtly, 'I've arranged for Romayne to sit at your table in my place.' Struan even more curtly said, 'Very sensible.'

In all Maria, and, she supposed, everyone else, was glad when time came to go to the luggage-room and rearrange their things, because it meant disembarkation was near. She wanted a horizon broken with hills and trees again instead of a purple line where sea and sky met; instead of a salt-tanged breeze she longed for the perfumes of a spring garden; instead of cabin walls that enclosed you in too small a space, she craved the wider walls of a home; instead of planking on a deck that heaved and dipped occasionally, it would be wonderful to find grass beneath her feet and tree-lined paths dappled with sunshine and leaf shadows.

The Landfall dinner and dance came, the last night on board, and next morning they woke to see islands dotted about and a growing coastline; they were almost within Waitemata Harbour, which meant water as smooth as the surface of obsidian ... and it was. It was a dream of a day. Here was a lovely shimmering city, spread round scores of bays, and in the centre of its blue waters, the symmetrical island of Rangitoto. Among the high-rise buildings rose small hills that were the cones of extinct volcanoes from the long ago, mostly clothed with green bush on their lower slopes. Even from here they could see it was semi-tropical, with houses with multi-coloured roofs rising from gardens clustered with giant tree-ferns and exotic-looking palms.

They came face to face with Donal just before disembarking and were glad Aunt Alberta was just with them. She boomed, 'Well, we might as well say goodbye now, Donal. I expect you're getting a plane immediately. Struan has a car booked for us. We'd get home quicker flying, but we want to show Maria the lie of the land, the contours of hills and mountains ... ten to one if we flew, we'd just look down on a floor of cloud.'

He nodded. 'Good idea. I wish the four of you a very pleasant journey, and happy reunions.'

Struan said, 'Oh, Romayne isn't going straight home. She wants to see her sister in Takapuna first, for a few days.'

Donal gave them a collective word of farewell, but Romayne wasn't having any of that. She said calmly, 'I do hope you'll give Alastair my sincere wishes for his future happiness, Donal. That comes from the heart. It would seem out of place to send a wire to the reception, but I'd like you to be big enough to pass that on and to tell your mother and father the same. Goodbye.'

Soon they were away from the immense harbour and sprawling city with its shining silver span of bridge that curved over the waters to link the communities on either side, and travelled south to stay at Cambridge as the day was, by now, far spent after their drive round the water-front and city. Aunt Alberta was determined Maria's first sight of Hawkes Bay should be by daylight, not in the featureless dark, so they turned in at a motel, delightfully furnished in the Colonial style, where they could cook their own evening meal, and relax in privacy after so long in the ship dining-room.

They travelled from early morning the next day, through the dewy pastures of the dairyland of the Waikato province, threaded through by the Waikato River, the longest one in New Zealand, running for two hundred and twenty miles from where it rose in the snows and ice-fields of the Tongariro National park, Struan told Maria, though it was known as the Tongariro River then, into the immensity of Lake Taupo, and draining that lake over the spectacular Huka Falls before meandering through green and pleasant lands.

Maria exclaimed over the differences all the way, and the similarities too, delighted to see so many English trees she could recognise, though it seemed so strange to her that, as this was October, they weren't changing colour ... that the hawthorn hedges were rosy and pearly with blossom, in-stead of red with haws, that clematis was starring garden trellises with white and pink, and wistaria drooping purple plumes over arches and that some daffodils still lingered in sheltered spots. The snowdrops and violets were over, but rhododendrons and azaleas were patching farm and town gardens alike. 'I feel it ought to be golden-rod and asters and chrysanthemums.'

They saw a signpost for Rotorua, and half-heartedly offered to divert and show her the exciting thermal area for an hour or two if she wished. Maria laughed. 'Your faces would change if I accepted that noble offer, wouldn't they? We can come here from Napier some time, I guess. You're just raring to get home now, aren't you?'

They chuckled and agreed. She said, 'Besides, I'm dying to see Hawkes Bay.'

Struan said curiously, 'How come you got so keen on this area?' Alberta seemed interested in her answer too. -

Maria laughed. 'Oh, you know how it is, a name crops up again and again after you first hear it. I had a patient who came from there, once. I imagined, because of the Bay, of course, that it would be on the coast, but now I realise it could be inland. Such a funny name—Why-puck-something.'

They grinned. Struan said, 'Waipukurau, the-stream-where-the-mushrooms-grow, but it's believed it should be Waipukerau which means many floods. It's fifty or so miles south from us, and yes, inland. Was this patient returning to New Zealand? Will you want to visit her ... or him?'

'I might, some time, if convenient.' (It could provide an excuse for roaming, for looking for the towers of Camelot.)

They swept on past Wairakei, the-place-where-the-pools-were-used-as-mirrors, but nowadays the hot pools were harnessed to geo-thermal power that occasionally billowed great clouds of steam across the road and notices warned drivers to be careful. Then they crested a hill to look down on an unbelievable expanse of water, Lake Taupo, the centre of the North Island, all two hundred and fifty square miles of it, with the Auckland–Wellington Highway skimming the shoreline.

Holiday cottages, bright with semi-tropical flowers and ferns, clustered the water's edge in the bays, scores of motels pointed to a huge tourist and holidaymakers' trade, and Struan said it was a trout-fisher's paradise. They lunched on takeaways Struan had bought on the way, sitting at the water's edge, watching small boats bobbing at the rim, and looking many miles over the water to where, at the far end, Mount Ruapehu, at times an active volcano, rose, its shoulders glittering with snow, against a cobalt sky.

As they drove off Struan said with a note of nostalgic satisfaction in his voice, 'The next turn left into the hills, and we're on the Taupo–Napier Highway, the road *home*. This used to be quite a risky road, but diversions and broadenings have made it a grand road now ... just two hours to Napier and even less than that to the Esk Valley. The most beautiful valley of all. Our place is almost to the junction with the road from Gisborne, but just before that you wind up to the top, and there it is, Heronshaw. We'll stop on the way at the Waipunga Lookout ... magnificent falls there, and you see them in the best way of all, slightly below you. It would be a pity to miss them.'

They passed the green enamelled bush of the Opepe Reserve that hid within it lonely graves, sad reminders of the ambush of a cavalry outpost a century before, dipped down huge hills, roared up the other sides, crossed and re-crossed rivers. Sometimes the landscape widened out giving glimpses of ranges that seemed everlasting, folding back in ridge after ridge against the sky, wild, untamed fastnesses where only deer and opossums and hunters roamed.

Then the landscape gave way to homesteads ringed and avenued with all manner of English trees.

'Ah, the beeches are coming into leaf,' said Struan. 'I love them best of all, the new and tender green of the young leaves. The beeches look so ancient till spring wakens them and then they seem just like infants.'

Maria knew a moment of enchantment. 'Oh, I like that. It reminds me of my mother. She always thought silver birches and larches looked much younger than their age. So many people have these thoughts but keep them to themselves. Which is a pity. I've always wondered why they speak of heroes as strong, *silent* men. I prefer them just as strong, but I'd rather have a talkative extrovert type, myself.'

Alberta laughed. 'Struan was reared by my sister-in-law, and nobody brought up in Johanna's household had a chance of being an introvert. Johanna just bubbles over with happiness and somehow draws out everyone else to be the same. Just as well she did have that nature, it helped her overcome a lot of sadness.'

'Deed aye,' said Struan. Odd how a Scots phrase crept into his vocabulary now and then. The two of them lapsed into silence as if remembering the sadness that ought to have overwhelmed Johanna but hadn't. Then Alberta roused herself and repeated what Struan had said earlier, 'How fitting that is ... I mean your description of the beech leaves, Struan. The new and tender green. It takes me back many years. I had a small nephew, Maria, who had the most astoundingly sombre taste for poetry, far beyond his years. He loved Shakespeare at an early age. That reminded me of him. I can see and hear him now, looking absurdly young with his cowlick of hair sticking up and his knobbly little knees above his school socks, proclaiming grandly that bit from *Henry the Eighth*. So strange a choice for a little boy:

' "This is the state of man: today he puts forth
  The tender leaves of hope; tomorrow blossoms ..."
I won't go on, the rest of it's too sad for a day like this.'

Struan's hand left the wheel, patted Alberta's knee. Maria said, 'I can just see him with his knobbly knees and cowlick. You have a way with words, Alberta. I don't know that passage, but even if the rest is sad, I like that. The tender leaves of hope and tomorrow blossoming.'

Struan's voice came in, 'And that's something you only realise when you're older. When you're very young you don't believe—if you're in the depths of despair—that tomorrow will blossom. I remember Gran telling someone that and adding that the trouble is that only experience of life makes you realise that time heals. So the second time round perhaps frustrations are more bearable.'

'As Johanna knew so well. She's had frustrations a-plenty, but it's never soured her. Not even that she never saw small Blaise's tomorrow blossoming.'

Maria realised he must have died young. For a moment a strange wave of sorrow for Johanna and her little boy with the knobbly knees swept over her. But Johanna hadn't lived on, resenting that her son had been taken from her ... instead she and Athol Mandeville had become adoptive grandparents.

Suddenly Struan said, 'There seems to be an extra-ordinary lot of traffic on this section of the road today. Anybody would think they were going to a fire. And look at all these parked cars!' A bend further on, and a road running off into some deep ravines, caused him to glance quickly back down it. There was a gap in the dense forestry that clothed those hills to the north. They saw a clearing, well in, and a mass of other vehicles.

'Oh, they must be having some sort of field day there. I wonder what for? Can't be a tractor demonstration or crop-spreading. Perhaps it's some new spray done by hand. Oh, well, they'll tell us about it when we get home. I wonder if Grandfather and Ramsay wanted to be there. Not that they will be, unless they looked in on it earlier. They'll want to be ready with the red carpet and the fatted calf. I wonder how many times Gran has been down the drive to see if we're coming.

'Maria, the hills are more open now, you'll notice, and we're getting near the coastline, but you won't see the sea till we breast our hill. Then you'll get the whole sweep of the bay. By the way, though the province is called Hawkes Bay, which intrigued you for some reason, spelled with an "e"!—the Bay itself is just Hawke Bay, a large sweep of shore.'

Maria said quickly, 'Are we coming into the village?'

They were ... so tiny, just the necessary buildings, then on through paddocks where grape-vines were twined on wires, greening now with promise of a good season to come; they passed a tiny beautiful memorial church, where the family worshipped, she was told, more paddocks of young green corn grown for the canning factories, hills above them dotted with sheep, then at a yellow fingerpost that said Mandeville Road, they turned right and climbed steeply past prosperous-looking new houses that had a Canadian air in their cedar paint and white facings and wide patios. The houses thinned out as they climbed on, they turned left, took a dip, then a very steep incline, breasted the homestead hill where the road curved on to a lookout and as Struan brought the car to a stop, the whole wide scene burst upon Maria.

To the north-east, a terrific scimitar of coastline ended in great bluffs and a misty horizon rimmed with lilac against a peacock-green sea. A plume of thick white smoke piled in cottonwool whorls from the Whirinaki Paper Pulp Mills close to the shore; nearer at hand the sun turned the hull of a ship making into Napier Harbour into a dazzle-ment of blinding light, and to the south-east gleamed like the white cliffs of Dover, those of Cape Kidnappers where two centuries earlier the famous navigator Captain Cook had saved Taiata, the servant of the Raiatran chief and priest whom the *Endeavour* had taken aboard from Tahiti, from being kidnapped.

'And it's the home of the gannets, remember,' said Struan. 'That's *my* particular view. From my room, which is a sort of attic up top, I can stand at my window and see the sunrise come up over there. Even though the hills run-ning back inland from this arm of them are higher, there's no house built on any crest from which you can see just that. Then from my room at Amber Knoll looking west I can see the snows of the Kaiwekas.'

'Your room at Amber Knoll?' queried Maria.

Alberta said, 'He often comes to keep an old woman company. I'm not nervous, never have been, but at times I'd be gey lonely if Struan wasn't always bursting in and out.'

Maria told herself it was absurd to feel such a wave of gladness wash over her at this bit of news. She told herself the next moment that as Alberta wouldn't be lonely now with a companion, he wouldn't come, naturally.

The engine sprang to life again and they moved off, rounded a corner. 'Oh, the peaches are in blossom,' cried Alberta. 'The loveliest of welcomes.' They lined each side of the narrowing road, with a translucency of pink where the sun shone through their frail petals. Ahead of them were the gateposts of Heronshaw, with between them not wooden bars or wrought-iron scrolls, but, as was com-mon here, cattle-grids set in the metal of the roadway to prevent stock wandering out or in—great time-savers com-pared with gates.

'If it had been after school-time, Timothy and Chris-tabel would have been sitting on top of the gateposts. What a rattle these cattle-stops make! That's going to bring them all rushing out.'

But it didn't. The front door was standing open, it was true, but the whole place lacked movement and noise.

Struan grinned. 'They must be getting impervious to that din. We've stolen a march on them. I won't even pomp the horn, we'll sneak in and give them a surprise. They must be still setting the table or decorating the pavlova. Don't slam the car door, leave it swinging.'

They crept in, expecting to hear voices. Not a murmur reached them. 'Odd,' whispered Struan. He turned his head on one side, in a listening attitude as he reached the foot of the stairs. 'They must be up there. But it sounds as if not a soul is home. What an anti-climax!'

They had all cocked their ears. Then into the silence came a chilling sound ... an unmistakable groan—a groan that had a striving effort behind it, a forcing sound. Struan said, 'What in hell's that? My God, someone's tied up, I think! Gagged ...'

A second similar groan followed. Maria clutched Struan's arm as he went to bound up the stairway, 'No, Struan ... it must be Judith. I mean, that's someone having a baby ... but I can't hear anyone with her. Oh, but there must be—come on!'

Alberta was just behind them as they took the stairs two at a time. The sounds led them directly to the master bedroom. Judith was on the big bed; she'd obviously had little warning, but had flung back a beautiful quilt and thrown a travelling rug across it. As they stopped in the doorway, she had hold of the top bedpost, and was bearing down, determination to help the baby into the world etched on her blanched features. Struan said, 'Sis, oh, Sis, we're here. We'll help. Where are the others?'

'Oh, Struan—oh, Aunt, thank God! I was all right when they rushed off. They're along Ranley's Gully. There's been a plane crash beyond there. I'm not due for another month. Ohh! But this one's doing very well, I can manage. But I was worried because there are two, about what to do with the first one, while ... ah, here's another pain!'

Struan said quickly, 'Tell, us, Sis, have you got a doctor on the way? Did you have time to phone?'

'No, no warning. I just flung myself on the bed—but try to get one, only not our doctor because he's gone to the scene of the crash—so any doctor from Napier.'

Maria said, 'It looks to me as if it'll be all over soon, though call one just the same, Struan. It's all right, Judith, I'm a midwife. Draw in your breath a little, it's coming a bit fast ... Struan, the phone, Alberta, get me some old pillow-cases....'

Judith said, 'Struan, you must tell this strange doctor there are two. I'm thrilled ... I can get two for the trouble of one this way.'

Maria could have cheered—there was pluck for you! Struan was back in no time. 'Didn't get the first doctor I rang, but his receptionist is contacting one for us. I said I was needed here, had to get back to my sister. Don't mind me, Ju, after all I've brought plenty of lambs into the world, and I'll act under Sister Willoughby's instructions.'

That was masterly, it gave Judith a feeling that someone of professional status and knowledge was at hand. Judith, gasping with her effort, said, 'As long as the babies are all right, that's what matters. I'd hoped to carry them full-time, but they were admitting me to hospital tomorrow to keep an eye on me. But this way, I'll be home again in no time. Much nicer for the kids ... they get so disrupted, poor lambs... here goes for another effort....' And then the strain prevented further talk.

A small blond head had appeared, was ushered into the world. Maria experienced that moment of rapture and wonder that had never yet failed her as a new little life with all its potential came into sight. The symbolism of that tiny uncurling body had a touch of the miraculous.

'A perfect baby,' she said gloatingly. 'Small but perfect, and a boy.'

Judith gave a huge sigh of relief. 'My small Stuart,' she said. 'I so wanted another boy to call him after my brother.'

Maria wondered. Oh, Struan must be the Gaelic form of Stuart, she supposed. There was no time to comment. She went on fixing the baby up, working gently, but with speed, wiping its breathing passages free, laying him on the mother's breast for that first wonderful moment of contact ... oh, what lungs, she thought thankfully, and hoped the second baby would be as healthy.

Judith gave a giggle of pure mischief and perhaps relief.

'Oh, poor Ramsay! He's going to be as mad as a meat-axe. He wanted to be present at this birth, thinks it's a wonderful idea. He'll be very jealous of you, Struan.'

Struan grinned, 'I'd sure swop places with him right now! Maria, how long do you think the other one will take? I've known the time vary considerably with ewes.'

'Yes, it can. Judith will be able to tell soon. I don't think it will be long, seeing it started so suddenly. Now, let's get on with it. Alberta can take this one over. Just roll him up in that pillow-case. Freshly-ironed linen is marvellous. And the room's beautifully warm. We'll think about baby clothes later. I want him here where I can keep an eye on him. Just sit down in that chair with him, Alberta. Ah ... Judith, it's starting. Struan, in my yellow case in the car, are some white uniforms ... get me one, will you?'

In ten minutes an equally fine baby girl was being welcomed by her mother. Judith, wan but radiant, was saying, 'Two little blondies! The others were dark like Ramsay, Maria. Oh, Aunt Alberta, I'm so glad they're fair. This one will be Sara for my—for Sara.'

Maria said crisply, 'Now, Struan, you can make us all, and especially Judith, a large pot of tea. I think Judith and I will be through by then, and I'll have her comfortable. And we'll do something about the babies—listen to them, they're certainly vigorous! They aren't much premature, I'd think.'

'And my doctor would agree with you. He thought I was a bit out. Oh, I do hope they don't whisk me into Napier in the ambulance before Ramsay gets here. I'd love to see his face. The children ought to be here soon. They were taken to the Aquarium on Marine Parade today to see the man-eating fish. Alberta, aren't my babies just beautiful? And Gran was so used to twins with us, bringing us up from scratch, that she'll be a great help. You all will be. I agree that two babies at once for your first must be a bit frightening, but with my other two at school, it'll be fun.'

'It'll be fun, she says!' said her brother hollowly.

'Their clothes are at our house, Struan, ready packed for my flit tomorrow. Perhaps you'd be able to get them soon. And what about their baths?'

Maria shook her head. 'That's for the doctor to say. If you've some baby-oil I'll just swab them till he sees them. Have you got carry-cots or anything? Or bassinets? Then when they've had some nourishment I can put them down. Struan, that tea.'

Alberta began to enjoy herself, now she'd got over the shock of the birth, and was drooling over the babies, and praising Judith sky-high for the way she'd managed. Maria worked over the infants with the sureness born of good training. She turned her head, said, 'Oh, look at Struan!'

He appeared with a gigantic tray, piled with food. Judith gave way to weak giggles. 'Struan, you idiot! I'm a nursing mother from this moment, and nursing mothers don't feed on crayfish salad and cream-filled pavlovas. You've raided the welcome home feast!'

'Well, it looked so good and I thought you deserved something special after all that effort ... I didn't dream it took so much energy to get babies into the world ... and if the doctor gets here and orders you in Arohaina, you'll miss out on all this. I thought you might be starving.'

'I am, but just for plain bread and butter and perhaps a slice of that jelly sponge, but gallons of tea. Down you go and cut some bread. That was the last job I had to do. But I came up here to see if I could see any smoke from the plane, if it had caught fire. I'd just raised the binoculars up when I realised something was happening to me. Thank heaven you were here early! I really panicked in those first few seconds, because of there being two babies. Oh, I wonder if they've got to the crashed plane yet. It was a small one—four people in it. Bob Ranley saw it come down and alerted everyone pronto. I heard an ambulance go screaming up the road some time ago but haven't heard it come back. What an hour!' She looked at her two babies cradled in her arms. 'Two little lives ushered into life here, and just a few miles away, who knows what?'

Struan bent over her, 'Sis, you mustn't dwell on that. We've got to take what comes. Let's just be thankful we had a trained nurse on hand to deliver these babies and attend to you. Let's take the babies for a moment and you have your tea. Gosh, they don't sound very happy about their arrival, do they? I wish they'd shut up, my ears are splitting.'

Maria turned on him. 'That's the sweetest of all music to any doctor or nurse. Safe and noisy landings on the shores of time, we used to call it. Now, give them to me.' The bassinets had been here at Heronshaw because Johanna had been draping them, and they were all ready for small occupants. Alberta had used some of the kettles from downstairs to fill hotwater bottles to warm the beds and when the babies had had some nourishment the bottles would be removed and the infants snuggled down.

It was an idyllic sight, those little fair downy heads against their mother's breast ... all travail done. No doubt Judith would have a reaction later, by the very suddenness of it, but at the moment she was radiant, all Madonna-like.

The baby that wasn't being suckled was screaming its head off so loudly they didn't at first hear the cars arrive. There was a lull, and into the welcome silence fell a man's voice. 'What *am* I hearing?' it demanded. 'That's a baby yelling ... a new-born baby ... Judith, where are you? Oh, my God ...!' and a sound of footsteps bounding up.

He came to a full stop in the doorway and lost all his colour. There, facing him, was his wife's great-aunt and her brother, looking absurdly smug, a stranger in a white uniform, with a swathed infant bawling in her arms, while there in her grandparents' bed was his wife, flushed, triumphant, stars in her eyes, with another baby at her breast!

He said weakly, 'I don't believe it, I just don't believe it. Oh, Ju, you weren't on your own, were you? I *knew* someone ought to have stayed.'

She laughed so merrily Ramsay knew she was all right. 'Oh, pooh, it's nothing to me. And I didn't have them on my own, the family got here in the nick of time with a mid-wife in tow ... this delectable girl is Maria Willoughby, the one who was travelling with Aunt Alberta.' But he wasn't taking it in. He had no eyes for anyone but his wife. She added, 'Another pigeon pair, a son and daughter, aren't we lucky?'

As he kissed his wife two other figures arrived in the doorway, a couple in their seventies, a broad, thickset man with sandy colouring so that if she'd not known differently she'd have taken him to be Struan's true grandfather, and a woman of striking beauty. Her hair, turning white now, must have been copper once, but her winged eyebrows were dark and her hazel eyes an attractive mixture of green and brown, gold-flecked where the westering sun opposite the windows lit them. She had a sweet mouth, curved, well-disciplined, and slightly concave cheeks that brought into prominence the high cheekbones that make for beauty. A personality, Maria surmised, of velvet and steel.

Everyone tried to tell the tale at once. Maria, under cover of this, removed the little girl from her mother and substituted the boy. She handed the girl to Johanna Mandeville. 'Your new great-granddaughter,' she said. 'I don't suppose you care which you greet first. It's six of one and two threes of the other.'

Johanna took the baby, then looked straight up into Maria's smiling face. 'Oh, it's so long since I heard that said! My mother used to say it, and my little boy, who picked it up from her. Most people say six of one and half a dozen of the other.'

Maria nodded. 'A patient of mine remarked on it once— said she thought it was a North of England way of saying it. My mother was from the North orginally.'

'Yes, my mother was from Northumberland. Blaise was the only one who picked it up. For some reason I didn't.' Blaise, the little boy who hadn't found his tomorrows. How sad! But here were babies aplenty to satisfy Johanna Mandeville. Her eyes were glowing.

They heard a car. A doctor from Napier. He singled Maria out immediately because of her uniform. The others, except for Ramsay, faded out. He made his examination of mother and infants, pronounced himself extremely satisfied with all of them. Both babies were nearly six pounds, so they wouldn't have to be treated as prems, but they'd be taken in to Arohaina where expert care would be theirs.

'You're in luck,' said the doctor crisply, to Judith, 'having Sister Willoughby arrive like that. Did you say she's to be here some time? Good. Save you getting a Karitane nurse in. I'm all in favour of the mother of twins having help, both practical and moral support for a month or two. It's a pretty tiring routine, as I know. We've twins of ten, ourselves. But somehow it's most inspiring. I'll ring the nursing-home from here.'

Ramsay and Athol had already told them that by some miraculous set of circumstances none of the four people in the plane had been killed, although all had suffered injuries, though it was thought not very serious ones. The saving grace, following a skilled emergency landing in very rough country, was that it had been seen so soon and hadn't been inaccessible.

Timothy and Christabel arrived in off the school bus, enchanted to find their longed-for babies already there, and only furious that they still had to be taken off to the nursing-home. Their father explained patiently that they wanted the new brother and sister to have the same good start in life they themselves had had. Athol himself rang the Sadie who had been mentioned, and it sounded as if she was going to be at Arohaina to await their arrival. A little unusual, Maria thought.

Judith said to her two older children, 'I feel I'd like to stay home too, but I must go. I'll feel right out of it, with Struan just home, and Alberta and Maria. I wanted to hear all about the voyage, and England, and everything. Now, I wonder if I could have Maria to myself for a few moments before going.'

'You want to thank her,' said Ramsay, shepherding them all out.

Yes, that was what Judith wanted, but then she said, 'Maria, with all we've come through together, I feel I can ask you this. The last few hours have leapfrogged time for us. I feel a friendship has been made. Romayne Averell's father rang us one day and said she was joining the ship at Tahiti—she rang him from Los Angeles. We felt disturbed. I don't particularly want her for Struan. I'd been relieved when I knew she was going to marry Alastair McFie, then it was all off. I don't want someone like her

for my brother. He deserves the best. Did you feel they
were ... well, close?'

Maria hesitated, then said, 'Judith, I must be fair. When
I met her in England, I thought she seemed—oh, how
shall I put it? Slightly artificial. I think now it was mostly
her appearance. But Donal McFie was on board too, and
obviously hadn't forgiven her for jilting his brother. The
way she reacted when he openly taunted her once made me
respect her. I must speak as I find.'

Judith said unhappily, 'I know she has charm—that's
the trouble. A man wouldn't see through that. I wouldn't
like to think she used Struan. He's a chivalrous fellow and
she's very like her mother who was abominably selfish.
Her father's a pet.'

Maria said gently, 'It could be she's suffered from her
mother's reputation, even Alberta thought that, but now
she's come to respect Romayne more. She told her she
had guts.'

Judith's eyes widened. 'Not really? Not Aunt Alberta?'

'Yes, she didn't approve of the way Donal had gone on.
A pity, because apart from that he's a nice fellow. So
Alberta more or less begged Romayne's pardon for her
judgment based on her knowledge of Mrs Averell. She
even said Romayne was very welcome to come to stay at
Amber Knoll any time she felt like it.'

Judith boggled. 'It's beyond me. You must all be be-
witched. But here's hoping she doesn't come, and that if
she does, my brother will be discriminating enough to see
you're worth two of her.'

It was Maria's turn to boggle. Judith laughed. 'Oh, I
know I shouldn't say such things, but I'm thinking them,
and I'm very like my Aunt Alberta!' She added, 'We both
say what we mean. And the moment I realised how fortunate we were to have you on the spot at this traumatic
moment, it flashed into my mind.'

Maria pushed back a strand of hair from her forehead.
She suddenly felt hot. Then she said firmly, 'It could be
very embarrassing to feel oneself the target of matchmakers, however flattering that might be. And anyway,
love's like the wind ... it bloweth where it listeth. It could

be that Struan sees something in Romayne that none of the rest of us do.'

Judith heaved a sigh. 'That puts paid to my hopes. You wouldn't talk like that if you fancied him. How crushing ... I shall just have to make myself happy with my two gorgeous babies and stop worrying over my big brother. But I would so love to see him as happy as Ramsay and me and settled in life.'

Maria said, firmly and thankfully, 'I can hear them coming back. We'd like you into that nursing-home as soon as possible. You'll need a lot of rest after the events of this afternoon.'

They all suffered a sense of anti-climax when a small ambulance arrived, with an attendant, and Ramsay, the babies and Judith had departed. Then they arrived and finally came to the celebration table Judith had set only three hours before, chivvied there by the impatient and hungry Timothy.

The first toast was to the new arrivals in the family, naturally, but the second to Maria. 'Not only do we drink to her health,' said Athol Mandeville, 'but to the hope that her days with us may indeed be long in the land ... she will always have a special place in our hearts and in our home.'

'Amen to that,' said Alberta, raising her glass. She wore an expression of smug triumph. Why? Oh, perhaps she thought it was all due to her that a trained nurse had been on the emergency scene so quickly. She saw Struan looked narrowly at his aunt, grin, and raise his glass.

A tide of feeling swept over Maria. A longing that was a physical pain that somewhere, in this lush province, lapped by a peacock-green-blue sea, rich with its orchards and vineyards, a family that might prove to be her own, might be as pleased as these folk to receive her.

CHAPTER FIVE

THESE were dear people. They could hardly have been other than fine, folk who in their forties had adopted twins. This must have been to fill the place of the grandchildren they knew they could never have, as their little Blaise had died so young. What a great job they'd made of rearing them. It was obvious Judith had a strong character; the way she'd striven to bring her own twins safely into the world without a soul to help her proved that, and Struan was evidently the mainstay of his adoptive grandparents. How nice that the little boy, as fair as his uncle, was to be named for him.

Maria knew a gladness that now she had a very good reason to stay at least three months. She had an idea that back in London Struan had thought it madly extravagant of his great-aunt to propose so long a stay with wages as they were. Not that she was going to take anything like standard wages, Alberta wouldn't consent to settling for her keep only, but they were going to compromise. That would give her the necessary time to explore the possibilities of tracing her father's beginnings. She must be cautious, though.

Towards the end of the meal she said, 'I have a yen to look up a patient in Hawkes Bay I nursed once. I——'

Struan butted in, 'You mean the one in Waipukurau?' She hesitated, but only fractionally. Better not be too specific about an area. This could be anywhere in the province. She shook her head. 'No, this was another one. But it certainly wouldn't be easy because——'

Athol came in. 'Oh, lass, it mightn't be as hard as you think. It's a sizeable area, but not closely settled as you know it in England. And even comparing it with other New Zealand provinces, it hasn't any cities the size of Auckland or Wellington. What was the name?'

She burst out laughing. 'That's just it—it was Smith.'

Even the children laughed. Timothy said, 'Oh, there are columns and columns of Smiths in the telephone books. But you never know, you might bump into this patient some day in a Napier or Hastings street.'

Maria continued, feeling fairly safe because of the name, 'But he lived away out in the country, on a pretty large sheep station—he kept us all entertained with his stories of dipping and shearing and so on.'

Struan grinned. 'Of course when you're thirteen thousand miles from home, even an eighty-acre farm can become a large sheep station. What's a thousand acres more or less when you can't be checked up on?'

Johanna looked askance at him. 'What a nasty suspicious mind you have! If this patient was the sort Maria would want to look up, I'm sure he wouldn't be that kind. You never know, Maria, even among hundreds of sheep stations from the sea to the Gorge—the Manawatu Gorge—and from north to south, we could find ourselves hearing of a man named Smith, who landed up in hospital when he was having an overseas trip. How old a man was he and what was his Christian name?'

'Oh, fiftyish,' she replied, guessing her father would be about that, 'and his name was Rupert.' Rufus was too unusual for her to say, but Rupert near enough for someone to muse that they'd once known a Rufus, but never a Rupert. Then she laughed lightly, said, 'Not that it's in the slightest bit important. It would be interesting, that's all.'

Alberta stood up. 'Well, let's get away up to Amber Knoll and unpack. I'm sure Timothy and Christabel are dying for us to show them what we brought them from London. I suppose they'll stay here with you tonight, Johanna?'

'Yes, and Ramsay too. We planned that for when Judith was to go into hospital. It saves Ramsay doing their cooking. He'll stay in town tonight with Sadie, though, and see Judith again tomorrow. We'll all come up. I'm as bad as the bairns, I'd like to see what you've brought for me.'

As they drove on up to the other house and it came into view, Maria said, 'Oh, another very large house, and just as beautiful.'

Athol said, 'Did Alberta tell you we had it fixed so it can be used as two flats? When we get Struan married off, he and his wife can have Heronshaw, and we'll come over here near Alberta.'

Struan looked sideways at Maria. 'Devastatingly candid, aren't they? Never knew such matchmakers! They take it as a personal disgrace that I've got to thirty without taking a wife to my bosom. It's enough to give me a complex. You'd better be on your guard. They're as bad as the families of long ago, arranging matches for their children. I *won't* be pushed into marriage!'

They had to laugh. 'As if anyone could push you into anything you didn't want to be pushed into,' said Johanna fondly.

Amber Knoll gleamed out against its dark background of trees in newly-painted sun-gold wood, with a dark brown tiled roof and dark brown facings to its sills and doors. 'It looks a newer house than Heronshaw,' commented Maria, 'yet not too new. I love oldish houses.'

'Well, it is newer. It was built after the 1931 earthquake. Heronshaw had to be strengthened after that, though we counted ourselves as lucky here. It was in the cities, Napier and Hastings, that the greatest damage and loss of life took place,' said Johanna.

'I was the only one in the house that morning and fortunately I'd just gone outside to make sure Blaise wasn't going too high on his swing. He didn't realise what was happening, and even I for the first startled seconds thought I was feeling dizzy. Blaise thought he'd achieved a height never known before. It was the way the earth was tilting, seemed as if he couldn't swing back.

'I'll never forget how I felt when it started to jolt, but he hung on, thinking I was doing it, and when it did come back, I stopped the swing. It caught me an awful wallop. I got him off, told him what it was, which didn't mean much to him at his age, and you know how it is with children, as long as their mother's there they think their little world must be all right.

'I hoped and prayed that this was the centre, that nowhere was faring worse than this, not knowing of the

cliffs that were falling down on Napier, the buildings
tumbling like houses of cards, and ground rising up out
of the swamps and harbours.'

For a moment those of them who had passed through it
were silent, remembering, then Johanna shook herself.
'Come, come, we'll scare the new member of the household to death! It was only once in a lifetime and long ago.'

Maria liked her new designation 'a new member of the
household', and knew that the fact she'd come to Judith's
aid with expert knowledge and experience in her hour of
need had bridged a gap of many weeks in a getting-to-
know-each-other sense.

The house had been aired for their coming, its windows
open to the cool spring air, early lilacs nodding in at the
sills, purple and white, the starry pink clematis blossoms
clinging to the verandah posts, wistaria wreathing the
ponga trunks of the loggia, daffodils on the kitchen table,
sprays of almond blossom in the big drawing-room, as
Alberta, true to her generation, still called the lounge.
Pots of indoor hyacinths on the sills and in the hall scented
the air, and tall lavender irises stood in a corner by the
stairs, in a huge vase brought out from England by the
first Mandeville in 1857.

Maria's spirits were high; she was still in a state of
exaltation after helping to deliver safely two of the next
generation for Heronshaw, who belonged by all ties of love,
if not of blood, to this estate. She felt that because this first
family she had met from Hawkes Bay seemed so conscious
of the past from pioneer days on, surely she'd be able to
trace her father's homestead. It looked even older than
Heronshaw. She'd heard that the first settlers built after
the fashion of the homes they'd left, and there was something very English about those tower rooms. Some of
them, even, not realising the import of living in a different
hemisphere, had actually built their rooms to the cold
south instead of to the sunny north.

No doubt her grandparents would be long since dead,
but there could be uncles and aunts and cousins who might
just welcome her. So many families had a black sheep who
left the family fold, and as it was so long ago, perhaps his

peccadilloes would be forgotten and forgiven now, and in any case not wished on to the child who had never known him. But she'd fathom it out herself. If she told the Mandevilles, they might get so keen they'd rush their fences, and she'd much rather find out what kind of people her connections were before revealing herself to them.

The cases spilled their contents on to the carpet, everyone oohing and aahing, and it gave Maria a Christmas feeling as gift after gift was bestowed. She had a shell necklace herself for Christabel and a Tahitian coral-boat carved in mother-of-pearl for Timothy. She was most surprised, though, when Struan suddenly handed her a parcel. 'For me?' Her voice almost squeaked with surprise.

He nodded. 'I got it for you in Cambridge yesterday. You were lamenting on board the ship that you'd left your Palgrave's Golden Treasury of Verse behind. We were trying to look up a quotation for a crossword, remember? You said you never went travelling without it as a rule, that it had accompanied you all over Europe on tours.'

It was a beautifully bound copy in navy blue leather, with gold lettering. Maria's fingers ran over it caressingly. 'Oh, if only you could see my tatty old copy back home ... I've had it since my schooldays.'

He said, 'Nothing makes you feel so settled in a place as having your very own books beside your bed.'

As Maria lifted her eyes to offer thanks, she caught a significant look pass between Alberta and Johanna. Two minds with but a single thought ... oh, dear, it could make for embarrassment. She must try, in some way, to disabuse their minds of this idea. But how?

She didn't need to. Christabel, pouncing on another parcel, long, slim, obviously a jeweller's packaging, said, 'And what's this? Who's it for?'

Struan took it from her quickly. 'Not to be opened here and now. That's Romayne's.'

Maria's eyes read the name of the firm on the elegant wrapping paper. Ciro's, Regent Street, London. No small gift this.

Alberta blundered, said, 'Why didn't you give it to her on board when she turned up?'

He hesitated, then said, crisply, as if he'd like to tell them to mind their own business, 'I had a reason for not wanting to give it to her yet, so no niggling at me, when she's over here, to bring it out, Christabel.' His tone forbade further questioning.

Maria thought, bending over some discarded wrapping paper so her shoulder-length hair swung forward to hide her expression, that obviously it was for a special occasion ... like a string of pearls to wear with a wedding-gown. He'd not been able to resist buying them in London.

That night, tucked up in the room Alberta had said must be hers because it had a view of the whole sweep of Hawke Bay, with the misty headland, far distant, of Mahia Peninsula, Maria thought of that jeweller's box again. It looked as if the family would just have to make the best of it. She said to herself automatically, *'And so will I!'* Every day deepened the knowledge that Struan Mandeville was the one above all others she'd wish to spend the rest of her life with, and it was evident he loved Romayne Averell, and was hoping that the prejudice against her would die down.

The opposition the family were bringing to bear upon them would have but one result ... that of pushing them into each other's arms. Love had always laughed at locksmiths and family feuding. It wasn't only in Verona, in the days of the Capulets and Montagues, that such things existed. She knew a sorrow for Romayne as well as for herself, because Romayne had jilted a bridegroom too, as well as her mother had done before her, and just because few people had liked the mother, she was classed as just as selfish and cruel. It wasn't fair to Romayne.

After an hour of tossing and turning Maria took herself to task, told herself it was all in her imagination, that instead of feeling this turmoil of mind, she should be thanking her lucky stars she was here, probably in the very province where her father was born, with kindly folk who were providing a home for her, which meant she had three months in which to pursue her quest. She ought to be able to trace Rufus Smith by then if she was really determined. And if, when she found those traces, she thought it better to depart without revealing who she was—well, England was just thirty-six hours away by air.

She need not see much of Struan. He'd be busy on the farm, she'd be looking after Alberta and, when Judith came home with the twins, there'd hardly be a moment to spare. Suddenly the energy-sapping hours of the day caught up with her and she dropped over the edge of sleep and oblivion.

Morning always brought fresh hope ... those tender leaves unfolding. Maria woke to light stealing through the chinks in the curtains, and awareness that she was at last on the Sunrise Coast, the first place in the world to be wakened by the sun, flooded over her. She flung back the cover and went across to her window, high in the east gable, and flung both casements wide. Oh, last night she hadn't noticed it opened on to a narrow wooden balcony, similar to Swiss dwellings. The rails were painted brown and a couple of tubs of geraniums added to the Swiss likeness.

As she looked eastward and southward to those faintly etched white cliffs, her lips parted with delight. In the centre, the sun wasn't quite above the horizon of aquamarine waters, a pale sun, with dazzling facets, beginning to strike rays upwards against the blue of the cloudless sky.

It seemed alive, with an entity of its own, a tremendous force not to be gainsaid, demanding that the world should rise and recognise that here was another day, with working hours and many needs, crises and culminations.

A voice, close at hand, startled her. 'Glad you woke, Maria.' Struan's voice. 'Aunt Alberta said she'd have my head off if I dared to tap on your door, but I think anyone coming from the other side of the world should see this as soon as possible.'

'I'd no idea you were sleeping next door,' she said. 'I saw you carrying your cases into a room at Heronshaw last night.'

'Grandfather thought it wiser. I don't suppose there's anything in it,' he added, 'but one of our neighbours, driving past last week, twice saw a man loitering about our top gates. They lead down to this house. So he thought it better I should sleep down here. Ramsay is at the big house. We didn't say anything to Gran or Aunt. Grandfather just said to them it'd make less for his wife to cook for if I stayed down here. Do you think you can stand up to cooking breakfast for me? We've two men working for us, but they come from Eskdale each day.'

Maria knew a traitor warmth at her heart. Struan added, 'Come on over the sill on to this balcony, there's a wider view. But you'd better put something on over that delectable garment, the early air is still chilly.'

(And he wouldn't want his Aunt Alberta catching them together if she was just wearing this primrose wisp of a shortie nightie!)

She grabbed an equally charming though more substantial velvet robe in deep gold, and stepped over the sill. A huge pear-tree, in a diaphanous dress of pollen-dusted blossom, grew close to the railing, and on the ground below, pink-tipped daisies starred the emerald lawn.

Even as she stepped over, that dazzling orb freed itself from the horizon and flung splendid banners of golden and rose light across the sky of the Southern Hemisphere. Nearer at hand the hill below them cut off all sight of the coast road and the edge of the surf, so that the sea was an unbroken limitless blue. Who could think that just a few miles away hidden from view were two cities and vast pastoral properties and orchards? From this particular point you were conscious only of sea and sky and sun.

Struan had a short towelling jacket over his pyjamas and a towel in his hand as if he was off to the shower. She could see a stubble of light golden hair on his chin and upper lip.

She said, 'Such peace! As if it had never known anything else. As if it was like this in the dawn of time and has continued like that for ever.'

He grinned. 'And yet it once——' he stopped.

She said, 'Go on, Struan. You mean that it hasn't always been peace and harmony. I'd rather know.'

'Really? You won't feel I'm taking the gilt off the gingerbread?'

'I like the truth about things. Tell me.'

'I suppose you know that back in the eighteen-sixties there was trouble between Maori and Pakeha—scenes of much heroism on both sides, a sad time of misunderstanding. But it was complicated by a religious cult, Hauhauism, tied up with the old beliefs but confused with many Old Testament teachings. The Hauhaus believed it was their destiny to free the land from the Pakeha yoke. A party of them moved down from Tarawera on that road we traversed today—at least the site of that road—and a skirmish took place just along from here. But there were days and nights of terror, when it was first whispered that the Hauhaus were coming.

'Ellaline Mandeville, the first wife here, had brought out some fine heirlooms of her family with her, Georgian silver, some jewellery, a turquoise necklace, a pearl ring, a bracelet set with emeralds. Among the treasures of her house was a very fine greenstone *tiki* given her by a friendly chief when she nursed his little girl back to life when she was at death's door. Many chiefs and lesser men among the Maoris were very friendly. When word came that it was no longer safe for the women and children to stay, Ellaline's great friend, Parehuia, buried the treasures after sending them on their way, caught up with them, and guided them through swamp and tussock to shelter and company. Then they went to Napier till things should settle down, and three days after they reached there Parehuia saw a runaway horse, dragging a trap in which were three terrified children.

'She sprang at the horse's head, turned it into a coach-yard, where its mad terror brought it up against a fence, and Parehuia was pinned against it, and died. The children were saved. So the secret of where she hid the heirlooms died with her. Oh, it's not of fabulous value, just sentimental, but we've always hoped it might yet be found. Many a time we've stopped ploughing at the sound of metal striking against metal. Ramsay's great-grandmother —he's one-sixteenth Maori, you know—prophesied that one day two daughters of the house of Mandeville would find the treasure. None of us are superstitious, yet we all carry a faint hope that this shall come to pass some day. I'm sure it was in Judith's mind yesterday when she welcomed another little daughter. She said once ages ago that she'd like another little girl just to give the legend a chance of coming true!'

Maria felt moved, then realised something. The family didn't seem to see anything strange in Judith hoping her daughters might find the lost valuables, even though they were not, in actual blood, Mandeville daughters. But wasn't it sweet to think the ties by adoption were so strong, it appeared quite natural to them? That was as it should be.

She looked up to find Struan looking down on her, a reflective look in his eyes. As if he was weighing something up.

She said, 'Yes?'

He hesitated, then said, 'I think I should tell you—no, better that Judith herself should tell you, as time goes on. I'm always rushing my fences. And I'd better go have my shower, then leave the bathroom clear for you.'

For Maria the next month passed so quickly she suddenly realised that if she didn't do something soon about trying to trace the Smith homestead in Hawkes Bay, her time at Heronshaw would have gone with nothing done.

The trouble was that existence here was so full and satisfying that the days slipped by uncounted. Judith and the twins were allowed home ten days after their birth, solely because Maria was at hand, and every morning she cycled over one of the house tracks to Hibiscus Hill to help bath the twins, rub their backs to bring their burps up, dress them, do their washing, and see Judith didn't exhaust herself.

Stuart and Sara were thriving beautifully, seemingly bent on catching up fulltime babies, and for a while the entire household seemed to revolve round them. That other Sara who had gone to the nursing-home when Judith was taken there often came out, and it was just as well she was usually called Sadie to distinguish her from the girl-twin.

Johanna loved Sadie, you could see that. They were

kindred spirits. Johanna said to Maria, 'She lost a wonderful husband three years ago, and her only son is studying
in Edinburgh just now, but she never complains. I
wanted her to come out here to live, but she prefers to keep
on her Napier home, which you can understand, and
does nurse-aiding at an old people's home three mornings
a week, so we like her to spend as much time out here as
possible, when she's not driving round with meals-on-
wheels for shut-in folk and taking them for outings.'

'It would be lovely if she married again,' suggested
Maria, 'she's such a striking-looking woman I should
imagine there's every chance of it, and she's got a nature
to match. She's quite Nordic-looking, isn't she?'

Johanna nodded, 'Naturally enough. She's descended
from the Norwegians and Danes who came out and settled
Dannevirke and Norsewood in pioneer days. New Zealand's like that ... Scots settlements in Dunedin and
Waipu, French in Akaroa, Yugoslavians away up north,
originally on the *kauri* gum-diggings, Chinese in many
places, and all kinds of nationalities round the old gold-
fields.'

Judith mentioned the old legend about the missing
household treasures to Maria one day. 'It's so foolish of
me, but just because Ramsay is descended from Parehuia
my heart gave such a leap when Sara was born ... it's the
dream of my life that Ramsay's daughters and mine should
find it.'

Maria said, 'If it's foolish, then it's a nice foolishness.
I happen to believe in believing in things, otherwise no one
would embark on adventure, or even live with hope.'

Judith gave her a quick hug. 'Oh, Maria, it's so marvellous having you here! It's for all the world like having a
sister. That was something I often envied girls at school
for ... I had to leave my playmates at the school gates,
though Struan was all that a brother could be. You'd know
how I felt because you were an only for long enough.'

'Yes, how lucky I was that when Mother married again,
I got a brother and a sister. My mother had married an
absolute rotter who deserted her before I was born—easy
for him to do, he was a seaman. She had a thin time of it

till she met my stepfather. Yet I never remember her before that as anything else but happy. It was quite an achievement not to yield to bitterness, to make a happy, if solitary, home for me. She had no one when he left her in Dunedin. She lost her own parents when she was about fourteen.'

'She must have been the same calibre as Grandmother,' said Judith. 'The trouble she had! Yet she never let it warp her. I've never even heard her envying other women who have several children, all living near them. But for her, and Granddad, Struan and I could have had a very different childhood. As it is we can remember nothing but love and security.'

It was the next morning that Maria came upon Johanna unawares. Judith had rung and said, 'I thought Grandmother seemed a little off-colour last night, so I wondered if you'd like to drop by and give her a hand. Not to say anything, but just to hint that I didn't need you this morning so you thought you'd drop in to see if there was anything she needed help with. We're always expecting her to slow up, but she's still a tiger for work, especially at this time of year with the men so busy outside.'

So when Maria saw Athol riding across the paddocks to join Struan, she went across, slim and tall in belted green slacks and a loose green and white checked shirt. She tapped, got no answer, went in the side door and heard Johanna singing softly to herself from the living-room. She went to the doorway. Johanna was busy with a duster. Maria was just about to call out when she saw her pick up the big framed photograph of Blaise taken when he was about four. He was standing by a collie dog, his little hand clutched tightly in its long coat, a toy train at his feet. Maria froze as Johanna, unknowing anyone was near, said, 'Good morning, Blaise, my darling. A very good morning to you, as always.' She flicked her lambswool duster over the glass, replaced it, then moved on, resumed singing, a light song from a Gilbert and Sullivan opera.

Maria took a couple of silent steps backwards, then turned and tiptoed outside. She'd come across again later.

She'd no idea when Johanna and Athol had lost their only son, but the poignancy of that greeting meant that to her, his mother, he was still a living reality. She found the tears were rolling silently down her cheeks. She turned the corner of the house and with her vision blurred bumped into Struan, whom she'd thought over the hills and far away with Athol.

'Whoops!' He steadied her, then said quickly, 'Maria, tell me, what's happened? Bad news?'

She said, putting up a hand to dash the tears away, 'Just that I witnessed something so touching just now. Beautiful too, but sad. Your grandmother seems so light-hearted, so content, but I came across her unawares. She was dusting Blaise's portrait, and she ... Oh, Struan ... she said good morning to him. I——' She looked up apologetically. 'You'll think me a great sentimental idiot, but it got me by the throat. So long ago, Struan, yet she still wishes him good morning. How long is it?'

His eyes went sombre, counting, then, 'More than thirty. I believe that she grieved so much at first that Grandfather was terribly worried. She spent so much time in his room he felt it wasn't healthy. Her cousin took her away for a holiday, and while they were gone Grandfather turned his room into a guest-room, packed all his things away. Poor man, he didn't know if he was doing right or wrong.'

Maria gave a cry. 'Oh, Struan, she could have felt he was being wiped out of memory even. But how did she take it?'

Struan said slowly, 'I think she saw, through his action, how concerned he was for her mental welfare. She pulled herself together then. He didn't burn Blaise's things. They're still behind a locked door at the end of the old loft. It had been used as living quarters by the stableman in the old days. All his toys and books are there, his school things, his collections of bird pictures. Then, of course, Grandmother found other things to take her mind off him.'

She nodded. 'Yes, once she adopted twins, she'd hardly have much time to brood. Did someone suggest just that or—oh, here she is. Struan, I want her to think I'm just arriving.'

Johanna appeared with basket and scissors, said, 'Oh, Maria love, you can help me. All the flowers inside have given up at once. Lilac never lasts long, nor do the snowballs, but I can't resist cutting them. Oh, Struan, you're tall enough to reach that rose at the top of the arch. I love November because the air is always full of the scent of roses.'

When it was picked, Johanna looked beyond them, her face changed and she said, 'We're about to have a visitor ... I can see a rider coming down the hill, must have come up from the other valley. Oh, it's Romayne.'

Maria wouldn't look to see Struan's expression. She said, 'Oh, how lovely—she's rung a couple of times when I've been out. Perhaps she thought she'd just surprise us today.'

Struan said, 'Yes, she's been busy helping her father.'

So Romayne had been ringing him. Well, naturally.

Johanna said swiftly, 'Struan, Donal's in Napier. I met him in town yesterday when I took Timothy in to buy his gym shoes. I told him to come out and have a meal with us, but I think he'd ring first, so if he does, see if you can wangle it so that Romayne isn't here at the same time. I can't think of anything more awkward after what you told me about the incident on the ship. Though for her father's sake, I'd not be sorry if she spent some time over here. I think he deserves a clear run now.'

'A clear run? What do you mean, Gran?'

'We think he's about to become engaged to Gertrud Holbein ... the woman he should have married long ago. It's all seemed so ideal. But if Romayne stays on to housekeep for her father, that could put a spoke in the wheel. I wish she'd stayed in England. Both Gertrud and John deserve nothing but the best for this autumn wooing.'

Struan said, 'Well, we can't have it both ways, keeping Romayne away, but having Donal here, or vice versa. I'm all for furthering the middle-aged romance myself. Romayne is big enough not to worry if he turns up. I'm not sure Donal is and quite frankly at the moment I don't care tuppence if he *is* uncomfortable. Well, I'll go and meet Romayne.'

The two women watched him vault a fence, gain the track that led down from the hill road, saw Romayne rein in, Struan's hands go out to assist her to dismount. Maria swung round. If they were going to kiss she didn't want to witness it.

She said, 'I'm thinking of going into town to buy me a little second-hand car. You've all been generous with transport, but I'd like to be a little independent. How would you like to drive me in, Johanna, and help me choose one?'

Johanna was delighted. Maria made up her mind she wouldn't be obvious and look as if she were running away, but she'd better get used to seeing Struan and Romayne together.

CHAPTER SIX

STRUAN was decidedly disgruntled at lunch-time when he found out Johanna and Maria were Napier-bound to look at cars. 'Can't you put it off to another day? Then I could come with you and give anything you take a fancy to the run-over.'

Johanna looked wicked. 'Despite all this Women's Lib business no man ever thinks a woman capable of buying a car for herself! It's a fact of life. It so happens, Maria, that I'm mechanically minded, but till this very moment I've never had a chance of looking a car over without the men butting in. You needn't worry about your protégé, Struan, she's getting the A.A. to vet it.'

Romayne said. 'You don't have to stay home on my account, Struan, I'll be leaving early, in any case. It's quite a ride back, and I'm just getting used to a saddle again. I'd like to call on the Merridews going back. I haven't seen them yet.'

Maria knew the same admiration she'd known for Romayne when Donal had been so cruel. She'd develop a complex yet, feel unwanted anywhere. She said quickly,

'I've lots of other shopping to do that would bore Struan stiff and I'll be as candid as Johanna and say I'd enjoy looking at cars without any males hanging about. But I feel so disappointed I'm going out when you've just arrived, Romayne. I wish you'd brought your overnight bag, and taken up Alberta's suggestion of staying here.'

Romayne laughed, said easily, 'Unless Alberta's regretting that gesture ... shipboard life makes strange bedfellows and....'

Alberta came in very decidedly, 'If Maria hadn't got in first I'd have been saying the same thing. You're going to be saddle-sore if this is your first long ride, Romayne. It must be all of ten miles. I'm sure Maria would lend you some night things ... why not give your father a ring and say you'll stay on at least a couple of nights?'

As Alberta wasn't known for insincere offers, Romayne accepted immediately. Maria said swiftly, 'My sister and sister-in-law bought me almost a trousseau for the trip, Romayne. You can have your pick, not only in night-wear but trews and dresses too, if you decided to stay longer.'

Already she felt so at home she could issue an invitation like that. Romayne's pale cheeks showed a flake of colour—pleasure. She said, smiling, 'I'd love to. I don't think there's any secret about this ... I'm pretty sure the whole district knows, because despite the fact I was feeling so guilty about staying away so long, I feel decidedly a gooseberry at the moment. Dad's leaving more and more to my brother and his wife and spends most of his time at Gertrud's. I'm sure they'd rather spend it at home, as down in the village her pottery and painting friends are always dropping in. She's so sweet. I can't think why Dad just doesn't get on with it and make sure of her.'

Struan said, 'Good for you. That would leave you free to live your own life.'

Romayne nodded. Johanna said, 'Any plans?'

Romayne's tone was light. 'Dozens of them, but none definite as yet. But I've dropped a hint to Gertrud that I'm not looking on Roahiwi as my permanent home.'

(No, of course not; things with Romayne and Struan could come to a head any time now, and away from close quarters with Donal McFie, they might cease to worry about any possible estrangement between Struan and Donal.) Maria knew a mixture of emotions; pity for Romayne caught up in a difficult situation, feeling no doubt, despite this healthy attitude towards her father's possible remarriage, that she wasn't needed in her childhood home; pity for Struan too, and, perhaps, pity for herself. Well, it would be good to get away into the city with Johanna this afternoon, and no doubt, Alberta.

Alberta declined. 'Nice for you and Johanna to be on your own and get to know each other without scads of other folk around. I'm driving up to Te Pohue today on Institute business.'

Maria was surprised. Alberta had surely changed her attitude. Time would have been when she'd have played gooseberry herself rather than leave Romayne and Struan together.

Napier was a gem of a town, rimmed by a glorious sea. They dipped down to Bay View, once called Petane, the Maori way of pronouncing Bethany, threaded along the coast road that had huge citrus orchards each side of it, blessing the air with the scent of orange blossom. Acres of apricot trees ran in orderly rows, plums, all tanged with salt air.

The small airport lay among its fields, with a backdrop of emerald hills curving to the west, with its lagoons lying about the railway, hinting at deeper inroads by the sea long ago, before the massive earthquake raised the land up eight feet or so.

They turned over the bridge to run through the port, the road Johanna so loved, past the small-boats harbour called the Iron Pot, skirted round the sheer clay-and-rock cliffs of Bluff Hill, once called Scinde Island, with the tall white buildings of the hospital crowning it and giving it quite a continental air. Shipping offices and stores were crowded together here, and wharves jutted out into waters that only rarely had any greyness, and sparkled now in opalescent colours.

Men were busy loading great containers carrying wool and dairy produce and timber and timber chips from the immense forests inland, to faraway markets. Yet withal, the city itself was small enough to be a darling town, intimate in that one hardly went into a shop where the Mandevilles weren't greeted as friends. The gardens along the seafront were so bright with flowers they were dazzling, with here and there stretches of billiard-smooth lawns to rest the eyes. Even yet, early in the season, they were obviously thronged with tourists.

Buying a car seemed very simple, merely a matter of Johanna taking Maria to the firm in Carlyle Street where the family dealt, sure of getting value and personal interest. Maria said, 'I need something I can sell easily again when I go back to England. I came out with Mrs Gregory Jensen, and after about three months here, I'm going to explore New Zealand, particularly the South Island. My parents came from Dunedin. Then I'll bring the car back to you before flying back to London.'

Johanna said quickly, 'Don't say that, Maria. You seem as if you've been at Heronshaw for ever. I can't bear to think of you returning. I like to think of you over at Amber Knoll with Alberta.' She turned to the salesman. 'She's a kindred spirit for Athol too, she's a devoted bird-watcher and you know what he's like.'

He grinned. 'Indeed I do. Last time he brought the Holden in to try to trace a whining noise in the engine, it wasn't just enough for him to run along Marine Parade for me to listen for it; no, as soon as he saw I was on duty in that department in an emergency, he had me running it along Hyderabad Road and out round the lagoon and before I knew what I was doing, I was out of the car tracking down some wading-bird you don't see often on your property. It reminded me of schooldays and him taking Blaise and me way back in the forests. We had a dream that some day we might even find a *huia* ... but I guess that one *is* extinct, unlike the *takahe*. The foreman said he'd never known anyone take so long to trace a fault that day, and looked very suspiciously at my muddy shoes.'

They chuckled. It was so like Athol. It didn't take long to narrow their choice. When they were nearly decided he said, 'By all means get the A.A. to check it out, but if I were you I'd take it back to Eskdale and get Athol and Struan to look it over—they'll never be quite sure of it otherwise.'

At that Johanna and Maria burst out laughing and admitted it was true. They filled in time by going along to Marineland, and managed to see the latter half of the dolphin, seal, and sea-lion display, then Johanna had difficulty in prising Maria away from the bird hospital where wounded or stranded birds were brought to be restored to health and freedom.

Johanna saw a friend leaning over the otters' quarters and went away to her, leaving Maria adoring the gannets, with their smooth swan-like plumage, the deep sienna-yellow heads, the bluish-grey about their eyes, the contrast of their black wing-tips. She shaded her eyes against the sun, brought the white cliffs of Cape Kidnappers into focus ... imagine thousands of gannets there! She must take one of those safari trips there before leaving.

A man said to Maria, 'Glorious birds, aren't they? Have you been to Cape Kidnappers yet to see the colony? So unusual for a mainland.'

'No, not yet, though I will while I'm staying here.'

'It would be a shame to miss it. Are you a tourist? Staying long?'

'Not exactly a tourist. I accompanied a patient out from England—she lives here—and I'm spending three months with her.'

'A patient? The lady you were with just now? Has she been very ill?' He glanced over towards the otters, almost nervously, she thought. But that was stupid.

'No, her sister-in-law. She became diabetic, otherwise very fit, but she was travelling by ship and needed a companion.'

'Well, certainly that lady looked the picture of health.'

What a strange man! In casual meetings like this one usually talked of the weather, or the tourist attractions. She said, 'She's the youngest seventy-year-old I've ever known. So is her husband.'

He said quickly, 'It's been nice talking to you. Goodbye,' and he turned and was lost among a crowd of children.

Johanna was bringing her friend back. They decided to go in search of a cup of tea. As they moved through the souvenir shop Johanna stopped so suddenly the group behind cannoned into her. She apologised and, off balance for a moment, caught at Maria's arm to steady herself. Maria said quickly, 'Johanna, are you all right? You've lost all your colour.'

'Oh, have I? How silly! It was just that for a fleeting instant I thought I saw—I mean I saw someone who—who was so like my—like a friend I had years ago, I felt quite—funny. A likeness can give you quite a turn sometimes.'

Maria said, 'I know. There was a man on our ship so like my stepfather that it really startled me the first time I saw him. But when he spoke his voice was so different it didn't seem half so striking.' She noticed Johanna didn't fully regain her colour till she'd had her tea.

They drove in Johanna's car to the sales depot. The salesman was chatting in his office, then came out with his caller. Maria stopped dead, then said, a little flatly, 'Oh, hullo, Donal. Johanna just said today you were here on business. How are you?'

He said he was fine, but he looked much thinner than on board ship. He kissed Johanna, said, 'Well met. I checked out of my hotel today. The firm's switching cars and a new one was to be driven down today, from Auckland. I'm to take it back to Wellington. The buyer of the old one wanted it right away, so I let it go, but there's been a hitch in delivery of the new one. I've finished my appointments and am at a loose end. I rang Heronshaw, but got no answer. I was going to ask if I came out on the Taupo bus could I stay a couple of nights. How about it?'

Johanna managed not to show embarrassment, though Maria guessed her thoughts were racing. It would have been too awkward to turn him down in front of the salesman. She managed to say brightly, 'That would be delightful, Donal. Then we could catch up on news from Wellington. We had so little time the other day. We're taking two cars back as Maria has one more or less on appro. Oh, there's the A.A. man bringing it back. Maria, let's hear what he has to say.' As they walked across the courtyard she said rapidly in a low voice, 'You take Donal with you, Maria, I'll go on ahead, and as you were present when he and Romayne clashed, you can explain she turned up today. I couldn't say anything in front of the salesman, and didn't want Donal to think the whole thing had been talked over at home, but you could say to him that if, because of this, he decides to just fill in time in town after all, you'll explain to me. He'll find other accommodation.'

Donal, all unknowing, said easily, after the report had been given, 'I'll have to pick up my luggage at the hotel. We'll be at Heronshaw not long after you, Johanna. See you soon.'

Maria waited till they were parked in Marine Parade opposite the hotel before she said anything. As he got out she said, 'Just a moment, Donal. I must tell you something. This morning Romayne rode over and we asked her to stay a day or two. It could be awkward. I think we ought to offer you the chance to change your mind.'

His lips tightened. 'For whose sake?'

She hesitated, then, 'I've got to be honest. I could try for tact and say for everyone's sake, including you, but to be truthful, it's for Romayne's sake. She won't hear a word said against you for the way you behaved on ship ... I mean not telling her earlier that Alastair was engaged to someone else, then telling her the way you did. She thinks it's entirely natural for you to feel the way you did.

'Now she's home she's found her father courting his boyhood sweetheart, and she's trying to give them time together. I like that. Not an atom of jealousy there. I think she's someone who was dubbed as like her mother and she isn't. Even Alberta has completely changed her mind about her, so you'd better try to book in here again.'

There, she'd said her piece and he hadn't interrupted her! She went to look up—and was completely disconcerted when he said, 'My main reason for coming to Heronshaw is to see Romayne and to apologise to her.'

She stumbled. 'I—why Heronshaw? Why not Roahiwi?'

He gave a strange laugh. 'She could throw me out of

Roahiwi, but not out of Heronshaw! I rang her home first, and was told she'd ridden over there. Even had she been gone by the time I got there, it's within reach, and I could ride over, speak my piece and disappear if she didn't want me there. I must find out how she feels about it. It could be she's more or less wiped it out of her mind. I can't. I was surprised at myself acting as I did. Struan and I have been friends for so long, so have our families. When I couldn't get Heronshaw on the phone either, I was deciding to take a rental car, instead of the bus, and drop in. When you two walked in, I thought it providential. I know you don't think so, Maria, but I'm coming, and I'll chance my luck that Romayne doesn't tell me she'd rather I went back to town; it's over to her.'

They gazed at each other reflectively, then Maria spoke. 'I think it's the right thing to do, Donal. If you apologise it will remove any restraint between you and Struan, whatever happens in the long run.' She thought he looked at her sharply.

She added, 'Relationships are always getting tangled up in life, and sometimes a word or two, said at the right time, *and in the right way*, can save a lot of tension, even heartache. I think it's touching to find an elder brother so devoted that he resented his brother's bride-to-be turning him down, though——' She paused. How easy it would be to say the wrong thing now.

He grinned, 'Though it shouldn't have lasted. You're quite right. It became too personal a thing to me. I must put it right.'

Maria knew it mightn't have rankled had he not suspected that Romayne had broken it off because of Struan, his friend. This might sweep away any bitterness that remained, but it wasn't going to be an easy meeting!

She dared not say Johanna wasn't now expecting him. She said rather breathlessly, 'I'll just get out of the car while you're picking up your things, for a breath of sea air.'

He slipped round, opened the door for her and as she got out her bag fell right at the feet of a passerby, who stooped, picked it up, returned it to her, said, 'Oh, hullo, it's you again.' It was the man who'd talked to her in Marineland.

He hesitated, said, 'I hope you'll forgive me, but I couldn't resist speaking to you back there. You've such a look of my wife.'

Maria felt an intuitive pang for him, though his look, for some reason, disturbed her. She felt it probably meant his wife was dead.

'Of course. These likenesses do crop up.'

Donal said, 'Maria, I won't be a moment. I'll just get my luggage.'

The man had silver hair but had been fair once, she thought. He was young-looking in spite of a heavily lined face. A sad face. He lingered. 'What a lovely name, Maria. It suits you. An old name grown popular since *The Sound of Music.*'

She nodded. She rather wished he'd go. Quite an ordeal was ahead of her and the sooner it was over the better. He cleared his throat, said, 'I've always been interested in names. Does your surname match it? Some are euphonious together, some not.'

She had a puckish thought that had she said Smith, he might have found it too short for euphony. 'It's Maria Willoughby.'

He nodded. 'A good running sound. Well, I mustn't keep you. Nice to have met you while I'm in Napier.'

Donal was crossing the road when she turned. He slung his case in the boot. 'Is that chap still going? Had he been younger I'd have suspected a pick-up, but they're not inclined to mention wives, I suppose! He looked a lonely sort of guy. Perhaps he's a widower.'

'I thought that, too. Well, let's get going.'

They had little to say to each other on the way out. Maria had an idea Donal was mentally composing his apology in his mind, and she herself was taken up with wondering just what sort of a reception they'd get at Heronshaw. Johanna would probably have told Struan on the quiet that they'd just avoided an awkward situation. In the midst of her unease an unhappy thought struck her. That man with the silver hair. Why hadn't she asked his name, asked where he'd come from, who his wife had been? Here she was, looking for relatives, and she'd missed a golden opportunity! Of all the stupid things ... she'd been too absorbed in the problem of Romayne and Donal. By the time they entered the vineyards of the Esk Valley and swung up the hill she felt as taut as a drum. If only they could see Romayne emerging from the stables on her own! Once Donal had his apology out of the way, things might be less sticky, but if everyone rushed out as they arrived, eager to see her new car, and they saw Donal emerging with her, it would be an ordeal.

The cattle-stops gave their fair warning, and as they came to a stop outside the front entrance Struan came out, alone, but as Maria expected, all eagerness. That look was wiped from his face as Donal got out. It was succeeded by a scowl as black as could be seen on a fair man, and it was directed at Maria.

Donal didn't hesitate. 'It's all right, I know Romayne's here and I'd like to see her alone, Struan. Where is she?'

Struan said, with evident relish, 'Well, being alone with her is just what you're not going to get ... she's at Amber Knoll with both my grandparents, Aunt Alberta, Judith and all the children. We're having dinner over there.'

Again no hesitation. 'Right, well, I've got to put up with what I can get. I insulted her more or less in public, so public it will have to be for the apology. Coming, Maria? Coming, Struan?'

Struan's jaw set. 'I'm not, and if you think a feeble sorry can put things right, you're due for a setback.'

Donal looked impassive. 'It won't be feeble. I think I'll apologise to you too, Struan. We've been pals too long to fall out over my churlishness—in fact worse than churlishness—my bitterness. I can understand how you feel. I took that long hard look at myself you advised and didn't like what I saw. If Romayne doesn't want to see me again, after the apology, okay, I'll take myself off. I'm sure Maria will run me back to town again, even if it makes her late for dinner. She's been most co-operative.'

Maria said hastily, 'Just get going, Donal. Get it over—without me.'

Donal disappeared in a spurt of speed. Struan, two lines between his brows, said, 'I'm surprised at you. I thought you'd have gone along to hold his hand. Just imagine, I said to Gran when she told me that she couldn't have done better than leave it to you ... that you had a way with you, but you turn up with him in tow. How do you think Romayne is going to feel, Donal turning up to apologise with half the Esk Valley in the room?'

'She'll feel a lot better than you seem to at the moment. I hadn't a snowflake's chance in Hell of stopping Donal McFie coming. I tried.'

'You tried! He could hardly hijack your car.'

'I reckon he would have if I'd refused. But more than that, he convinced me this was the only way. He'd rung Roahiwi to find out she was here. What's more, I reckon that for her sake he wants to make amends before the very people who were there when he tore a strip off her ... I've changed my mind, I'm going to be there. I'm taking that farm-truck standing there so conveniently, and though I may miss some of the apology, I'll be there to see the result. Are *you* coming or not?'

She made a dive at the truck, rushed round to the driving side, found her arm wrenched back. 'Get in the passenger seat, you're not familiar with this.'

She wasted no time arguing, but on the way up the winding hill track she said hotly, 'I'm as good a driver as you ... *you* learned on country roads, *I* learned to drive in London, and don't charge clean up to the front door at the Knoll, you could dent my new Mini before it's even paid for!'

He made no answer. Donal must have slowed down after his initial standing start at speed, perhaps remembering it was Maria's car, because he was just getting out as they took the last bend. He looked back over his shoulder as he mounted the steps, said, in a don't-care voice, 'Didn't want to miss the fun after all, Struan! Going to enjoy seeing Romayne throw me out on my ear? Not to worry, I'll have cleared my conscience, anyway.'

Maria felt like wringing her hands. The apology might

clear Donal's guilt and probably make Romayne feel better, but it wasn't going to improve the situation between the two old friends any. She saw Tim and Christabel and the twin pram on the lawn, so that would reduce the audience!

Donal never paused. Struan and Maria were almost running to keep up with him. Voices from the dining-room guided him. They entered with Donal only slightly in lead. Johanna and Alberta were sitting by the fire winding wool; Athol was reading the *Daily Telegraph* by the window, and at the rush of footsteps, Romayne and Judith, busy setting the table, looked across it, cutlery in their hands, at the combined entry.

Maria just had time to notice that Romayne looked beautiful in a blue linen dress of Maria's own. It had a long slender scarf of filmy white slotted through epaulettes, and tossed over each shoulder, and had a wide belt studded with pearl beads, clipped in at the waist. A bright coral brooch held the scarf in place at her throat, and she'd found a coral ribbon to tie back her smooth black hair. Her eyes were startlingly blue and as they met Donal's, her colour rose, betrayingly bright, enhancing her loveliness.

Donal came up against the table opposite her. His eyes went right and left to the others. 'It's a bit public for an apology, an unconditional apology, but you're to know I insulted Romayne on the ship, also publicly. Maria tried to prevent me coming out here tonight, with the best possible motives, I believe. She wanted to prevent you being more hurt, Romayne. But it made no difference. I'd already tried to get in touch with you, only to be told you were here. I believe now that you broke your engagement to Alastair for the wisest of reasons, honestly and courageously, and I admire you for it. I was a brash fool, and darned near spoiled other relationships too. How about it, Romayne? Friends? Or would you rather I didn't stay?'

There was just one moment of tension. Romayne's lower lip quivered for a fleeting scrap of time, then, somehow, she managed to laugh. 'Well, now you've got all that out of your system, I'd like you to stay. Yes, friends. And Struan and Maria, you can take those awful looks off your faces.

It's forgotten from now on. If it's mentioned again I'll scream! And I might just tell you, Donal McFie, you're lucky there's enough dinner to go round.'

The next moment could have held an awkward silence, a sense of anti-climax, but it hadn't a chance. Small Christabel tore in, 'Mum, Tim's at the top of the gum-tree, and the branch he used to step there from has broken—he's stuck!'

It emptied the room in a moment, Struan in the lead seeing he was nearest the door. He gave a yell to Timothy to stay where he was, and it was quite evident that with his great length of arm and leg, one broken branch wouldn't matter. Donal climbed up behind Struan and took Tim from him when he was plucked from his lofty perch, and in turn Donal handed him to Athol.

Dinner became a merry affair, their relief making them lighthearted, and Ramsay wondering a little at their high spirits. When the dishes were done, the babies played with, Ramsay and Judith disappeared with their children and when twilight fell, after a short whispered sentence or two, Romayne rose. 'Donal and I are going for a walk. His parents have been sweet enough to send some messages I'd like to hear, so we'll climb the hill. Don't worry, quarrelling is at an end.'

Struan, standing by the French window, noted the direction they took, turned and said, 'Come on, Maria, I've a bit of humble pie to eat myself, the way I bawled you out when you arrived with Donal, but unlike him I don't mean to do it in public.' As they left the room, he looked back, said to his grandparents and great-aunt, 'Poor Maria, she's got herself involved with a mad, mad family, and I did promise her stepbrother I'd look after her in New Zealand.'

At first it was of Romayne he talked. 'I'm glad Alastair's parents have sent her messages. It was for their sakes she didn't break it off sooner. Must be maddening for a girl to find she has the ideal prospective parents-in-law, then find she can't, after all, marry the chap. She found Alastair just a little too immature.'

He took her up through the wattle grove, through a larch

spinney, to a gate where you could gain the road and have access to more of the Heronshaw property by way of a stile.

He helped her over, birds twittered, disturbed in their slumbers. The moon hadn't yet risen, so they had to pick their way. Now the air was aromatic with the tang of the pines, their needles cushiony under their feet. Below them, out to the east, they could hear the distant thunder of heavy waves crashing on a shingle beach. A sheep coughed in a paddock below, and presently the sky darkened and became pricked with stars, letting the heavenly light through.

Maria stumbled, was caught and held. 'We're almost to the top, Maria. We call it Blaise's Eyrie. He was a great little lad for naming things, Gran says. This was his place. He hollowed out all the rotten rock from round these big rocks and made a seat out of it. I suppose he thought the long, long thoughts of youth up here. Pity it all ended as it did. He had such promise. Poor Gran and Granddad!'

'Indeed,' said Maria, 'yet out of their natural grieving, they found solace in you and Judith. Some people would have taken it quite differently, allowed themselves to become bitter, would never have thought of becoming adoptive grandparents.'

Struan said slowly, 'Hasn't Judith told you about that? How it came about?'

'No. No reason why she should, I suppose. Neither do you have to tell me, Struan. You both belong here by all the ties of love.'

The silence that fell then wasn't a strained one. Finally she looked up at him, seated beside her on the Eyrie. It was dark enough not to worry lest she gave away her feelings, light enough to see his fair profile, strong, craggy, faintly silvered by the starlight. Yet his face looked gentled, as if his mood was tender, whimsical. He looked down on her, smiled, said, 'You feel it really doesn't matter I'm not a true grandson of the estate?'

'How could it matter when there's such a strong bond?'

'I like that,' he said. 'I like it very much. And I like this.'

His arm came round her, he swung her across him,

laughing. She lay back in the crook of his arm, looking up into his face. She had a moment of wondering about Romayne before his lips found hers, then all other thoughts except the delight of the moment were blotted out. She hoped Struan couldn't feel the quickened tempo of her heartbeats, though she could certainly hear his thudding, held like this, her right ear hard against his breast.

When they needed breath he lifted his head, said laughingly, 'I've not apologised for bawling you out, have I? Would that do instead? Or does it need words?'

Her voice was low, husky. 'Sometimes words are clumsy. Naturally you were angry.' But that brought the thought of Romayne back. Was Struan, in spite of his nonchalance, rather pipped that Romayne and Donal had gone off by themselves? Was this a sort of 'two-can-play-at-that-game' attitude? She mustn't let it go to her head. She said, mock-severely, 'Time we went back. For someone sworn to dodge the matchmakers' wiles, you play with fire, Struan Mandeville!'

Maria felt that the next twenty-four hours passed in a dream. There was no reality about anything. Had anyone told her two days ago that Romayne would be here, borrowing her clothes, Donal staying too, and the pair of them apparently at great ease with each other, she'd have thought them crazy.

Athol, Alberta, and Johanna were wonderful people, taking it all in their stride. She said so, to Johanna, helping her in the kitchen. 'Most people of your age would be saying you didn't know what the younger generation was coming to, but you've taken it just as if it was a children's quarrel, a flare-up, blows, and then forgotten.'

Johanna laughed. 'That's as it should be. There are worse things than broken engagements. It's when kids take sides that the quarrels get hotter and last. The two main combatants get it out of their systems. And Struan aye fought everyone else's battles. Poor Donal, he doesn't know yet, I'm thinking, why it affected him as it did.'

Maria knotted her brows. 'What do you mean, Johanna?

Wasn't it the same with him? Fighting his younger brother's battles?'

Johanna chuckled. 'At the risk of sounding smug, I'll leave you to work that one out. I don't think it'll be long. I feel it's best left to work itself out, without any of us putting a finger in the pie.'

Maria felt intensely curious and a little dismayed. Could Johanna mean that Donal had suspected all along that Struan was interested in Romayne, and he'd felt angered at so tangled a web? Strange, though, that while in Britain they hadn't resolved things one way or another. Yet, with Struan's love for his foster-grandparents, you couldn't imagine him marrying over there. Maria felt a sense of desolation. Last night, in the closeness of Struan's embrace, those tender leaves of hope had uncurled a little, but so soon the doubts had returned.

Oddly enough, she couldn't resent Romayne. Romayne had suffered enough and deserved a happy ending now. That lightheartedness of hers had carried her over a bad patch. It had become a habit, perhaps. Was that why she seemed so at ease with Donal now? Might she still, beneath it, be on her guard with him? Was she accepting his olive branch for Struan's sake, for the long-time friendship between the two men?

After lunch Struan proposed that they went swimming in the lagoon. 'You'll keep down the far end, I'm telling you,' said Athol. 'Maria and I don't want our nesting birds disturbed.'

Struan laughed. 'You and Maria are a pair! Donal, since she came here, Grandfather's always missing when I want him to help me. And if he's not crawling round the forest floor with her, miles away, or stalking the swamps, he's got her in here listening to the bird-calls on the radio, so she can identify them.'

'Well, the lassie can identify so many of our English birds, I wanted her to have a fair go on the bellbird, the *tui*, the *kereru*.'

Struan went on, 'He's such a crafty beggar. He gets out of all sorts of jobs he's not so keen on, spreading manure, and using the big-end loader, on the pretext that Maria has never seen a warbler's nest yet, or that he's found the welcome swallows are building under the old humpy-backed bridge. As if swallows are a novelty to folk from England, anyway, but only to New Zealanders!'

Maria said, 'It's always a minor miracle, Struan. I found that in England. One day, in Cambridge, I thought it even more wonderful than the Tudor roses under the arch of the entrance to St John's, to see house-martins building there, with supreme cheek and confidence.'

'And we're getting far fewer mosquitoes since the swallows have arrived,' said Athol. 'But Maria loves the *pukekos* best of all. I'll have to stop grizzling about them rustling my potatoes next season, I can see. And I'll probably be coaxed into planting a few extra rows for them the year after next.'

Maria blinked. 'The year after next? Athol, I'll be back in England in some hospital long before that!'

His grizzled sandy brows rose, his deep-set blue eyes looked directly into hers. 'Will you, lass? I dinna think we'll let you go.' The sheer affection in his tone made her blink again. She'd realised by now that Athol only dropped into Scots intonation, the tongue of his mother who'd been a Blair, when he was deeply moved. The first time he'd mentioned Blaise he'd said, 'He was a little de'il, a thrawn wee laddie, one hint of opposition and he was off widdershins. But for all that I'd never ha' thought it was going to mean such sorrow for us, that rebellious streak.' It hadn't been a time for words. Maria had merely squeezed his arm, then said, 'There, in the reeds . . . a grey heron!'

She'd looked up widdershins. It meant anti-clockwise. Small Blaise had been a rebel. She wondered what his father had meant. Had some foolhardy, wilful act of disobedience brought Blaise to his death? It could be. He must have been about twenty when he died, seeing Struan had said when she'd seen Johanna bid his photograph good morning, that it had been thirty years ago. Perhaps a shooting accident when hunting, no safety-catch when climbing through a fence. Perhaps tackling some dangerous mountain face when warned not to attempt it. It must be something like that. Some member of the family would talk about it some day.

It was a glorious late November day, a promise of all the days of summer ahead, a stretching from December to February. The bignonia flowers hung in burnt orange clusters where it had climbed, bougainvillea flaunted its gaudy splashes of colour from trees it had wreathed around, from trellises and arbours; canna lilies were growing tall, the blue of the plumbago was attracting the bees. Maria loved the luxurious plumbago, she thought it looked like blue geraniums in the shape of its flower clusters; tree-ferns dotted the trees in the shrubberies with green star-like formations, a hundred mosses and ground ferns enriched the leafy bowers where streams trickled down the hillsides; oleanders reminded her of a holiday spent in Italy, yet all the long-loved blooms of English gardens could be seen here too, spicing the air with nostalgic drifts, roses, lavender, cinnamon pinks, carnations. A lovely, lovely world.

The water, shallower now, was unbelievably warm. It was rimmed with willows and this end was pellucid and still. Romayne had to wear a sun-dress of Maria's, in blue jersey silk. It was brief and served very well. Maria used her coral bikini, and hoped it wouldn't remind anyone of that disastrous scene near the ship's pool. But it seemed as if the water had purged away all enmity and misunderstanding. No one watching would have dreamed these four had ever been anything but the best of friends.

There were cedar-painted garden chairs up here and a long seat, beside a barbecue that was used in the long hot summers of the Hawkes Bay Province. They towelled themselves and flopped on the seats, the sun caressing their skin.

Suddenly Donal said, 'So Athol thinks the Sunrise Coast won't let Maria go too easily. Great chap, isn't he? So much in the habit of adopting people he can't bear to let her go. But what about you, Romayne?'

She looked across at him. 'What about me? I'm only here a day or two. My home's at Longridge, remember?'

The Averell homestead was often called by its English translation of Roahiwi.

His look was intent. 'But for how long? Didn't you say a marriage was in the offing? Your father's? Would you feel comfortable staying on? Would there be enough to satisfy you? This Gertrud will have her own ideas, perhaps?'

Maria felt indignant, stirred a little. What was he up to? This could disturb Romayne, so newly restored to some sort of contentment. Was he purposely being awkward? She sat up. Struan was beside her on the long seat. His arm came round her shoulders, his hand squeezed the far-away shoulder in what she thought was a warning gesture. She sank back. Was it that Struan himself was most interested in the answer to that?

Romayne was gazing over the lagoon, 'Oh, I shan't be home long.'

'Why?' Donal's voice was sharp.

'Gertrud's such a marvellous person I've got the idea she's just waiting to see what I want to do before saying yes to Dad. I feel the years, for them, could go by so quickly, too quickly now. I've applied for a post as a physiotherapist in Tauranga. It's not available till the end of January and if I set my mind to it I ought to be able to get them married before then. If my coming away like this hasn't springboarded his proposal by the time I get home, I'm going down to Gertrud's to let her know I'll probably be going North in the New Year. I'll say I feel a bit selfish leaving Dad without a housekeeper again but I've got to take what offers. I only hope the Napier Hospital stops advertising for one before either Dad or Gertrud see the ad.'

Struan's voice was sharp this time. 'Why on earth don't you apply for that? Must you go so far away?'

'Yes, I think Dad and Gertrud ought to have as much time as possible to enjoy each other, on their own. They had their lives spoiled for each other long ago.' From the way Donal and Struan shut up, Maria guessed it was Romayne's mother who'd been the rift in the lute. Maria broke the silence.

'I saw in the telephone book that Gertrud's name is spelt without an "e" as is usual. Why is that?'

Struan answered. 'Because she's of German extraction. If it had the "e" it would be pronounced Gertruda. Haven't you got a sort of complex about "e's"! Why?—She was astounded to find Hawkes Bay was spelt with one, Donal.'

Maria's cheeks grew hot. Romayne, noticing though not understanding, said quickly, 'Let's go back to the house thataway, over the stile.'

Maria said, 'We can't. It's sheer bog. Athol told me Blaise learned that the hard way—he went in up to his armpits.'

Struan stared. 'You mean Grandfather actually mentioned Blaise to you?'

Now Maria stared. 'Yes, why shouldn't he? He talks about him a lot when we're bird-watching. What——'

'Because he never mentions him to anyone else. All that grief is sealed up in him. Gran often does, to Judith and me, never to Athol. It hurts him too much, she thinks. I think it's very healthy that he's done it to you. Any chance of you encouraging it, Maria, but not obviously? The fact that you've come in from the outside and it happened long ago makes it easier, I guess.'

She said slowly, 'Don't tell Johanna. She could say something and he'd turn in on himself again. Or she might feel hurt it wasn't to her. I must do it naturally, as you say. That car salesman mentioned Blaise to Johanna, used to come out here with Blaise in the school holidays. I'll mention that to Athol.'

Struan had a reflective look. 'I saw him coming out of the loft quarters where he stored Blaise's things, the other day. He didn't see me. It must still hurt. Oh, sorry, this is a sad subject for a glorious day like this. Come on, everyone, I'm starving and Gran was getting the pikelet girdle out before we left. I'm all for pikelets with elderberry jelly and cream!'

On Thursday Donal got word his car had arrived, so Maria drove him in to pick it up and make for Wellington, and she paid for hers. Now she'd be able to take time off to

cruise round Hawkes Bay Province on her mammoth task
of trying to find a homestead with twin towers and a row
of dark pines behind.

She'd need some sort of help. By now she'd gone
through Miriam McGregor's volumes of pioneer women,
with their pictures of early homesteads, but there'd never
been one that even faintly resembled the cutting she'd
found, or mention of a Smith pioneer. She slipped into the
library and began poring over indexes at the back of
volumes of local history, but drew a blank there also.

Nobody here would connect her with the Mandeville
family, so she asked for help. She asked a librarian, 'If I
wanted to do some research on early homesteads still in
the hands of later generations, how would I make that
search?'

The librarian came up with the answer promptly.
'Simply go to the Post Office and ask them for Rural Mail
delivery maps for all the districts, say, covered from
Napier, Hastings, Waipawa, Waipukurau, Wairoa Post
Offices, and so on. The names of the farm owners would
be on them. Take a bit of doing if you couldn't pinpoint
the area, but not impossible.'

'Oh, thank you. That's marvellous.'

'I suppose I can't help you? I've lived here all my life,
and know many outlying areas as well.'

Maria chuckled, 'I was trying to trace someone for
friends in England, but the trouble is, the name is Smith.'

The librarian laughed too. 'Not easy in that case. Unless
it was someone well known, or with an unusual Christian
name ... like Thaddeus or Hezekiah.'

Maria decided to take a chance. 'Well, the man I wanted
to trace—present day—had a not very usual name. Rufus.'

The woman pursed her lips. 'M'm. Not unusual enough,
and there's another snag. That can be a nickname, like
William the Conqueror's son, William Rufus. A redheaded man.'

'Oh, I'd not thought of that.' Then she cheered up. 'Oh,
I've just realised it wasn't a nickname, it was on m——
it was on the birth certificate I saw. His daughter's.'

'Did she not know where her father came from? Most people talk about their childhood.'

'He died before she was born. And her mother wasn't exactly—communicative.' Maria felt singularly detached, as if indeed she was acting on someone's behalf.

'Well, all I can say is she's saddled you with a mighty task, but the only thing I can suggest is the Post Office.'

Maria made for the Post Office. She stored the maps at the back of the top shelf of her wardrobe. If anyone at Amber Knoll saw them, they'd think it very odd.

She pored over them late at nights, taking notes of what Smiths she could find on the mail routes, and began plotting the excuses she could make for taking long days off by herself. Athol and Johanna and Alberta couldn't have circumvented her plans more if they'd tried. They were always suggesting Struan should accompany her on her days off, or inviting themselves along, picnic hampers and all. Twice Athol carried her off in a completely different direction, because there were no birds other than those she'd already seen, where she'd planned to go.

Even when she cunningly managed to take some route, stopped near a mailbox and said, 'There's an interesting-looking house among those trees, I'd like to look at it,' he'd say, 'We'll do that on the way back ... I think we should get to this patch of native bush early in the day,' and ten to one they'd come back a different route. Maria almost gave up. It was so easy as the days grew hotter and the flowers brighter, to let things slip. And life was so pleasant here, why bother to try to find people who wouldn't be half so kindred?

CHAPTER SEVEN

ROMAYNE was often across at the Esk Valley, sometimes driving the distance, sometimes riding. It seemed impossible that it was so near Christmas. Christmas in high summer was absurd. It wasn't till Timothy and Christabel began anticipating it with great glee and the shops began appearing in the old-time decorations that it began to have any reality at all for Maria. It seemed so wrong that they were picking strawberries, making raspberries into jam, seeing the very early peaches beginning to colour on the homestead trees, making gooseberry tarts for the deep freeze against the time when they'd be so busy with shearing and haymaking, that they'd be glad of them.

Struan took Maria in to Hastings, to hear a local choir put on an opera, and as he swung round past the Iron Pot to the port, a hundred Christmas trees against the darkening sky sprang into festoons of coloured lights. Oh, far more than a hundred, because the lights started at Ahuriri where the shipping lay, and continued along Marine Parade, twined in each gloriously symmetrical Norfolk pine as far as the eye could see.

'At last I feel as if Christmas is really here as well as in England,' she exclaimed. Then she added ruefully, 'I'm being silly. In England Dickens made Christmas individually and typically English. But it belongs to the whole Christian world, doesn't it?'

He said slowly, 'Yes, I suppose it can't be a matter of geography. No snow or mince-pies in the Holy Land. It's one of the intangibles. Christmas is in the heart, I guess, wherever you are.'

Maria was swept with magic. 'Oh, Struan, I like that, I like it. My stepfather used to say things like that. So many people think them but are too shy to come out with them.'

'Well, there are some people I wouldn't dream of saying them to, but I find it easy with you—and so does Athol, evidently.'

'Thank you, Struan. That's the nicest compliment I've ever had. And it's brought Mother near too. She used to sing a song I never heard anyone else sing. It's about Christmas. I brought it with me, along with a few more things she composed. I was playing it for the children the other day. Mother was quite gifted. I can only play, but she often set words she liked to music. The last line is almost identical with what you said, about Christmas being in the heart.'

Struan said, 'You seem so much a part of Heronshaw that I tend to forget you had a life before you came out here with Aunt Alberta. Rather selfish of me.' His hand came to cover hers lying on her lap. 'We forget you must sometimes be homesick, that often you must feel very alone. But never mind, Maria, you've more real roots than I have, even if those roots are back in England. Oh, I forgot, your father was a New Zealander, wasn't he? Do you know anything about *his* relations? Most families run to one black sheep somewhere on their tree. Even if *he* was a waster, as you seem to think, you might have people here who would welcome you. Don't you know anything about them at all?'

He felt her hand shake beneath his, but she said sturdily, 'Not a thing. Mother said very little about my papa. She said he never talked about his early days. She had just one sister, a lot older. She died not long after Mother went back to England. So that's it. My life, like yours, is what we make it ourselves, and we were both lucky in the people who brought us up.'

'We were,' he said. 'You in your stepfather, I in Johanna and Athol Mandeville.' He chuckled, 'Johanna and Alberta would think our conversation had taken a very sombre turn! I was told to give you a gala night, in case you were missing the bright lights of London.'

Was that all it was? Struan obeying their suggestions? He certainly didn't seem to be making the pace with Romayne. Could it be he and Romayne didn't want to be too definite so soon after the breach with Donal had been healed?

Nevertheless, the magic still lingered, the local company putting age-old bewitchery into song and acting. They had supper in Hastings, with friends Struan met, and came back to Amber Knoll in the early hours, creeping quietly into the house not to disturb Alberta. Moonlight shone whitely through the landing windows, and pooled silver radiance on a white sheepskin rug at the foot of the stairs. As she paused, one foot on the first step, her long brown and gold skirts trailing back, a green silken shawl about her shoulders, he put out a hand to detain her.

'I've something to ask you. I've been trying to make up my mind about it all day.'

She was glad she had hold of the newel post. She felt as if she were poised in flight. What *was* he going to ask her? Could it possibly be what she most longed to hear? But would a man like Struan be different in love? She didn't think so.

'Yes, Struan?' she said on a thread of sound.

'Donal rang from Wellington today. He said Jeannie, Alastair's young wife, is making a trip with him—and Donal is coming too—they're both in the same stock firm, you know. Jeannie has it in mind that seeing the two families were such friends the most sensible thing to do would be for her to meet Romayne, that it would make for less awkwardness all round. They want to know if they can stay here, meet Romayne across at Longridge. I've not asked Aunt or Gran or Grandfather what they think yet. I thought you—being nearer Romayne's age—might have more idea of how it would affect her. I simply said to Donal I'd discuss it with everyone and ring him back.'

What an anti-climax! One moment filled with hope, with wonder and delight, the next, in the depths. This was just one more evidence of his concern for Romayne. And she must appear unaware. She said, stepping down, 'Let's get away from the stairs. We might wake Alberta.'

She stood by the kitchen table, feeling as flat as ditchwater. She managed to say, 'I think I should ask Romayne straight out. I'll do it tomorrow. Goodnight, Struan, and thanks for a very pleasant evening.' She went swiftly out of the room, unwilling to look as if she had expected a goodnight kiss.

Maria drove over to ask Romayne. She'd never seen her so animated. She'd seen the car from an upstairs window and rushed straight down the stairs and out of the open front door. She leaned in through the car window. 'Guess what? I was just waiting till Dad left the house before ringing you so I could let myself go. He and Gertrud are getting married on Saturday. This Saturday, mark you! Just the family and the Mandevilles ... that includes you, at St Paul's in Napier.

'Gertrud's going round with stars in her eyes and looks positively beautiful. She's lost twenty years. So's Dad. I landed that job in Tauranga. Start beginning of February. This happened overnight. I went to my brother's, Gertrud came over, there was a moon over the Ridge—the very place where they quarrelled thirty years ago. There's romance for you, Maria. Can I come over to Amber Knoll while they're away? They won't hear of me staying here alone, though I wouldn't be nervous. Not with the dogs. But my brother's house is half a mile away, so they're fussing.'

'Alberta will love it. She's always scared I'll miss people of my own age, like in hospital nursing.' Maria hesitated, then plunged, 'That is, if you don't mind that Donal and Jeannie and Alastair will be out at Heronshaw a good deal of that time. It's not a coincidence, it's Jeannie's idea. Donal rang up.' She told her the story.

Romayne said, 'Is Donal keen? Or is he just falling in with what Jeannie wants?'

'Donal was disappointed that Struan just didn't say okay right away. Does that satisfy you?'

'I think so. As far as meeting Alastair and Jeannie it's fine. I only hope Donal has nothing ulterior in mind. I don't feel—ever—that I fully understand him.'

Maria was dismayed. 'Do you mean you didn't accept his apology wholeheartedly? I mean, can't you forget what he said on the ship ... and earlier, after you broke it off? Both you and Struan told me you had a clanging row over that.'

'That does still hurt a bit. He was more upset than Alastair. I'd looked for, hoped for, a different reaction. For more understanding.'

Maria said, 'I feel I've quenched the happiness you felt when you came running out to tell me about your father and Gertrud. But it had to be said, seeing Struan is to ring Donal back. Romayne, are you sure? I think you've borne enough. I could ring Donal and say you just couldn't.'

The expression on Romayne's face changed again, lit up. She put her arms about Maria, hugged her, said, 'I've never had a friend like you before. I can get through anything when I know you're around. I've come alive since we met on the ship, lost my diffidence. Because of you Alberta unfroze, and for some reason I always wanted to stand well in her regard. Oh, here's Dad, all beams.'

Jeannie proved a delight. She was so naïve, so outspoken, had such warmth in her nature, that restraint just melted in her presence. Romayne had managed to meet the two of them on her own, something engineered by Maria, and told her afterwards that Jeannie had swept away all stiffness by dimpling and saying, 'I ought to be madly jealous because you're so classically beautiful and I'm all freckles and snub nose, but I'm not. I'm eternally grateful that you ditched him and left him free for me. Oh, I do hope you meet the right man soon. I like being married awfully. It's fun. Before I got married everyone went round saying, "Don't expect it to be a bed of roses, mind," and I made up my mind that I'd never, ever, say such a horrible thing myself. Anyway, who'd want to lie on roses, they've got thorns. I'd rather have pine-needles. It's all right, Alastair, I know I talk too much, but I'm not going all stiff and shy on it just because you and Romayne were once engaged. Your mother wants us to meet and be friends and what your mother wants goes with me.'

The three of them stayed in Napier till the business was done, but at the weekend they came out to Heronshaw, and had a gay time, swimming, having sessions of baby worship over the twins, worshipping together at the little memorial church at Eskdale. They took Monday off and all drove over to Longridge to have a picnic among the hills.

It was pastoral perfection, with here and there gorse blazing goldenly from hollows, sheep gleaming in white-fleeced flocks against pastures so emerald from this wonderful season of sun and rain, that it looked like an over-painted landscape. It was an ideal morning and noontide for a picnic, and after it they lay, replete, in the long grass under the shade of some native trees.

Maria turned on her back, gazed up at a tall *totara* whose bole rose innocent of branches for two-thirds of its height, said, 'I like the way the English trees are interspersed, so you get the perpetual leafiness of the evergreens, but a splash of colour in autumn as well. Autumn will be in April, won't it? How strange! To me it ought to be the time when the beech leaves are greening and the bluebells coming out in the Surrey woods ... remember "April's in the west wind, and daffodils".'

Jeannie was lying on her tummy, very absorbed in something, a little distance away. 'What is it, my love?' asked Alastair. He sounded half asleep.

'It's a ladybird. It's being so busy. Makes me chuckle. My little niece asked me the other day if a he-ladybird was a daddy-long-legs.'

'Talk about west wind,' said Struan, 'that's a nor'-west wind that's sprung up, and a mighty strong one. To say nothing of a hot one. Look at the tree-tops swaying. That'll be gale-force in exposed places.'

Romayne was sitting on the stump of a poplar that had been felled last year because it was rotten to the core. 'It was like finding an old friend had died,' she'd said earlier. 'It had such lovely hollows in it. I used to hide all my treasures there, the things Mother thought were rubbish, bits of driftwood from the shore, coloured stones and shells. I hope none of the others develop rot.'

Now she thought of it again and glanced up affectionately at Tall Tom, as she called the one set on the very rim of the dell they were in. 'My word, that wind is swaying him!' Then she gave a yell of real urgency, *'It's coming down ... it's coming down!'*

She had the advantage of the others, they were all lying down and weren't looking up, but she didn't run from the danger, she ran clean into it, under it, because it was going to fall on Jeannie. Romayne was tall and she ran like Atalanta, almost horizontally across the ground, and flung herself over Jeannie, pushing her down into the long lush grass.

The others were out of range, had no more time than to spring to their feet when before their horrified eyes, the tree crashed down and the two figures clutched together as one disappeared from sight beneath a heaving, swirling mass of leaves and branches.

They reached the subsiding mass as one, began tearing at the branches with their hands, uttering names as they did so. They saw the gleam of Romayne's white skirt, the glimpse of a pink Indian muslin blouse, but nothing of Jeannie at all because Romayne had completely covered her with her own body.

Donal worked like a man possessed, forcing branches apart, giving intense intructions to the others to hold them back as he worked. He saw the back of a black head lying very still and forced out of him came words he hardly knew he was uttering, 'Romayne, my darling, my darling ... Romayne, speak, say something, move, please, please?'

Her head moved very slightly to one side, brought into view a cheek from which blood was pouring, and the faintest of whispers said, 'Just winded ... I think,' then, 'See to Jeannie.'

Alastair was scrabbling in front of them under Romayne. Jeannie's voice, much stronger, said, 'I'm all right. Romayne saved me ... oh, *is* she all right?' Her little gamin face peered through the network of leaves.

At that moment Donal kissed Romayne. Struan said, 'For Pete's sake, we don't want kisses, we want these branches off them ... come on, man. ...'

Maria was helping too, parting, holding back, gasping as she worked. If the trunk had got them nothing could have saved them from fearful crushing, but it was bad enough and until they got them out, they couldn't know how bad. It became evident that they would get them out without having to send for more help, but the fear was that there might be internal injuries.

Romayne got her breath back ... not only the falling tree had been responsible for the lack of that ... and both she and Jeannie began to reassure the others as they worked. Then suddenly Romayne groaned involuntarily. She said instantly, 'Sorry, it's just that my back's bruised. I——'

Donal said savagely, 'Well, I'm glad you can feel pain. I was terrified all feeling might have gone. Tell us how best we can handle you.'

'Turn me on my side a little, but hold me firmly, and Alastair and Struan can try to draw Jeannie out. I think she's in a hollow. But stop the moment she cries out, in case her legs are hurt.'

Grimly, the men began their task. Maria noticed Donal had his lower lip clenched tightly between his teeth. They edged Jeannie out inch by inch. Maria leaned over into the depression so that when Jeannie was fully out, Romayne's back didn't give way. There was no question of Romayne being lifted off first, she was much further under the weight of branches than Jeannie. Donal had his arms right under Romayne's shoulders now, and drops of sweat rolled off his face on to hers. Another groan escaped Romayne as Jeannie came free, but she said quickly, 'It's all right, just wrenched and bruised muscles. Is she all right?'

They'd dragged Jeannie away to a clearer spot of grass. Alastair said, 'She seems to be ... thanks to you, Romayne.'

Romayne, with her one free hand, made a deprecating gesture, said, 'I had to. For Alastair's Jeannie,' and fainted.

It was Donal who groaned then. Maria said crisply, 'Better she should go out to it for a few moments. But we must be extra careful ... move her inch by inch.' They did it as she said, supporting her body as much as possible, Alastair and Maria lifting the mass off her. Then she was free and they could see her legs weren't broken, though they were hideously scratched. Her extreme pallor terrified them, though. They rushed the picnic rug over, the cushions, thankful for that much comfort, covered her over. She opened her eyes, didn't seem to see anyone but Donal. 'Did I dream it?' she asked, blood trickling from her lip.

'Dream what, my darling?' said Donal, leaning close to her to catch the words. The others stared, their fears stilled for the moment.

Her eyes lit up, focused more accurately, she smiled although painfully, 'Oh, you did it again! It wasn't a dream. You called me darling.' The lip trembled. 'But it's just because I'm hurt, I know. I'm not really, am I? *Your* darling?'

His hand went to her uninjured cheek, 'It's not because you're hurt. It's because you *are* my darling. I've cared against my will. But——'

She almost giggled. 'But me no buts. Oh, I've stopped you ... go on, go on, Donal.'

'I was going to say, but if you'll have me, I'm yours. I've cared against my will—ever since Alastair brought you to Wellington.'

She wasn't in the least embarrassed because they had an audience. 'You idiot! That's why I gave Alastair up. That's why I came on board the ship. Ask Struan.'

Struan said, 'I'm loving this, but it's not the moment. You can do your billing and cooing later. We've got to get help from your brother's, and a doctor, to both of you. To be sure we can move you. Get cracking!'

'*You* get cracking, Struan,' said Donal. 'I'm not leaving her. I died about a thousand deaths. Struan, get the lot, doctor, ambulance, and get her brother's wife up here with the first-aid kit.'

Jeannie was obviously just shocked and bruised, Romayne had taken the damage she should have taken. Romayne was too covered with surface wounds for them to be confident there was no internal harm done, and even though she seemed to be making light of it, Maria wondered if it wasn't merely that the knowledge that Donal loved her was causing her to ride the crest of the wave and ignore her physical hurts.

While Struan was away Maria and Alastair left Donal with Romayne, whispering to her, while they got Jeannie comfortable. Jeannie said in a low voice, 'As long as Romayne suffers no lasting harm, I'm glad the tree fell. Fancy it taking that for those two to get their wires uncrossed.'

Alastair said in a bewildered tone, 'I never dreamed of this ... how could I? Maria, did you know? You were on the ship with them.'

She had to conceal how much it meant to her personally.

She managed a chuckle. 'Not I! In fact, I thought she came on board because of Struan.'

Jeannie's voice squeaked with surprise. 'Oh, how could you, it's clear he——' A fierce look from Alastair stopped her in mid-stream. But Maria knew what she meant, and was glad.

Romayne's brother and his wife came tearing up in a Land Rover, with everything needed in this emergency, including a stretcher, mattress, bandages. The hastily-tied handkerchiefs were removed from Romayne's arms and legs, her face sponged, a warm drink given her, because in spite of the day's heat, her teeth were chattering with shock. She couldn't lie on her back. She lay half on her side, half on her stomach, her face turned so she could see Donal's.

Maria wanted to laugh at the expression on Beth Averell's face when she realised something had happened between those two. When she'd finished her ministrations she came across to Maria and said, 'Am I mad ... do I dream? Or have my eyes deceived me?' Maria whispered what had happened. Beth cast her eyes up. 'What it takes to get some people to make up their minds! But thank heaven it's not as bad as it might have been. Oh, here's Struan, now we'll know what's happening.'

He reported they'd been very fortunate. A doctor had been at Rissington, and was on his way. He would be here before the ambulance, which of course had to come from Napier.

The doctor pronounced Romayne lucky, even though a few uncomfortable days lay ahead of her. He stitched two cuts on her arms, cleaned her up, told her she'd still have to go to hospital to be under observation, have X-rays, etc.

Donal went with her, as of right, but making sure by saying 'I'm her fiancé.' Jeannie was taken in by car, with Alastair, but just treated and discharged.

Maria was astounded at Johanna's reception of the news. She'd looked for great astonishment, but Johanna merely said placidly, 'Well, it saves me tiring my brain trying to think of ways to get that pair to see what was inevitable.

Mind you, I'd never have thought of chopping down a tree to achieve it.'

Even Struan boggled. 'I didn't dream *you*'d twigged it. I wouldn't have, if Romayne hadn't told me when we met up in England, that she gave Alastair up because she found it was the elder brother she really cared for. It was an unwelcome idea at first, one she fought against, but finally she had to break her engagement. When Donal dressed her down so bitterly because she'd jilted Alastair it nearly killed her. But fancy you knowing. How?'

'She and Alastair were here one afternoon and I happened to be watching Romayne when a car arrived. She looked out of the window and for an unguarded moment when she saw it was Donal it was a revelation. Then she dropped her eyes, but I saw her hands clench till the knuckles showed white. Two weeks later the wedding was off. When you came home and said you'd all been on the ship together, I knew hope, only to realise they were further apart than ever.'

Maria said, 'So that's what you meant, Johanna, when you said you didn't think Donal knew yet why the broken engagement had affected him so strongly. You knew he was in love with Romayne, and she with him. What an idiot I was not to see it myself!'

Struan looked surprised. 'But you knew Romayne cared for him. I said she came on board because she'd seen him on the ship at Southampton, and that she was so scared he'd think she was keen to see him, she pretended it was because of me. It put me in a lovely position with you, and Aunt Alberta. Made me look a downright liar. Of course you knew.'

Maria blundered. 'Oh, I thought she wanted to sort of reinstate herself in Donal's eyes so that later on it wouldn't make a breach in the friendship between you and him.'

The deep blue eyes widened. Johanna might not have been there. '*Later on?* What can you mean?'

The betraying colour ran up from Maria's throat. No inspirational excuse flashed into her mind. 'Well, I thought —that is—I—well, it looked as if ... anybody would have thought it.'

Struan's big hand grasped her wrist and shook it. 'Come on, I mean to know. You're forthright as a rule. There've been misunderstandings enough. *What* would anyone have thought?'

She tried to make her tone matter-of-fact, as if it hadn't been vital to her. She even achieved a shrug. 'I thought Romayne had jilted Alastair because she found out that, after all, she'd been ... er ... more attached to you than she knew. It often happens. Girl meets someone new, mistakes novelty for love, and finds out that after all she loves the boy-next-door ... in these great open spaces, sixteen kilometres is practically next-door!'

He whistled, eyes alight with laughter. 'I'd have credited you with more intelligence. You absolute nit!'

Johanna said sharply, 'Struan, you go too far. What makes you think *you're* incapable of giving a wrong impression? Men are like that. They're single-minded and fail to see anything but their own interpretation. Maria was probably fair mazed.'

Maria was recovering. 'Yes, and all that guff about letting Donal think you were interested in *me* put me further off the scent. If it wasn't to lessen strain between you and an old friend, what was it?'

Struan looked a little disconcerted now, glanced at Johanna, who said promptly, 'If you're wishing I'd take myself off, lad, you can keep on wishing. We've had misunderstandings enough ... carry on, I find it intriguing.'

His lips twitched. 'I could deal with it a lot better without my grandmother standing by.'

'I'm here to stop you blundering further, and I will not have Maria hurt.'

'There's favouritism for you! Anybody'd think she was your grandchild, not me.' There was no resentment in his tone.

'She's as dear to me as if she were. And don't dodge the issue. Answer her.'

'Well, with poor Romayne vowing she came on board because of me, I thought we were steering for a situation where Donal *would* think just that and as I knew he'd never spoil my chance with any girl, I made up to you.'

Johanna burst out laughing. 'Some girls would smack a man's face for that, for less than that. But I can see through it, it gave you a good excuse for philandering on the boat-deck in the moonlight, didn't it? I don't blame you.'

He grinned. 'That was it, Gran. That's why Maria hasn't slapped my face. She enjoyed it too.'

Maria's eyes flashed greenly and for a moment it looked as if Johanna's prediction of the slap might come true, but laughter bubbled up in her and she was overcome. 'For sheer effrontery, Struan Mandeville, you take the biscuit! Look, could we change the subject? We got muddled, so let's forget it. How about talking about the weather?'

They didn't need to. At that instant Athol came in, a sheaf of papers in his hand. 'Ah, Maria love, there you are. I've found them—Blaise's sketches of the *wekas*, the *pukekos*, and the stilts. Look, these are what I was telling you about.' He spread them out on the table behind them and quite missed Johanna's transfixed expression, then, as she came to, her startled glance at Struan or the way those two slowly smiled at each other.

The sketches were exquisitely done. Young Blaise must have been quite an artist. Each reed, each bullrush was finely drawn in detail. They could have graced any nature book. The ripples on the water suggested the faintest of zephyrs. Maria, looking more closely, said, 'Were these all done on the same day?'

Athol shook his head. 'No, not even the same season. Why?'

'Just that there's the same dragonfly in each. Look—well, it can't have been the same one, then, but——'

Johanna and Athol laughed. 'The dragonfly wasn't always there, even. It was a little—um—foible of our son's. We had a picture of a flower arrangement—well, still have, up in our bedroom. That artist always put a tiny ladybird somewhere in his paintings. Blaise liked the idea and copied it with a dragonfly. It's his signature tune in a way.'

'What a charming idea! And of course these are very well done. What infinite detail in the striation of the wings on the *wekas*. Oh, what a paradise this place is for bird-watchers!'

Athol said quietly, 'Then why ever think of leaving it, lassie? Must you go back, or am I being selfish? If you felt you must continue with the work you were trained for, you could get a position in Napier Hospital and even if you had to live in, you'd be here at weekends. Think on it, for an old man's sake.'

Maria's eyes were bright. She put an arm about him, hugged him. 'Athol, I'll remember that always.'

Struan said, 'Better still, will you *consider* it? It needs an answer.'

Maria looked not at him but at Johanna. 'It's a habit with you two, adopting people. It looks as if you'll have Romayne here till she and Doñal marry. The house'll burst at the sides yet.'

'Aye, that's what we'd like,' said Athol. 'It was a house built for the big families of the old days, and in our day this family had dwindled. We like to keep adding to it. That's why Alberta brought you back.' He shuffled the sketches together. 'I'll take these back to the quarters, unless . . .' he turned to his wife, 'I've a mind, now I've seen them again, to get them framed, as a set. Perhaps all in one long frame. What do you think, Jo?'

Johanna looked ten years younger than half an hour ago. 'Why, Athol, I'd love it. I'd have loved it long ago.'

He looked startled, 'Then why didn't you say so, lass?'

'I thought it would hurt you. You haven't mentioned them for so long, and you and Blaise were the ones who shared such an interest in birds.'

'Aye, that we did. And it's all been revived since Maria came. Though I've been thinking of hunting these up ever since I went to that exhibition of bird pictures in Auckland, last Easter.'

'You went to an exhibition, Athol? You never said. When you stayed on after that wool sale?'

He was quiet for a moment, then, 'I had the feeling that if Blaise ever carried on with his painting, he might some day exhibit—even under another name—and that could lead us to him.'

It was surprise and shock that held Maria from speech, strong feelings that checked Johanna and Struan from uttering. Then Struan took the sketches from his grandfather's hand and said, 'Come on, Maria, we'll return these to the quarters meantime. I'll put them on Blaise's desk, Grandfather. You can see to them later.'

He whisked Maria, still stupefied, out of the room. He said to her as they crossed the stableyard, 'We won't go back for a bit. He's not mentioned Blaise for so long, they could have quite a lot to say to each other. You've done this, girl, it's sheer magic. He's talked to you so much about Blaise that it's become natural. It will set Gran's mind at rest. She thought the bottling-up of all his disillusion wasn't good for him. Watch your step here, Maria, these wooden stairs are too narrow.'

They were into the upper room before Maria gave voice to her bewilderment. As Struan laid the sketches down he said, 'A bereavement wouldn't have hurt half as much. That heals. This has been a closed wound, still hurting. What are you looking like that for, Maria?'

She brushed back her hair from her forehead. 'I feel so stunned. I thought Blaise *was* dead. Dead thirty or more years ago. Where is he? What happened?'

Struan looked aghast. 'I suppose we thought Aunt Alberta would have explained She knew you some time in England. She and Blaise were sucl ends, from all I hear. He gave great promise, but there seemed to be some flaw in his make-up. He couldn't take responsibility, was very wilful. In his late teens he got into trouble—bad company. A pity he wasn't brought to book for it, but he always just avoided prosecution. Oh, he could charm the birds off the trees, literally and figuratively.

'When he was about twenty, he had, they thought, got into such trouble with the crowd he was in with that he lit out. They suspected he'd stowed away, or got taken on as a crewman, on a certain South American ship that was in port just then. All efforts then, and through the years, failed to trace him. Now it seems as if Athol has never given up hope. The worst feature was that they've always felt they must in some way have been to blame.'

Maria had tears in her eyes. 'Struan, so many families have one black sheep. You don't often hear of a whole family going wrong. If they'd had three or four and seen the others turn out well, they wouldn't have tormented themselves. But when your eggs are all in one basket, it's disastrous. But there's one matchless comfort they must have.'

'What?'

'The way you and Judith turned out, of course. What else? They may not have brought three children into the world, but they reared three!'

The blue eyes lit up. 'Maria ... that's a gift from the gods, a nice compliment, even if not wholly deserved by me, but certainly by Judith.' He chuckled, 'But I can hardly say to Gran "Don't whip yourself, look how I turned out!" can I?'

'Of course not, but sometime I'll make that point on your behalf, Struan Theodore Mandeville, but don't get bigheaded.'

'I'm sure you'd soon take me down a peg or two. You're good at that.'

'What do you mean?'

'Lady, you've a short memory. You cut me down to size, and serve me right, very early in the piece. You said I wasn't the tall, dark, handsome man of the average girl's dreams. I was broad, stocky, and had, above all abominations, sandy lashes! And that you wouldn't marry me if I was rich as Croesus and had diamonds on all my fingers and toes!'

Maria caught her breath in, then said sturdily, 'I did *not* say *above all abominations*. I *don't* abominate sandy lashes. I think——'

He shook her. 'Go on. I've a feeling this could be complimentary, and until today I've never had a compliment from you.'

She wouldn't.

He said, 'Were you going to say you think sandy lashes quite attractive?'

She pulled a face at him and a dimple flashed out. 'I was

going to say I think they're quite attractive *in their own way*!'

'Spoilsport! You deserve to have your ears boxed ... or be kissed.'

'Either punishment fills me with dread,' she said, slipped from his grasp and rushed towards the stairs. He shouted a warning, too late. Her speed on the narrow steps took her out into space, she shot over the hand-rail and pitched headlong very neatly into a huge vat filled with fowls' mash, dry and powdery, that stood below.

He was there in a minute, hauling her out. She was a sight to behold, the cloud of dark hair a mass of sawdust-like particles, her brows and lashes too, and she was coughing and spluttering and sneezing.

His moment of horror gave way to relief and he was overcome with laughter. 'Maria, that was poetic justice. Now *you've* got sandy lashes!' He thumped her on the back, brushed madly at her hair. 'Look, there's a tap on the wall. I'll hold my hands under it, and you can have a drink.'

She bent over his cupped hands, drank deeply, used his handkerchief, dampened, to wipe her face, and said crossly, 'I feel such a sight, and it's all your fault!'

'Women! What does it matter? Nobody could expect to feel glamorous under such circs. You're always in trouble, a mixed-up kid, despite all those nursing medals. Fancy thinking I was in love with Romayne! Never mind. I've a lot of leeway to make up, I know. That interview I had with you when I first heard Aunt Alberta had asked you to accompany her to New Zealand! It would have served me right if you'd led me on, then turned me down flat. What a crass idiot I was! But now——' he noticed a strange look on Maria's face, interpreted it in his own way, pulled himself up, said, 'But I'm not crass enough to go too far with this conversation, with a girl who's just been pulled out of a bran tub! It's not the setting in which to murmur sweet nothings, is it?'

Maria said faintly, 'All I want at the moment is to get under the shower and shampoo my hair. Don't you dare tell your grandparents I was running away from you.

You're in a mad mood. Let me go. It's nearly lunch-time.'

His fingers bit into her arms. 'But still time for this,' and he bent his head and his mouth found hers. She could feel the warmth of him through her silk shirt, worn loose over her cotton trews, the ripple of the muscles under his skin, the compelling force of his whole personality. Not a punishing kiss, but a passionate one for all that. Struan lifted his head. 'Well, not as glam as the boat-deck in the moonlight, but still a touch of magic, wouldn't you think?'

She was suddenly shy, and he knew it. 'It's all right, Maria. You've only just got over the idea that I was in love with Romayne. I'll give you time to get used to the idea that I'm not. I'll let you go back to the house and explain the state you're in. I'll get chipped as it is for letting you fall over the banister.' Before they parted he said wonderingly, 'You know, I still feel Aunt Alberta was up to something when she asked you to come. Not matchmaking, but something.'

She looked up at him saucily. 'But you ought to be more careful just the same. All this kissing and other nonsense could put ideas in Aunt Alberta's head. You know perfectly well they're dying to get you married off, and if she *was* up to something, what else could it be but that? What other reason could she possibly have for wanting me out here in New Zealand?'

'What indeed?' said Struan. 'But there's something. Even yet she has the air of one biding her time. I know my aunt.'

CHAPTER EIGHT

ROMAYNE came home with stars in her eyes and a big sapphire on her finger. 'Donal's mother rang me at the hospital and said as far as she was concerned, she'd like me for a daughter-in-law whichever of her sons I married. She's such fun—exactly what I'd like for the grandmother of my children. I never felt *she* classed me with Mother.

Poor Mother, she was a flibbertigibbet. On all counts now I'm fine, except for the scratches on my face—people look at me as if I've been attacked by a tiger.'

Johanna said, 'Donal's mother must come here for a few days soon. We could fit her in nicely before Christmas.'

'Lovely, she wants us at Wellington for Christmas, so we can go house-hunting. I feel we need it too, to get to know each other properly. Till now we've spent most of our time fighting each other, or cooing at each other across a hospital bed. The wedding's to be end of February. Maria, what do you think of green for your bridesmaid's dress? Judith suits it too, and Christabel, with her gorgeous dark colouring, could be in copper bronze.'

Struan said, 'And the bride will wear a triple row of pearls.'

Romayne looked startled. 'Oh, I'd forgotten. How miserable I was that day! We were walking down Regent Street and were just passing Ciro's when he said, to cheer me up, he was so certain it would all come right, he'd buy me a present there and then to wear the day I married Donal! And he did. I thought he was clean mad!'

Maria was glad Struan had never known what she'd thought, about those pearls. Romayne went on, 'Gertrud is having the time of her life, says she always dreamed of having a daughter and planning her wedding, bell, book, and candle, so I'm giving her her head.'

Maria said, 'You're going too fast! I only meant to stay three months, that's five. I thought I'd have January here, then go on down to Dunedin, and go home shortly after.'

'Sheer nonsense,' said Struan, 'you've no reason to bustle off. Of course she'll be your bridesmaid, Romayne. Otherwise I'll be escorting Judith down the aisle, and where's the romance in that?'

Judith pulled a face at him.

'Why Dunedin?' asked Donal.

Maria turned to him. 'I was born there. Six months later, when my mother realised my father wasn't coming back—he deserted her not knowing I was coming—she went back to England to her sister. I've got my birth certificate. I'll trace the nursing-home if possible, look up

the records, find the house in St Clair, and if any neighbours still exist, I may find out something about my
father's relations. Not my father himself. I don't want to
meet up with him, ever.'

'Very sensible,' said Aunt Alberta briskly, 'but there's
no need to do it yet. You can have all the time you want
after the wedding. Anyway, if you find your relations, they
may not let you go back to England.'

'I shouldn't think they would,' said Judith. 'Any family
lucky enough to be able to claim Maria wouldn't want her
to disappear to the Northern Hemisphere again. We certainly don't. Forget about going back, Maria. I keep saying twins aren't half as much work as I'd thought, and then
I realise that's because you're here. We need you at
Heronshaw.'

Maria felt a rush of tears as she looked at Judith, and
as she did, she surprised a strange look on Aunt Alberta's
face. Almost one of triumph. She *was* a funny old thing!
No wonder, if Struan had caught some such look on her
face in England, he'd wondered what she was up to. But
how sweet to be wanted. A wave of love for Alberta swept
over Maria.

She raised her head, listened. 'I can hear the children
coming. As soon as Christabel has had a snack, I want her
to start her music practice. I want her to be really proficient
in her songs for the Sunday-school break-up.'

'Bless you, Maria. I'd not have had the time this year and
I do want her to stick at this. I don't want her taking up
things in a wild burst of enthusiasm as I believe Blaise
used to do, then tire of it.'

'Oh, Judith, there's something of that in all children.
The main thing is to keep their interest stimulated. She
said yesterday it was an awful lot of practising for such a
short time on stage, so I told her we'd put on a wee concert
of our own, on Christmas Night. I'm making Struan do
those conjuring tricks he did for the children on board,
and Alberta will do some monologues. Isn't Johanna getting a big time out of hunting out the decorations and
refurbishing them?'

'Yes, she's always the same. You never hear her moaning

about the work it makes. I hope we're going to have a couple of carols from you, Maria. I always stop and listen if you're singing to Timmy and Chris.'

'Yes, they've kidded me to do just that. I'm going to use a song my mother always sang to us at Christmas, at the end.'

Judith said softly, 'And by doing that you'll feel she's close to you still, this first Christmas without her,' and went swiftly out of the room.

A singing happiness pervaded Maria these days. She recognised it for what it was. No guilty thoughts now stabbed at her when Struan was about, because Romayne meant nothing more to him than a childhood friend who was going to marry another friend. She even let herself dream dreams at times; in that deliciously drowsy hour verged close on sleep, when all things seemed possible, when she didn't care any more about finding her father's family, she would admit to herself that this family could become her own if Struan ... if Struan ... here she would check her racing thoughts, her compulsive dreams.

The days were too busy for much time to be together. Everything in the garden was coming to fruition, berries to be snatched before the birds could get at them, cherries, early peaches, gooseberries by the kilogram to be bottled. New potatoes, small and waxy, were being dug, peas picked, the surplus frozen; there were endless social occasions, for every single group seemed to have a Christmas party, and once the school year ended Maria spent much time with Judith, organising the children's time.

Sometimes Maria blinked as she opened her windows wider in the mornings, and saw the symmetrical fronds of the phoenix palms silhouetted against the sunrise, looked down to see scarlet and vivid pink and rose-pearl hibiscus blooms opening their cups, the gaudy canna lilies unfurling orange and red banners above their purple-veined fleshy leaves; lemons hanging like yellow lanterns against their enamelled foliage—was there ever a time when a lemon tree didn't have ripe fruit, tiny green fruit and waxy, perfumed blossom? She loved the big thick borders of what she called pampas, and was called *toe-toe* here, and which she found was pronounced toy-toy. The silvery plumes were like magic wands to her, though she loved, of all the trees, the purple jacarandas best. To see the ground carpeted with lavender petals was like walking in fairyland.

'You'll have more time to yourself after Monday,' Judith said, 'because Sadie will be here from then. She always spends Christmas with us since she lost her husband and Gerald went overseas.'

'How the children will love that! I notice they always call her Nanna-Gray; she must love that, seeing Gerald has no family.'

'Yes, she's always been Nanna-Gray to them. She's eternally young. The children never feel she's descending to their level. They know she enjoys their romps as much as they do. She was like that with us too, all those years ago, once she regained her health.'

'Did she have some long illness?' asked Maria.

'Tuberculosis. There was a lot more of it then, of course, in the days before all milk was pasteurised. Tragic really, when so small a thing could all but eradicate it. She was in a sanatorium for three or four years. That's partly why she's still nurse-aiding; she feels she owes the nursing profession so much. When she retires, if Gerald doesn't come back to Napier, Ramsay and I would like to build a granny flat on to Hibiscus Hill. She would be separate but near. Maria, have you noticed that Grandfather even talks to Sadie about Blaise now? He's lost all his inhibitions.'

'Yes, and Johanna makes no secret now of going up to Blaise's Eyrie to sit. She and Athol have even gone together. Judith, how could he do such a thing to parents like that?'

'I've never been able to understand, or forgive it. I dread the thought that if he were destitute or in really grave trouble, perhaps healthwise, he might come back to disturb their lives again. I hope it never happens. I only want them to remember the dear little boy everyone seemed to love.'

Maria looked at the time. 'I must be away. I promised

to take the tea-basket to Struan, he's busy on the fences beyond the Eyrie.'

As she crossed the crest of the hill road to the other side, Maria was surprised to find a man sitting on the stile, and a car parked near. She hesitated for a moment—it was quite lonely—then she smiled, said, 'Oh, hullo, fancy meeting you here.' But her voice held a question. It was the man who'd spoken to her at Marineland, and who'd retrieved her bag for her.

He said, indicating his camera, 'I've been taking shots of the house and farm. I hope you don't object. I do a bit of amateur painting, and I take a basic sketch, and colour slides, and do most of my actual painting inside.'

'Oh, fair enough. I'm sure no one would mind. Take it as a compliment, in fact. Are you taking in the horizon too ... that ship coming in over the sea, and the coast road?'

'No, that makes for too big a canvas.' He held up a tiny cardboard frame, such as might mount a photograph, and put it to his eye. 'I take as much as I can get into this small compass.'

Maria was most interested. 'I can imagine that would make a more intimate, endearing picture. Will you be exhibiting round here? The Mandevilles—the people I'm staying with would be interested.'

'No, I'm not a local man. I live in London. I've business interests in New Zealand and visit often. I thought I'd take some subjects back with me. I've taken the bridge at Rissington, and some of the fascinating bends on the Taupo Road.'

Maria smiled wryly inwardly. So much for this man saying she was like his wife! He didn't even come from New Zealand, much less Hawkes Bay.

He said, 'But I'm holding you up. I take it that's lunch for someone?'

'Yes, for Struan Mandeville, the grandson. He's busy fencing past here.'

Did she only imagine a note of real surprise in his voice?

'A grandson? How? I mean——' he seemed to stumble

over his words. 'I mean, I thought a young couple had the place.'

Her brow cleared. 'Oh, you've seen Struan's sister and her husband. They have another house on the estate. The Mandevilles, Johanna and Athol, adopted twins when they were in their early forties, as grandchildren. They're a wonderful family, very close, even if there aren't ties of blood. It warms the heart to see them together.'

'I'm sure it must. Well, I must be getting along. But you're English, aren't you?'

'In bringing up. I was born in Dunedin, in actual fact, but my mother took me back home when I was six months old. My father had deserted her. Oh, I don't know why I'm telling you this. I don't usually mention it.'

'I take it as a compliment that you did. Perhaps one should pity him, losing a daughter like you.'

'He never even knew he had one. At least, not then. He did know later, I believe. But I had a gem of a stepfather. His family were all I wanted. But he's gone, and so is Mother now. Mother died earlier this year. So I was glad, when Mr Mandeville's sister came to stay next door to us at Osterley, and wanted someone to accompany her out here, to come.'

'Osterley? On the road to London Airport? I know it quite well. It has a stately home I've visited—Osterley House.'

'Oh, we lived quite near there. Willowfield, the guest-house, had a view of Osterley Park from its top windows.'

He chuckled, 'Soon we'll be saying, "small world"— people always do. Where did you live in Dunedin, or don't you know?'

'Oh, do you know Dunedin too? It was St Clair. I hope to see it before I go back.'

'Oh, are you really going back?'

'Well, I've a stepbrother and sister there. I've already stayed longer than I meant to, but I'm to be bridesmaid to a girl who was on the ship with us—Romayne Averell.'

'Of Longridge.' He added quickly, 'I've heard of him at wool sales.' He must be a wool buyer.

'Then New Zealand hasn't cast a spell about you? You've no real reason for staying?'

He was making her feel a little odd. Yet she felt compelled to answer him. 'No, what reason could there be?'

'Oh, I thought this woman who brought you here might have wanted you to stay.'

'She doesn't really need me now she's home. Well, I must get on with my basket, or Struan will be starving. Bye-bye for now.'

He helped her over the stile, released her elbow quickly, and strode off to his car. Struan said, 'Did you bring the car to the top of the hill? I thought I heard one.'

'No, it was a man taking photos. I spoke to him. He's an artist and works at home from slides. A strange sort of man I bumped into in town the day Johanna and I bought the car. He's an Englishman and a bit of a world traveller. Business brings him here. He seems to know the Averells, or of them. He mentioned seeing him at wool sales.'

Struan frowned. 'Bit odd, taking photos. They said there was a man hanging round before we came home. Grandfather was worried about a possible burglary.'

'I think it would be him. He said he'd been here before. But I liked him, Struan. He's just lonely, I'd think. He had rather a sad face. He's going back to England soon.'

'Well, if you see him hanging round again, tell me. I'll chat him up, even invite him down. I'd rather know more about him. And I'd rather you didn't stay chatting to him when you're on your own.'

Maria found that Christmas was Christmas the world over and had a magic all its own here. Judith informed her that the early summer dawn was a decided drawback, because the children woke with the first light and there was little sleep for anyone after that, at Hibiscus Hill. She loved the nine o'clock service at the Eskdale church, surrounded by the peace of the everlasting hills, the slightly Biblical air of the vineyards about them, the bleating of sheep, the lowing of cows, and all the scents of the summer stirring the air. 'A stable atmosphere, after all,' said Aunt Alberta, with deep content. 'We've got gold of gorse, and clove pinks instead of frankincense, and balsam instead of myrrh. What more could we ask?'

'What more?' said Maria in return. 'Oh, Alberta, you're such a kindred spirit. I do wish my stepfather could have known you. I do miss him.'

'Yes, and Christmas is the time to remember the ones we've lost. But at least I don't have to think Gregory is somewhere in this world, as Johanna and Athol do about their Blaise. I miss him too, I loved that boy so much. It doesn't bear thinking of.' Maria slipped her arm through hers and squeezed it.

Home to the Christmas tree, and the exchange of presents, all gathered now in the big house. The children had brought over all the small things from the stockings they'd opened so early, the place was a-foam with tinsel and tissue and bright wrapping-paper. Their own turkeys graced the table, fresh peas, new waxy potatoes, roast pumpkin, a little different from the vegetables at home, but there was the traditional pudding, something which meant their swim would have to be postponed till it was digested.

At last the long day of a semi-tropical Antipodean Christmas was over ... the sunbathing, the barbecue tea, the babies had been tucked down to sleep upstairs, and they began their carol concert, compèred by Maria. It went well, the monologues, the songs and recitations, Struan's few conjuring tricks, greatly successful because they were such an uncritical audience, he said.

Maria sat down at the piano, said, 'Because I want to remember my mother at this time, here's a song she set to music herself. She was quite gifted that way. We always had this to finish up with at Christmas parties. She had a lovely lilting voice. Mine isn't nearly as good as hers.'

She was underestimating herself. They'd turned out all lights except the ones above the piano. The light caught the chestnut glints in Maria's hair, tied back with a piece of emerald gauze, to fall in a bunch of turned-under ends over the simple scarlet and emerald patterned dress she wore, sleeveless and cool. Beyond her was an urn of holly, which lacked berries at this time of year here, but in which Judith had cunningly placed scarlet Shirley poppies to provide the right splash of colour. It was a light tinkling tune, that had within it the sparkle of tinsel and the chime of faraway sleigh bells. Maria's fingers rippled the keys.

> 'You love it all, I know, I know,
> The gilt, the imitation snow,
> The Christmas cards, the tinselled string,　•
> The parcels, one and everything;
> The fir trees twined, the rosy glow
> Of Yule-tide logs, the mistletoe,
> The frosty-spangled Christmas tree,
> The banter and the revelry;
> The holly berries bright and red,
> The hay-filled manger for a bed,
> The angel-songs, the guiding star,
> The Wise Men travelling from afar;
> The bairns that find with glad surprise
> The gifts your clever hands devise....
> You'll never lose the shining joy
> Of choir and carol, book and toy,
> For you have found the matchless art
> Of keeping Christmas in your heart.'

Maria knew they would love it. She swung round from the stool as she finished, and was instantly aware that the atmosphere was charged with some emotion she couldn't define. Her eyes widened, her lips parted. Struan and Ramsay and Judith looked exactly as usual except that they too seemed puzzled by the reaction of the four older people. Athol's face had graven lines down his cheeks, Johanna's eyes were full of tears, Sadie was so still she didn't appear to be breathing, and Aunt Alberta looked—of all things—apprehensive.

Athol tried to speak and failed. His look at Johanna was a mute appeal for assistance. Someone had to say something, it seemed to say ... here was a lassie singing a bit of a song, and none of us can say a word!

Johanna responded immediately. 'Maria, where did you get that song? Where *could* you have got it?'

Maria swallowed. 'Like I said—Mother set it to music.

I don't remember a Christmas when we didn't sing it. It was a favourite. But what's the matter? Why is it important?'

'Where did she get the words?'

'I don't know. Out of some magazine I'd think. It's yellow with age. She's got it clipped to the sheet of music and she's copied the words out again beneath the notes.'

Struan took it from her shaking fingers, and said, 'It's only stuck on by the top. There might be something on the back that'll tell us where it came from, but why, Gran? Why is it important?'

'Because our son wrote that poem. He wrote it when he was seventeen. Wrote it to me. It was his Christmas present to me that year, copied out so beautifully as a centrepiece in a border design of Christmas things, candles and mistletoe and ivy and fir-cones. It was ruined when we had that torrential rainfall before we had the new roof on. He must have got it published after he left here. Struan, where was it published?'

Out of the corner of her eye, Maria saw Judith cross to Sadie and take her hand in hers. Why? Struan said, 'There's an advert on the back, some shop in Princes Street, Edinburgh. Must have been in some periodical there. Very little hope of tracing it, I'm afraid. There's not even a name beneath the poem.'

Maria crossed to Johanna and knelt beside her. 'I'd never have sung it had I known. I couldn't know. It's a cruel coincidence. I——'

Johanna's hand came to Maria's dark head. 'Maria, don't take on. It's not cruel, it's a minor miracle. The music is so right for it. It somehow lifts my heart to know he cared enough to submit it to a magazine. Maybe his life hasn't been all waywardness and wrongdoing. His art, his writing, have still been part of him. There now, dear. I always feel at Christmas-time as if Blaise is shut out, but not this year. Sadie knows it and we sometimes have a little chat about him, as he used to be. But when you sang that it was as if a little bit of him was still here. God bless him, wherever he is.'

Aunt Alberta cleared her throat and rose. 'Now it's time

we had a last cuppa and Struan and Maria and I will away
to Amber Knoll. I'm glad we were able to hear that poem
again, Maria, and you must never have a single regret that
you sang it for us.'

Back at Amber Knoll Aunt Alberta pleaded weariness.
'Don't keep Maria up late, Struan. We've a big month
ahead, harvesting the small seeds, cutting the last of the
hay, bottling and preserving and freezing.'

He laughed when she had gone. 'Off with the motley, on
with the hard labour, that's Aunt Alberta!'

Maria went across to the uncurtained window, looked
out beyond the sweep of the shadowy hills to where she
could see the odd light winking out from down the
coast and said, 'They took it magnificently, but oh, how I
wish my mother had never come across that poem, that I'd
not brought it with me.'

Struan came up behind her, slipped his arms about her.
'Maria, don't. I've a feeling that the best gift Christmas
Day brought my grandmother, all of them, and especially
Sadie, was your song.'

She turned a little in his embrace, to look up at him. Her
hands covered his. 'Sadie especially?'

'They were childhood sweethearts. She broke her heart
when he slipped away with never a farewell word. He did
leave a note for his parents—said he felt he must get away
and live his own life or he'd be smothered. He said he
didn't want to marry and settle down and never see the
world. That was his only reference to her. Oh, it probably
went deeper with her than with him. But Judith and I
have always thought that despite her very happy marriage,
Blaise remained for her the Prince Charming of her
idealistic years.'

Maria said passionately, 'I hope he never comes back. It
would make havoc of their lives again. To a certain extent
it's healed. They've never had a single word in all the
years, have they?'

He said slowly, 'There was only one thing ever, and only
Gran believed in it. The rest of us thought it was wishful
thinking. We had a spectacular flood. It was widely reported, ten years ago. Despite Government compensation,

it was a terrific setback to our estate, and others. Completely anonymously a very large sum was paid in from somewhere overseas. We were never told where. It came through a solicitor in Wellington and he said he had to preserve the complete identity of his client. Johanna believed Blaise had made good and this was his way of reparation for causing them sorrow, though evidently he had some reason for not wanting to return, or be thanked. I think she thought he couldn't come back to New Zealand. But it was a comfort to her.'

He turned her round to face him. 'And now, Maria Willoughby, you look much too sad for Christmas night, and earlier, you looked like a Christmas tree yourself in your green and red dress. You're not to lie awake milling over this. How about me giving you other things to think about ... like this ...?'

She saw the well-chiselled lips smile, the light from the lamp turn the sandy hair to a bleached silver, pure Nordic, she'd say. Maria had never known such emotions sweep over her. She was almost afraid of them. It was nearly New Year ... this year with its sadness and misunderstandings and moments of sheer joy would soon be behind them. The glad, glad thing about it, looking ahead, was that Struan didn't love Romayne as she'd thought so long, never had loved her. Just before his kisses blotted out all coherent thought Maria offered up thanks that now nothing barred the way to a deeper relationship between herself and Struan Mandeville. If only she had known!

Boxing Day wasn't a holiday on the farm. They dared not tempt fate on this day of soaring temperatures by not baling the hay that had been cut a day or two ago. The men were out early, had made their own breakfast, the baler rolled out into the paddocks and the work began. Alberta and Maria went across to the big house to help with the batches of scones and pikelets, to cut thick wedges of fruit cake and to prepare a lunch that, with long knowledge of hayfield appetites, was as substantial as a dinner.

Maria was to take the smokos out, picking up Sadie on the way, who would have the flasks filled. The paddocks lay beyond Hibiscus Hill, looking towards the sea. She took the car. A track of sorts led to where they were working. It was idyllic, with never a cloud in the sky to worry the men. The scones and mini-pancakes disappeared like magic. Sadie looked a lot younger, out here among the hills. Her fair hair was only slightly silvered at the temples and she had an exquisite complexion. They were sitting in the shade of an enormous beech tree, planted, Sadie said, by Ellaline Mandeville more than a century ago. 'It's odd, but of all the history that belongs to this estate, Ellaline was the one who was always most vivid in character to me. Nothing so satisfied me as when Judith married Ramsay, a descendant of Parehuia's, Ellaline's best friend.'

She laughed. 'I still hope it may be Judith, or perhaps little Sara and Christabel who'll be the Mandeville daughters to discover the buried heirlooms. Oh, perhaps it's naïve to believe that long-ago prediction, only somehow Johanna and I have always clung to it. If it does come true, may it be in Johanna's lifetime.'

Words tumbled on to Maria's lips. 'I think that's the loveliest thing of all, that an adopted daughter is looked on as a possible part of that prediction. Judith mentioned it when Sara was born, that perhaps here was another daughter to share with Christabel the finding of it.'

At that moment she turned to look at Sadie, sitting beside her on the daisy-sprinkled turf. She blinked. What was Sadie looking like that for? The clear blue eyes had darkened with emotion. 'Judith hasn't told you? She's Blaise's daughter ... *and mine*. The children *are* our grandchildren, his and mine. The Mandevilles' great-grandchildren.'

There were no words. For courage and candour, Sadie Gray deserved a medal. Maria moistened her lips, tried to speak. Sadie put her hand over Maria's. 'I thought you knew. I thought Judith would have told you. Even Struan, though he's not quite so likely to. Alberta wouldn't, she's always felt it was over to us, but most folk round here knew. Blaise's parents legally adopted the twins so they could bear the name that should have been theirs.

'Maria, don't think too badly of Blaise that he didn't

marry me. He never knew the twins were coming. Not till after he'd gone did I know myself. Blaise isn't to be blamed any more than I am. I've never felt that. We let our feelings get out of hand for so brief a time. We met too young, we fell in love too soon, we grew too serious.

'My parents and his were wonderful. The worst blow was when it was discovered I had tubercular trouble. It was not long before the birth. My parents were considerably older and not as strong. I saw very little of the babies for two years because of the risk of infection. That was the hardest to bear. But I regained my health completely and ten years later I married Sylvester Gray, who'd been a school friend of ours, and I had another son. He knows all about it, and Judith has never hushed it up from anyone.' (She must mean that Struan feels it more.) Sadie added, 'Oh, Maria, don't cry. It happened so long ago, and the greatest sadness was for Johanna and Athol. Theirs was more cruel than if they'd lost him as a little boy.'

'I can't help it, Sadie. For *you* to bear all that! I thought for so long Blaise had died. The way they talked of him I could just see that darling little boy. Alberta, who had no child of her own, talked of his cowlick and his knobbly little knees and reciting poetry far beyond his understanding. She quoted him as rolling out that bit about the state of man ... "Today he puts forth the tender leaves of hope, tomorrow blossoms." I liked that. It's so hard to reconcile that little boy and the youth who wrote that lovely poem to his mother with the one who left them, and you, without word so long.'

Sadie looked out to the shimmering blue sea. 'I know. That's how Judith feels. She hopes he never crosses our path again. And yet I——' she paused. 'I've never said this even to Judith, but although I loved Sylvester deeply I sometimes feel I wouldn't like my life to end without having at least a glimpse of Blaise. I hope he married and settled down and had a family. I hope he's never been lonely or ill without someone to look after him. That's all I'd ask, just to know he was well and happy.'

Maria said, 'Sadie, I hope if ever I'm disillusioned as you were that I'll be as free of bitterness. Thank you for telling me. I admire and love you more than ever now.'

They picked up their baskets, moved towards the five-barred gate, drove back both aware that in those moments they'd forged a friendship as enduring as these hills.

Later, pondering, Maria wondered that Struan hadn't told her. True, he had hinted that Judith might. She thought of something read a few months ago. A woman had written of her own life as an illegitimate child and what comfort it had brought to countless others. She had found, strangely, that men were more embarrassed by it than women. Yet Struan was so well balanced. They'd talked along that line once. She'd mentioned Leonardo da Vinci. But he'd not told her the whole truth then, he had skirted round it. Possibly he loved his mother too much to want her talked about. Yet he hadn't seemed to mind the possibility that Judith would some day tell her. How had Sadie stayed so sweet? In spite of admiring her attitude, Maria herself knew resentment against Blaise Mandeville for all the sorrow he'd caused, even havoc.

Suddenly she thought with horror of the poem she'd quoted. Thank Heaven she'd not stumbled on ... 'to-morrow blossoms, and bears his blushing honours thick upon him; the third day, comes a frost, a killing frost. . . .'

Sadie had known that frost.

Now the real heat of a Hawkes Bay summer was upon them. Sometimes it seemed to quiver tangibly on the air, sometimes it seemed too hot for even the birds to sing. The pansies in the garden would flop their leaves to the parched ground, the delphiniums and hydrangeas hang their heavy heads. They spent all their evening hours soaking the gardens. They had to be careful not to get hideously burned and sought the shadiest pools in the river for swimming.

Sadie stayed most of January, helping her daughter with the babies, taking the other two children off Judith's hands, revelling in being a grandmother. Maria loved to watch her with Stuart and Sara, changing them, singing to them. As Sadie looked down on them, Maria knew she was seeing in them the little helpless infants she'd had to leave to Johanna's care thirty years ago.

One night as Struan and Maria and Alberta were walking home from Hibiscus Hill, Maria said, 'What a pity Sadie is going home this week. She loves the children so.'

Struan said, 'Has Judith told you of the relationship, then?'

Alberta seemed to stumble on the moonlit path. Struan steadied her.

Maria said, 'Judith didn't. It was Sadie herself. What I thought loveliest of all is that she bears Blaise no malice.'

Struan said, 'She leaves it to us to feel bitter on her behalf.'

Alberta said, 'You never knew him, you see, Struan. When I look at Sadie I always think of: "Love is not love that alters when it alteration finds." That's Sadie's creed and she lives by it. But I still love Blaise too.'

Maria changed the subject. She was the outsider. *Her* life hadn't been affected by Blaise. It was evidently a sore spot with Struan, and no wonder. Old sins cast long shadows, and it was the children who were the innocent victims.

Time, she felt, was rushing by too fast. To compensate the children for not going away for holidays this year because the twins were too small, they took them out for as many day trips as they could, to river and beach, to all the delights of the Marine Parade with performing dolphins and magnificent aquarium treasures. Once when they could spare a really long day away, they went right through Havelock North, and beyond, under the carved splendour of Te Mata Peak, that looked like a recumbent giant on the skyline, to an almost limitless stretch of beach, Waimarama. 'It means moonlit water,' said Struan to Maria, 'and by moonlight it's really something out of this world. I'll bring you here alone some night.'

The wind whipped her cloud of dark hair back as she rose from the water to face another big roller. 'Isn't it a long way to come to see a moon?'

His eyes glinted audaciously. 'Could be worth it. After all, a moon can engender a mood that makes one forget to watch it. Much more romantic than barrels of bran, my lass. You've spoiled some of my best moments ... thinking I was in love with Romayne, running away and the next moment spitting chaff at me! As for this month ... phew! What with Romayne bringing her mother up, kids under one's feet all the time, dressmakers popping in and out ... every time I'm free of farm work, you're either hosing the garden, baking, ironing, or bringing in armfuls of nappies; or building dams in the creek with Timothy and Christie! Or, heaven help me, like yesterday, when they told me you'd gone for a walk in the oak wood, and I found you hosing down the pigs because you thought they were suffering from heat exhaustion! The only thing those pigs were suffering from was their usual gluttony!'

Maria's laughter rang out. 'Don't waste these lovely rollers, Struan ... see you on the other side!' She dived clean through as the green water reared up to curl over. He dived after her, ducked her as she came to the surface.

'At least in February the children will be back at school and not your constant shadows.'

'The wedding will be nearer, we won't have a minute to spare. I've had to postpone going down to Dunedin till March.' She flung her wet hair back out of her eyes.

'March is the best time of all for Otago. Or April, when the colours are at their best. I'll come with you, Maria. You mightn't like what you find down there. You might need someone with you.'

They were standing waist-deep in the water. She gazed at him. 'Would you do that, Struan? But I haven't any illusions about my father, so 't won't hurt me.'

'Then that makes two of us. His voice was rough, almost angry. 'So it means I'd under nd o one else could.'

'Except Judith.'

'Yes, Judith, of course.'

Maria swallowed. In that moment, because of the resentment in Struan's voice, she hated Blaise Mandeville for what he'd done to his son. Struan cared, cared horribly. He'd had loving grandparents to bring him up, but he'd never known the completeness of a family that was mother, father, children.

She said softly, though no one was near, 'I'd like you to come, Struan. I'm not trying to find my father, just word of his people. It's a long shot, that anyone in the street might know where he'd come from originally, but I must try. But if I don't like them, I won't let them know of my existence. It will cease to matter.'

'It will cease to matter when you've a home of your own, a husband, children. You'll start a new dynasty, new traditions. Look out, here comes a monster! ... turn your back and ride it in.'

They held their hands in front of them, launched themselves as it broke, came up on the beach in shallow water and joined the others.

That night Maria knew a deep content. One thing she wanted, and that was to find that her roots did indeed lie in Hawkes Bay, that that torn-off caption would lead back here, because this was Struan's province. But she wouldn't involve him in trying to find the source of that picture till she was fairly certain it was here. And anyway, suppose she never found out, she was fairly sure now that she was going to find the happiness of her life on this glorious Sunrise Coast.

The February days were even hotter, the red gums were still burningly scarlet, there were whole avenues of them in town, the sea was sapphire, frilled with white, a tame dolphin came in to Westshore and frolicked with the bathers, followed the fishing-boats out to their grounds each day; the paddocks scorched to tawny-gold, the cicadas never ceased their shirring, the dragonflies by the lagoon glinted like living rainbows among the reeds, and at night they were grateful when at last the sun sank down behind the forests of the Kaimanawas.

Aunt Alberta had a Gisborne friend to stay with her and Maria recognised her immediately as a woman who'd stayed in the Willowfield guesthouse last year. She said to Alberta, 'Did you know she'd stayed there?'

'For sure I did. That was why I came to Willowfield, because Ruth mentioned how well she'd been looked after there.'

'How odd you didn't mention it to me.'

'I didn't realise at the time how often you were in and out of the guesthouse.'

Struan took some more mustard. 'But that was how *you* met Maria, the fact that she *was* in and out of the place.'

Alberta said, 'Well, you know what I mean, it just didn't occur. Ruth, don't you think that boysenberry jam is extra nice this year? The berries were really luscious up here. I've bought a lot and frozen them for pies.'

Struan, wiping dishes for Maria, said, 'Why was Aunt being cagey?'

'Goodness, what a suspicious man you are where Alberta's concerned! It just didn't get mentioned, that's all. They're great friends, I can see. Were they at school together?'

'No, I believe she lived in Dunedin, till she went to Gisborne to live nearer her daughter. Aunt met her at an Institute conference, and I think she stayed with her when I was away. But how strange she should go to Osterley to stay. Odd how lives criss-cross, isn't it?'

'Yes,' Maria agreed. 'I ran into that man who was taking photos of Heronshaw the other day in town. I was having a cup of tea in the Balcony tea-rooms and so was he, so we shared a table. He's been back to London since I saw him last. He's so attractive, but seems so lonely. He was rather interested in the family set-up here. I did what you said, asked him would he like to come out and see over it, perhaps sketch the house at closer quarters, but I think he thought the rest of the family might think it rather pushing.'

'M'm. I remember I did suggest that, but why's he always turning up where you are?'

She chuckled. 'You sound like a Victorian papa! He's old enough to be my father, for one thing, and for another, in a town the size of Napier, with only two main shopping streets, one's always bumping into someone one knows. I don't even know his name.'

Maria looked in on the two ladies. 'I'm off with Struan for another riding lesson. I may not be sitting down for the evening meal! Perhaps I'll make curry and rice, that I can use one hand for, and eat standing up. He's determined to make a horsewoman out of me, but it's hard going. I'm sure I take after my sailor father, but Struan won't have it. I've told him he'd better buy a boat and sell his horses.'

'I think you'll find you've got horsemanship in you,' said Alberta comfortably. 'Nothing to stop a sailor from riding.'

'You've more confidence in me than I've got myself,' said Maria darkly, departing unhappily.

CHAPTER NINE

MARIA had just caught up with Struan when she thought of something. 'I'll just run back and get something to tie my hair back with—I clean forgot. I like to see where I'm going, not have my hair in my eyes, to make sure no trees or pylons are rushing across the landscape towards me. You said Shanks was only an ambler, but he goes far too fast for me. I suppose you wouldn't settle for a bathe in the lagoon?'

'I wouldn't. On a property as big as this you need to have quick transport to places where even the Rover can't go. And come the autumn muster, you'd be handy on horseback. Right, off you go.'

The French windows on to the balcony were open and evidently Alberta and Ruth had moved to the patio below, and their voices were clear on the still air.

'For once in my life,' said Alberta, 'I'm afflicted with indecision. It's got to be told some time, but it's the question of picking the right time. It's been on the tip of my tongue for so long, but always some instinct has made me hold back. There are so many people to be considered, especially Sadie and Judith. I've a feeling I've meddled once too often. The others would love it, I'm sure. I've never been one to sit back and say I'm waiting for guidance—I think that's a lazy way. I've always felt God gave us our reasoning powers and He expects us to have gumption. But no amount of reasoning or gumption tells me how to deal with this. I feel so unsure of myself. Responsible too.'

Ruth's voice sounded unhappy. 'Not as responsible as I do. I started it. But perhaps time will show us the way.'

'Perhaps, and if what I hope comes to pass, then in a way that would solve it. It would seem so fitting. As if Fate had taken a hand. Yet by every ethical standard she has a right to know.'

Maria suddenly realised she was eavesdropping and that it seemed something very private. She must creep away so that neither of them suspected they'd been overheard. She wouldn't even tell Struan. It was probably some Insitute business, and not a family matter at all.

This lesson was more successful than the previous ones. When at last it was over and they came back to the horse-paddock, Struan said, 'You're getting the hang of it at last. You were master of your mount today, and he knew it. I'm looking forward to some early morning rides when you're more proficient. Nothing like an autumn morning with dew on the hill-grass and a sea-breeze coming from the east. We could certainly do with some dew right now. These are drought conditions all right. Much longer and the Prime Minister will declare this a disaster area. When it does break, it'll probably bring floods. That's what usually happens. Just to even things up the rain forgets to stop.'

He swung down, flung the reins over a post, held up his hands to her. Maria wrinkled her short straight nose at him, with its smattering of freckles thicker now since she'd been so exposed to the sun, and said, 'If I'm as much improved as you condescendingly remarked, I think I'm capable of getting down myself ... as long as he doesn't move off while I'm in the middle of it.'

'Well, don't risk it. And don't be such a spoilsport. This is the nicest part of the whole lesson ... for me.'

She swung down and was held in a hold there was no breaking. Struan's hand went under the short ponytail of hair, kept her head steady. It was a long kiss. She didn't want to move, told herself she was afraid of startling Shanks. He lifted his mouth a fraction, said, 'Let yourself

go, Maria. You can, I know. Like once on the boat-deck.'
She was aware of those feelings stirring within her that
were strong, gloriously right, a little frightening in their
intensity. When breath became essential he released her a
little, but his arms were still about her. The blue eyes between their thick sandy lashes looked down into the hazel-
green ones.

Then the sound of a smack upon a rump startled them,
and simultaneously a voice said, 'Move on there, moke,
I've an idea that without you, the view of the doings on the
other side would be much more interesting!' They gasped,
turned. Athol, grinning from ear to ear. 'That's better. I
could just see two pairs of legs, but they were very
eloquent. I'd say television's taught you a thing or two, old
son!'

Struan burst into a great guffaw of laughter. 'You old
devil! Sneaking up like that! You ought to have done the
decent thing and faded away into the spinney, or at least
coughed. This is the first time Maria and I have been on
our own for ages. It's like living in a glasshouse, Heronshaw just now. Visitors, visitors everywhere and never a
place to court in.'

Maria had a high colour. Struan went on, 'Anyway,
Grandfather, what did you want?'

'Maria—I wanted Maria. I've discovered a wax-eyes'
nest hung by horsehair on one of the pines on the knoll.
I've got the motor-bike over at the sheds, she can come on
the back with me.'

Struan flung up his hands. 'If it's not callers, it's birds
and grandfathers! A fellow can't get a chance. All right,
I'll unsaddle the horses and rub them down, I know when
I'm beaten.'

Maria sounded apologetic. 'You see, Struan, I've never
seen a wax-eyes' nest. Your grandfather tells me they
suspend them from the undersides of branches by horsehair and they look like fairy baskets. If they can't get
horsehair they've been known to use spiderwebs, and I can
only hope I see them at it before I leave, because how they
can do it without getting gummed up, I can't imagine.'

Athol scowled. 'Time you stopped talking of leaving.

Lassie, we canna let you go. I've never seen Alberta so happy. If it's selfish, I canna help it. I'll pay for your step-brother and sister to come out to see you some time if that'll help you settle.'

'It won't take that,' said Struan, unbuckling straps. 'My technique will beat yours hollow, Grandfather,' and he was smiling to himself as they turned away.

Despite the desperate need of rain, they were unashamedly rejoicing when Romayne and Donal's wedding-day dawned with cloudless skies and the promise of great heat. Maria, out early in the Amber Knoll garden cutting roses for the vases before the temperature could pale their petals and droop their heads, said so, then laughed as Struan said, 'There's a Chinese proverb that says if it didn't rain for three years someone would be bound to want it to stay fine for just one day longer.'

'How true! Good job that none of our wishes can cause a raindrop to fall, or the sun to appear.'

He laughed. 'That's got a Biblical sound, O sage.'

'No wonder,' she said dreamily, adding some sprays of gypsophila to the rosebuds. 'In a setting like this, you haven't got to be a psalmist like David to be inspired to poetry.' She waved her hand. 'I could quote the Bible for ages, this morning, like: "The little hills rejoice on every hand."' She added, 'I don't remember ever learning that, but it suddenly popped into my mind. No wonder! In scenes like these, I often think of the title of that book: *All This and Heaven Too*.'

He grinned. 'Ever hear of the old lady who couldn't remember that title and asked in the library for Rachel Field's *Heaven and Then Some*?'

Maria's laughter rang out on the clear air. Alberta, upstairs, heard it and was glad. Surely a happy ending was coming to all her doubts.

Struan said, 'I'm glad you're wearing green ... to match your eyes. It suits Ju too, with her copper hair. But she's got Sadie's blue eyes. Otherwise, had she had Gran's eyes as well as her red hair, she'd have been her living image.'

This was the nearest he'd ever got to talking of the relationship. She said, 'Was Blaise redheaded too?'

'No, he had Grandfather's colouring—sandy like me. Look out, Maria, those dahlias are full of earwigs, shake them out.'

She laughed, 'The serpent in the garden! Anyway, I must go in.'

As Maria, with Judith, walked behind Romayne and her father up the aisle, Romayne in white lace, with palest pink rosebuds, she was reminded of seeing her come towards them on the ship at Tahiti, in oyster satin, shot with silvery pink. Then Maria had known doubts, and envy, because she had thought Struan was in love with her. Then there had been that horrible moment of naked malice when Donal had taunted Romayne about Alastair's wedding ... oh, how time healed things. Now, here, Alastair was standing with Donal, so was Struan, and happiness was ahead of everyone. As Romayne moved forward to stand beside Donal, Struan turned his head a little and his eyes met Maria's, a smile at the back of them. In that moment she knew that her future lay here in the Esk Valley, that she wouldn't be taking that flight back to London....

It was a long and beautiful day, with the lovely rooms of Roahiwi flung open to guests and sunshine. Mercifully a faint zephyr came up from the sea and stirred the hot air, though guests still fanned themselves with their souvenir hymn sheets and sought patches of shade where seats were scattered under the trees.

Sadie seemed particularly radiant. She said to Maria, 'I'm so proud of Judith. Nobody would think she's the mother of four children. Look at Ramsay's face, he's just bursting with pride. I feel as I felt when they married that Parehuia knew and was glad that her family and the Heronshaw family were united in matrimony. Is that too fanciful?'

'It certainly isn't. We talk of the unseen world as being all about us, so why not in moments of special happiness? By the way, you're not only looking beautiful yourself in that soft blue, Sadie, but every time I look at you I think there's a sort of ... well, something about you. An aura, as if you'd heard good news.'

Sadie's eyes, as blue as Struan's, widened. 'I didn't think it would show. I—oh, it's stupid, but I'd love someone to share it with. I dreamed of Blaise last night. It hasn't happened for years. Perhaps because I was thinking, just before I fell asleep of how beautiful Judith was in that green dress, and I thought with intolerable longing how I'd love Blaise to see her. Even if he doesn't know about her she's still flesh of his flesh and bone of his bone. And mine. *Ours*. I dreamt we were both among the wedding guests, and Judith was standing behind Romayne and she turned and smiled at her father. She thinks she hates him, but if she knew him, she couldn't. And I woke, and it was dawn, and I lay there warmed and comforted. It was just as if it had really happened.'

Maria's hand took hold of Sadie's. 'Sadie, perhaps for some reason Blaise was thinking, or dreaming, of you. I think some things can set time and distance away. I'm so glad.'

It was all over. Romayne and Donal, shining-eyed and serene, had departed for their Norfolk Island honeymoon. Guests from Napier stopped off at Heronshaw to talk over the wedding, managed, in spite of the excesses at the feast, to do justice to a large supper, and it was one-thirty before Struan shepherded Maria and Aunt Alberta to Amber Knoll.

At three the drought broke in a spectacular thunderstorm that brought them all out of their rooms and downstairs, to watch the vivid flashes of sheet lightning, the zigzags of the forked lightning split the darkness, while thunder rolled and crashed fearfully among the hills and valleys. They rang the other two houses to make sure everyone was all right, because they could see lights coming on in them, but all was well. There would be damage done, of course, but nothing could be done till daylight.

They found to their surprise next day that the damage was surprisingly light. They sorrowed over a couple of

trees that had been struck down, but they still had power
and the telephone. Some areas were without both, some
roads blocked, but on the whole it had been spectacular
rather than disastrous. Alberta went across to Judith's to
do some ironing, Maria to help Johanna clean out her
storeroom. The men were out inspecting fences and cul-
verts.

She found Johanna in the drawing-room, on her knees
examining the carpet where the jutting-out wing com-
menced. 'What is it?' she asked, dropping down beside her.

'The guttering must have been blocked with leaves at
this corner. Athol hadn't got round to her. It used to be a
very bad corner for blocking in the old days when the
pine-trees were there. Before the earthquake there was a
whole row of them right behind the house. Some crashed
then.'

'Was there really?' asked Maria idly. 'I thought those
other trees looked as if they'd been there since pioneering
days. They look almost as ancient as some of the oaks and
beeches of England.'

'Oh, they grow so quickly here, and of course, in any
case, it's just on half a century ago. See, Maria, the water's
seeped right down that wallpaper and under the carpet.
Something to be said for the days when we had carpet-
squares and polished round them, they were so easily
lifted. This'll get mildewed if we don't lift it. I'll go and get
another screwdriver and you can help me prise it up. Oh,
there's the phone.'

Maria took the screwdriver off her, went on yanking
tacks out. Johanna seemed to be having a long conversation,
about the wedding. Ah ... good, that lot came away very
easily. She'd peel it back, and prop it against a couple of
chairs to dry. Oh, heavens, the floor was sopping here.
She'd have to get a bucket and cloth.

Next moment she was staring at the floorboards. What
a peculiar way of laying them for a room that was rectangu-
lar! They went round in a huge octagonal shape. What was
it? Certainly years ago, floors were mostly waxed, with
scatter-rugs, but ornamental ones were usually parquet ...
they didn't have octagonal insets in the corners. Sud-

denly she felt as if a tremor passed over her entire body
... she took a quick comprehensive look at the whole
room, that opposite corner; it looked the same as this.
They'd both been altered, and although there was no
wing at that end, the skirting-board showed squared-up
joins too. As if ... as if there had been towers here, one
at each end. Oh, but that was absurd. Crazy. Because that
other house had had a verandah in front, between the two
towers. And a row of pines behind it. A row of pines?
There *had* been a row of pines behind it. Johanna had
just said so.

She said to herself, 'Sheer coincidence, Maria Willoughby. It will just be that your father's boyhood home
was designed by the same architect. It's an English design,
and all the early architects would have come out from
England. You must be sensible. Coincidences do happen,
but don't expect me to believe that fate could step in and
you be offered a post as companion to a woman on the
same property as your father was born in. Anyway, this
property has never changed hands ... no Smiths.'

At which point Johanna came back, 'Oh, how clever of
you, you've got it all up. But there's far more leak than I
thought.'

'Yes, I'm just going to get a bucket and cloth and slosh
it all up. Johanna, that floor, it looks as if this room had
towers once.'

'How quick you are to guess that! It did. This side was
much weakened during the earthquake. Half the tiles were
hurled off both towers. So we stripped the old verandah
away, that joined them, and it was all shored up, and that
wing of two rooms added. I was rather sad because those
towers gave it character. Did we never tell you? Oh, I
suppose that, as usual, we didn't want to talk too much
about earthquakes to a newcomer, specially one we'd like
to stay. Blaise did a project on this estate when he was at
High School, and it's over in his room. I'll show you. He
did a very good sketch of it as it was. Not that he could
remember it, he was just a toddler, but we had an old
photograph of it from the *Weekly News*, a very good
pictorial magazine of those days. In fact, Blaise did sketches

from all our old photos, from pioneer days up. I'll show you as soon as we mop up.'

Maria wouldn't let herself believe anything. Probably when she saw the sketch she'd see it was only the same type of house. She mopped up almost feverishly. She wanted to see it for herself.

As they were halfway to the stableyard, Donal's mother and father called in, on their way home. Johanna said, 'It's in the top drawer of his desk—have a look, dear.'

Maria was never so thankful for anything in her life that she could look at it alone. She had a nameless dread. She wouldn't let her mind put it into words yet. It would be ghastly beyond all imaginings if ... if ... she cut the thought off at birth. Nevertheless it drove her to rush up to Amber Knoll to take, from the bottom of her case, the folder with the picture.

She didn't open it there and then. She didn't want to recognise it. But if, when she looked at Blaise's sketch, there was any doubt, she could compare them. Her whole mind seemed a formless prayer. She didn't want to say: 'Don't let it be Heronshaw, please! Don't let it be Heronshaw!' She was clamping her lips tightly together. It mustn't be. It mustn't!

She sped up the rickety stairs where so short a time ago she had come to grief, had tumbled into the bran, had been kissed.

Every nerve protested against having to open that top drawer of the shabby old desk. The project book was right on top and inscribed in printing was: *The History of the Heronshaw Estate*. By Blaise Mandeville, Form Five, Napier Boys' High School.

She brought it out, quite a thick book, covering all those generations. She flicked the pages over, came to the sketch of a little cob hut first, thatched with raupo reeds. Even in her distress of mind she saw that the work was exquisite. The next one had a timber addition. Another showed the unpretentious beginnings of the homestead, probably a sitting-room, bedroom, lean-to, close to the cob hut. Then a long verandah with just one upstairs room above it, where presently the dormers would be added.

She turned two more pages and there it was. Even before she opened her folder to lay them side by side, she knew it was one and the same.

Because the schoolboy Blaise had painted his picture, drawing it from this, she now saw it in its pre-earthquake colours. It seemed ridiculous when this was a shattering experience for her, that she even said to herself she'd been right, the window-facings *were* green, the tiles *were* orange. The wooden weather-boarding had evidently been covered with today's blocks of Hinuera stone, in pearl-white, but there were the two octagonal towers, with their curlicues of wrought iron. There was the verandah, the flight of steps leading down to the first terrace, the hydrangea bushes, the thick clumps of redhot pokers, the blue clumps of agapanthus, the bougainvilleas wreathing round the verandah posts, the squat chimneys, the row of pines forming the backdrop.

The fact that the house had become L-shaped with the two-room wing added had blinded her to any thought that this could be the house of her forebears, but had she had any suspicions at all, there were features she *could* have recognised. The corner of that roof peeping from behind those liquid ambers was surely the summerhouse roof, only by now you'd not be able to see it from this angle, they were so huge. That fence running down the hill was brick in this, so would have fallen in the 'quake, because she'd heard the brick buildings were the first casualties. Then it had had fruit trees espaliered against the warm bricks, now it was corrugated iron hidden under a tangle of jasmine and honeysuckle.

Those trees she'd thought of back in England as exotic-looking were, of course, smaller editions of the phoenix palms that rose against the skyline now, in a fronded symmetrical pattern of beauty, and when they had bulldozed into the hillside for the foundations of the Hibiscus Hill house, it had altered the contours of the land altogether.

Her mind scurried from one detail to another, but all the time it was shrinking from a real confrontation with the facts, the true recognition of what this meant to her. She noticed that by the fountain were water-reeds. The fountain itself was different. The one that tinkled its silver music now through all the lovely days at Heronshaw was just a cairn of rocks and ferns, down which the water fell. This belonged to a more ornamental day, an iron heron spouting water from an open beak. Beside the heron in the sketch hovered a gauzy-winged dragonfly, with which Blaise had signed all his pictures. She didn't know why that small thing pierced her consciousness and made her admit that dreadful knowledge that had come upon her out of the blue, that Blaise Mandeville was her father, her rascally, irresponsible father ... and Judith and Struan's father too! *She was Struan's half-sister.*

Maria dropped into the dusty old chair beside the desk and stayed there, huddled, frozen into a sort of immobility of misery.

It must have been a quarter of an hour before she roused herself. Even then she just got up and stared out of the window at that far horizon she had loved so much. No wonder she'd felt so at home here, as if she belonged. She *did* belong, but because of the manner of her belonging, she couldn't stay.

This whole setting was bound up with relationships, which ought to have grappled her to the homestead, to Athol and Johanna, her grandparents; to Alberta, in very truth her great-aunt, but because Struan was her half-brother, the position was hideous. She loved him with a love that should be given only to a man not bound to her by ties of blood.

Why, oh, why had Aunt Alberta ever come to Willow-field, ever been smitten with the idea of asking her to accompany her to New Zealand? That had been a cruel chance. In a detached way Maria wondered what the odds were against such a thing happening. It must be a colossal figure, millions to one, perhaps. She gave herself a little shake. Stop thinking along those lines! What does it matter? It *did* happen, so what? The question is, what do I do? Where do I go from here?

There was but one answer to that. Back to England, and the sooner the better. She must be careful, though, that they didn't suspect anything. It mustn't be too sudden, but as soon as was feasible. Because in her heart she knew that any day now Struan would ask her to marry him. Struan felt bitter enough about his birth, about his father, he must never know that final humiliation—that the girl he'd wanted to marry was also his father's daughter.

She crossed back to her father's book, looked down on his name, said, on a thread of sound, 'I think Judith hates you, Blaise Mandeville, because of her mother, and Struan must because he couldn't even bring himself to tell me about you—he left it to Judith. Though in the end, it was Sadie who did. Sweet Sadie. Yes, Judith and Struan hate you, and probably my mother did too, but none of them could hate you as I hate you, and I've never hated anyone in my whole world of people in all the years of my life!'

She felt better for having uttered the impassioned whispered words. She closed the book, put it away, went out of the room, down the stairs. Now to tie up the ends, all unknown to her dear, dear family. They must remember her only as someone who came here, stayed from the late spring till the early autumn, then faded from their ken.

She was glad the McFies were there. Chatter about the wedding put up a defence against any breaking-down, any unwary word such as might have been spoken had they been alone; helping Johanna prepare a salad, carve meat, all put it further away, except when Johanna said, asking her to get more tomatoes from the glasshouse, 'What did you think of the sketch? Could you trace the alterations from it?'

'I could. I was amazed at the difference it made with the pines felled and the fountain altered and the brick wall gone—to say nothing of the height of the trees.'

Her worst moment was when they heard the men coming, pausing to scrub up on the back porch. Her heart gave a sickening thud. How could she meet his eyes? She felt as if her guilty knowledge was written in her own.

But just as Struan came to the table, the phone rang and he turned to answer it. He hung up, said, 'I'll just have to have this and go. That was Bob Ranley. That storm was centred right over their property, back in, and they've just discovered a slip partially blocking the gully. They can't risk leaving it, in case of another. They want me to bring my front-end loader over, to cart debris away. They've got half a dozen men on the job now. Reckon there's two days' work ahead of us. I'll stay over there. You and Ramsay can manage, Grandfather?'

'Of course. Water can do a powerful amount of damage if it gets into the wrong channel. Have your lunch and away with you, son.'

Maria thought inconsequentially how she loved the way Athol called Struan son. As if the years rolled back and he had his own son by his side again. Pain stabbed at her. His own son ... their mutual father. She felt sick.

When the visitors left she went back to Amber Knoll. She had to be alone to think things out. Athol gave her the mail as she left. She said, 'How lovely, both Shona and Merle have written.'

Athol looked at her from under his shaggy sandy brows. There's a hint of homesickness in that, he thought. 'Have you told them yet, lass, that I want to pay their fares out here for a trip? Get them to make it soon. It's a short distance these days in hours, if not in mileage.'

Maria put her arms about him, kissed him and said, 'Did anyone ever tell you you're a darling, Athol Mandeville?' and knew a wild wish she could have said, 'Grandfather,' just once.

She read them in her room, lovely chatty letters, full of family doings. Getting them today could give her an excuse. She would invent an illness for Shona, say that if the next letter didn't report an improvement, she'd feel she must fly home. She could even pretend she'd rung her and found she was worse.

Then she could slip out of the lives of the folk at Heronshaw without dealing them any more cruel blows. They need never know their wayward son had deserted a wife, that another child had come into the world without his knowledge. But how glad she'd have been to have claimed kinship with them, if she hadn't loved Struan.

Suddenly she thought of something. Even without that complication how would Judith have reacted? Yes, she'd said once she'd love to have her as a sister, or something like that, but would any illegitimate child, given full status in a household like this, welcome the daughter of a true wife turning up? She'd lost sight of that aspect in the more devastating one of herself and Struan.

Well, it needn't exercise her mind; Judith was never going to know. In years to come Heronshaw folk would remember her only as someone from the other side of the world who'd stayed here a few short months, then returned to her own place and, in time, hadn't even bothered to keep up a correspondence!

Aunt Alberta brought Athol and Johanna to Amber Knoll for the evening meal. Johanna and Maria washed up together and Maria couldn't get Johanna off talking about the alterations and the earthquake. Finally Maria was relieved when she began talking of her own girlhood home at Te Pohue. 'My grandmother lived with us, had her own rooms and was an adept at never interfering. We were the greatest pals. I always hoped I'd have a daughter to call her after her, Louise.'

Maria was surprised into saying, 'Oh, my second name is Louise,' then wished she hadn't. How stupid, anyway, her father hadn't known she was coming, much less picked her name. To cover up she said, 'Louise who?'

'Louise Smith. I mean Smith was her maiden name. When Blaise was born she said, "Now, if only I'd had a maiden name like Claridge or Montmorency or something, you could have made that his second name, but no one seems to think of Smith as an in-between."

'So I said, "Why not?" So he was Blaise Smith Mandeville. I like family names retained.'

Maria nodded. She couldn't resist a further probe. 'Was he ever called Smithy for a nickname? Blaise is unusual, and boys often resort to nicknames.'

Johanna wrung her dishcloth. 'They called him Rufus. Not that he had red hair like mine, but Blaise sounds red-hot. But we never called him that of course, nor did Sadie.'

Maria thought only her mother had, of all his relations. When Blaise Mandeville had needed an alias, he'd used his second name and a nickname. Goodness knows what names he'd used since or where he was. She thought of Johanna saying good morning to his photograph every morning and an immense pity swept her. Never to know where your son was, the baby you'd brought into the world after hours of travail, the one you'd guarded against physical dangers, loved and taught and suffered with, must indeed be hell.

When she did sleep, after hours of trying to dismiss from her mind the turmoil of thoughts, she woke unrefreshed, with nausea swooping down on her as remembrance returned. Then she pulled herself together. While Struan was away she'd go into Napier and book her flight back. Better far to have a trip to town on her own, it didn't often happen.

Judith rang. 'Maria, Sadie wants me to go in to see her urgently, on business. Gran's going to the Institute with Aunt Alberta, and I've got Christie home with a slight cold. She's not in bed, it's too hot, but I wondered if you'd look after her? If she could come to Amber Knoll for lunch she'd be fine. Sadie said bring the twins, of course, but when I said Christie she said the business was private and she didn't want little ears pricking up. You will? Oh, bless you!'

Maria, in so far as she was capable of enjoying anything at the moment, loved having Christie to herself. She was a delight, that child, with the loveliest nature, with the faintest hint of Parehuia's chiselled features and patrician profile, and a creamy brown skin. They had a portrait of Parehuia over at Hibiscus Hill, and the likeness fascinated Maria. It had been done by one of the famous early artists of the colony.

Christie busied herself all morning drawing, and Maria could see that this grandchild of his had inherited Blaise's skill with pen and paintbrush. It gave her a strange feeling. My own niece, she thought, inheriting this from my father!

It was a sparkling day. Soon the year would slip into autumn and mornings become dewy and pastures spangled with cobwebs, but today every delphinium and rose shouted that summer still lingered.

Christie tired of pencil and paints. 'Maria, could we go and tidy the playhouse? You know, the old summerhouse.

Mum gave us some extra china the other day, old stuff. She gave me some contact to line the cupboard shelves with but said it was too hard for me to do, I'd get all stuck up, but not to put the dishes away till she had time to help me. Then we could use it for winter picnics. Would you?'

Christabel's chatter took Maria's mind off all that lay ahead of her. They took some cookies with them, and a flask of ice-cold orange cordial, and worked with a will. They scrubbed and polished and even cleaned the windows, and set out the dishes on the shelves.

'I'd like to clear this junk out at the far end,' said Christie. 'Aren't men awful? The minute they see a place on a farm, that isn't being used, they fill it up with rubbish. Those are old barrels we used to have standing round with geraniums in till the hoops fell off them and Mum got those stone urns instead. Ugh ... look at the woodlice under them! It's all damp, it'll rot the floor. And that pram's no good. Dad took the wheels off for Tim's trolley. If we got a barrow we could trundle it off to the dump.'

Maria hid a smile. Christie had heard Johanna going on like that. 'I'll get the barrow, Chris, you start hauling it out, but anything heavy leave for me. Good job we've got old jeans on.'

She was nearly back with the barrow when she heard a splintering crash and a yell, and ran. Christie had been right about the damp rotting the floor, it had given way and the child was half in the hole, half out, her arms spread out on each side, but not hurt because she was laughing her head off. 'Dad's going to be mad with me, but it serves them right.'

Maria tested the floor carefully, edged towards her and hauled her out. 'What's all that clanking noise underneath you?'

'I fell on to a lot of tins, old teapots and tray and things. I think they must have built this old place over a rubbish dump. Just shows, men were always the same, even in pioneer days.'

Maria had to laugh at her old-fashioned air. Christie

thought of something. 'They won't be *too* mad at me, will they?'

'They'd better not be. That floor ought to have been renewed long since. See, the rest of it's been done, though even then a long time ago. I suppose they just never got round to it. I'll tell them about it. I saw some planks in the stable the other day. We'll get them and put over the hole, though of course that corner's never walked on. I won't tell them there's a job here for them, for a few days, having Struan away has put them back as it is. I'm only too glad you weren't hurt, love.'

She woke at two o'clock in the morning with her mind instantly alert. Christabel had said she'd landed on old teapots and trays. Could it be? Was there a chance it could be the old treasure? What if, fleeing down the hill, Parehuia had stuffed it under the summerhouse? She'd do it from the outside; it was dug into the hillside. She might have known of the cavity, had probably watched them building it. On that night of terror, Parehuia wouldn't have had time to dig a hole to bury it. She'd have used a hole that already existed.

She got a chance to examine it because when Alberta said she was going into Napier to see Sadie, Maria decided to stay home. She didn't want anyone to see her going in to book her flight. Once she had it, she could make up some story of having to go home because of Shona. It was a little odd that Alberta didn't ask Maria if she'd like a day in town, but perhaps Sadie wanted to see her on the same private business Judith had gone in for.

Christie was back at school, and the coast was clear, so Maria slipped unnoticed into the summerhouse. She had to be really careful; the wood was ready to give way at the edges. She laid the planks so they were firm on the better boarding, and lay down. She saw a box on which she could faintly discern a ship's chandler's name. Oh, this belonged to the old days all right. The rough lid had rotted away and exposed the very blackened silver. It would clean up wonderfully ... a tea-service, a tray, an épergne of beautiful design, she could just see it in years to come gracing the big oval dining-table at Heronshaw; the turquoise necklace, the pearl ring, the bracelet set with emeralds and the priceless greenstone tiki were in a carved wooden box, thick with fungi, but safe. She didn't know tears were running down her cheeks as she handled them with reverent fingers, thinking of Parehuia.

Well, this was something she could do for her dear, dear family. It had been true that the treasure had been found by two daughters of the house of Mandeville, but they would think it was only one, Christabel. That would be enough to satisfy their romantic hearts. She arranged the planks back over the hole. It was a terrible temptation to tell them now, but it would mean a big fuss ... the whole district would be astir, reporters would come out and Maria felt she couldn't face it. Before she flew out of Auckland she'd write them a letter and say it had just occurred to her that the old teapots Christie fell on to could be the buried treasure, how about investigating?

That night Alberta and Maria shared a quiet meal. Normally they were such kindred spirits, conversation never flagged, but Maria put the restraint down to her own abstraction. The sunset was painting the sky behind the far forests and mountains inland with colours that clashed vividly and splendidly with each other, staining the blue bowl of the sky above the Pacific to the east with reflected paler hues, so that the world was one huge palette of colour.

She said to Alberta, 'I'm just going to the top of the hill to get that view from the Eyrie. It's too good to stay in.'

'You'll come down before darkness sets in, won't you, girl? It's tricky coming down the hill paddocks in the dark.'

'I'll be careful, don't worry.' She bent forward and kissed Alberta's cheek. Dogs barked hopefully, looking for a walk, horses whinnied softly as she went through the gates, trotted after her, the steers in the paddock came towards her in a bunch, curious as always. She went over the stile into the spinney, came up to Blaise's Eyrie. No, not Blaise's, her father's Eyrie!

This was to be her farewell tryst with this great sweep of

land that had belonged to her family since 1857. She wanted to imprint it on her heart for ever, because to-morrow, if they could offer her a very early flight to London, she was going to take it, pretend she'd phoned England about Shona's illness, hadn't said anything to them sooner because she hadn't wanted to worry them, and she would take off.

The sunset had paled now, and the sea was indigo, with just faint silver lights on the edges of the clouds above. The phoenix palms were in almost black silhouette to the north. Westward the last rays of the sun were striking up from the ranges, deep and mysterious. What was it Struan had called the Kaimanawa Range? The Heart-eater. Maria's *manawa*, her heart, was certainly eroded. Eroded, long ago, by her father's selfish ways. Yet all she knew of him as a boy made her yearn towards him. She faced it now, it wasn't hate, any more than Sadie hated him, Sadie who had most reason of all. She herself couldn't, because of her relationship to Struan, look back happily on the times that should have been lovely memories to take with her into lonely days. The sunsets they'd watched from the rail of the ship, the dances when he'd held her close, the first kiss, the long days here working side by side, coming out of the vestry of the valley church arm-in-arm as brides-maid and best man, it was so short a time ago ... now all that was tarnished, with a certain sort of shame ... but she couldn't hate her father, only sorrow for him....

A twig cracked sharply under someone's foot in the spinney. Maria knew a moment of intense alarm. Someone might have seen her come to this lonely hilltop. She stood up, poised for flight, listening, then Struan's voice said, 'Maria, Maria, are you there?'

The relief was enormous, but she didn't run to him. He came swiftly to her. 'Aunt told me you were here. I thought it couldn't be more ideal. I hoped you'd not already left.'

He'd showered and changed, into a thin jersey-knit crew-necked top in blue, over elegant walk-shorts and knee-length walk-socks. His light hair was darkly golden now with water, slicked down. His skin was ruddy, he glowed with health. Very Scandinavian-looking, very like Sadie, his mother.

Maria had changed at dinnertime into a simple sleeveless dress in white, bound with emerald green, and she wore scarlet sandals on her slim brown feet, and his Tahitian shell necklace was twisted round her throat. But it didn't escape him as he looked down on her that she had an unusual pallor, that there were violet shadows under her eyes, a wistfulness. Why?

'What is it, love?' he asked, reaching out for her shoulders. 'Aunt said you'd been very quiet tonight. She thought ... hoped ... you'd been missing me. I hoped so too. Maria darling, the wedding and all that flummery is behind us, so is the aftermath of the storm, now we've got time to ourselves.'

He swung her round, 'Look, Maria, they've just put the light on in the moon, over the sea. You could hardly see it, it was so pale when I climbed up. Don't you think that moon far outshines any Caribbean moon? Because this land belongs to us. I never want you to leave here. You'll marry me, Maria, won't you?'

His eyes were looking down into hers, very seriously, but suddenly he laughed, exultantly. 'I think I've actually taken your breath away! But you *must* have known it was coming ... it's too good *not* to be true, isn't it, sweetheart? We belong to each other. I won't wait for you to say yes, I can't.'

His lips were on hers, blotting out any answer, any protest, and she was held tightly against him in a closeness of embrace that held within it all the promise of what life together would have meant.

She was powerless to struggle, she could only stem the tide of feeling within her that threatened to submerge her, destroy her will-power to deny him what he asked. All of a sudden she went so limp, Struan lifted his mouth from hers and said, 'Maria, what's the matter? What is it? Have I——'

She brought her free hand up in a gesture that to him was curiously like trying to wipe his kiss away. He steadied her, then his arms dropped to his sides with the shock of the repulse. She saw the lines of his lips straighten, the light in his eyes die out, but he waited in silence, his eyes burning into hers with fierce questioning in them.

She said tonelessly, 'Struan, I didn't want it to come to this. I hoped to be gone before you said anything, before we got ... more attached. It's only living in close quarters that has triggered this off. We've been caught up into the romantic atmosphere of a wedding just lately. Wedding bells are in the air, but not for us. I can't stay, I can't.'

'For heaven's sake, why can't you? What's to stop you? You love it here. You love New Zealand. You love Hawkes Bay, the heat, the flowers, the citrus orchards, the vineyards ... I think you love my entire family, and oh, how they love you! How can you give it away? What can you mean?'

The moonlight seemed to have blanched her face even more. 'I mean that I'm homesick, deadly, terribly homesick. That's why I was quiet tonight. I've stayed too long. I'm weary for my old life, my own folk. I've got to return. All I love is back there.'

He said in a bewildered tone, 'I thought a new love had come into your life. That's the way it is between men and women. A new force, new loyalties. I can't believe——'

'You've got to believe it. My mind is made up. I haven't told Alberta yet, but I will soon. Don't let her see something's happened between us, Struan. It would spoil my last week. I must go on down now. I'll go over to Judith's, do some ironing for her. I'd rather not be at Amber Knoll tonight with you and Alberta.'

All he said was, 'I'll see you through the spinney and over the stile. I'll go for a walk after that.'

When at eleven Maria came home from Judith's, Alberta was in bed, reading. She called out that Struan was sleeping across at Heronshaw. 'He and Athol are going to be moving sheep at the crack of dawn.'

That suited Maria. Nothing must prevent her making her booking tomorrow.

CHAPTER TEN

SHE decided to park in Tennyson Street. In the car park there was a big kurrajong tree and it would keep the car cool. She felt forlorn, desolate, as never before in her life. This was what happened when you loved someone, when they filled your waking and your dreaming hours, then suddenly you had to tear them out of your life.

She crossed to the exit, saw St Paul's Presbyterian Church, rearing up against the bush-clad hill. On a sudden impulse she opened the gate, went up the steps, tried the door and entered into the solemn stillness of the long building.

It was modern, yet with all the hushed atmosphere of worship of the more ancient shrines of the Old World. Few churches in Napier were older than the earthquake. Maria knew the story of this one. During the lean times of the 1920's, the parish had worked towards a new church, and finally a worthy church arose.

By 1931, though the pews were still in the workshop, it was near enough to completion for the opening ceremony to be arranged for the end of February, when the Governor-General, Lord Bledisloe, would officiate ... but on the third of February the earthquake struck. Miraculously, though it was situated under the heights of Bluff Hill, it escaped demolition, but it didn't escape the fire that broke out in the city, following it. It must have been a crushing blow, after the years of endeavour, but when the parish people had recovered from the sorrow and horror of it all, they began to plan once more, to raise their temple in the midst of the desolation.

Maria sat in one of the back pews for quite some time, looking up at the glass Iona Cross set in the wall above the communion table. In its touching simplicity it let in the blue light of the sky beyond. Everything of the history of this place of worship spoke of resurrection, of hope putting

176

forth its tender leaves ... the falling down of masonry, the timber charred to ashes, then the patient rebuilding. This whole lovely city breathed of dauntless effort, sturdier, safer buildings, rising from the debris of the old. They had done their mourning beside the mass grave on the island cemetery now surrounded by green fields where once had been swamp, then returned to restore essential services so that people could, in time, move back to their houses from the sea-shore, the parks, the open streets. So, when hopes were shattered, once the numbing shock was over, you began to build your life anew.

Maria knelt, said a wordless prayer, came out into the street, crossed over, and there, directly opposite, was a travel agency. She went in, said quietly that she wanted to book a flight to England as soon as possible and produced her passport.

How simple it all was ... some phoning, some writing. All efficiency. Oiled wheels. Suddenly her attention wandered, then she swung back into the awareness of having been asked something twice and begged the agent's pardon. The dark young man opposite her didn't repeat his question, instead he asked, 'Are you all right? Would you like a drink of water?'

She said gratefully, 'I would. It must be the heat. Thanks so much.'

He was back in a moment with it, said, 'My wife's going to make you a cup of tea. Perhaps you've been overdoing it, not used to this heat?'

Maria agreed she had. The small human contact made her feel better. She was taken into a private office at the rear; she found the wife was from London, they chatted about places there, and she felt quite restored. The wife accompanied her to the door, said, 'Some bracing sea air is just what you need. What about walking along to Marine Parade and sitting on one of the seats under the trees?'

It was a good idea. It postponed going back to tell them she was booked to leave next week. The sea air lifted the dark hair from her temples and cooled them. There weren't so many people round now. The school holidays had seen this place crowded. There were a few tourists, one or two mothers with prams, and one man, sitting on an artist's stool with a collapsible easel in front of him, painting the gnarled trees, that twisted back from the force of the Pacific winds, year in, year out.

Something familiar about him caught at Maria. She stood up, tall and slim in her white dress, her scarlet handbag swinging from one shoulder, and walked across to him. She'd last seen him up in the Balcony Tea-rooms.

'Hullo,' she said. 'We meet again. Does it bother you to have anyone looking over your shoulder?'

'Some I mind. The ones who say: "Is that supposed to be that tree over there?" That's happened more than once.' They both chuckled.

'How very deflating!'

He said, 'Don't go, because I'm nearly finished. The light will change soon. Midday's no good for this. Besides, I'm particularly pleased to see you. I hoped to see you again soon.'

Strange! But she was well content to wait. Talking to someone who'd no idea of the cross-currents affecting one's life was somehow therapeutic. It had a steadying effect. There was a little stone stool like a mushroom just near. She sat on it, not talking in case she disturbed his concentration. She wished she could buy this picture, to remember the Bay by.

He began putting his paints into the portable kit he had. Maria went on studying the picture. What meticulous detail, something you didn't get often these days. The tiny tufts of grass were outlined exquisitely at the foot of the trees. Then she saw it, with an intake of the breath ... a tiny dragonfly, poised above the grasses.

She said quite clearly, 'A dragonfly ... your signature symbol ... *you're Blaise Mandeville!*'

He straightened up, met her eyes with a clear blue gaze, said, 'Yes, *and Rufus Smith, your father, Maria Louise.*'

He held out his hands to her. She didn't want to take them, but she did. He said, 'You have a lot to forgive me for, perhaps too much. If you feel you can't, for your mother's sake, I've just got to take it. But we were going to tell you tomorrow, when we come out home.'

She felt for the second time this week as if her world was crashing round her. Then she fastened on one word. 'We?'

'You won't be able to believe this ... Sadie and me. We——' He was unable to go on.

Maria swayed a little with the intensity of her feelings. Then she said fiercely, 'Above all people *Sadie* mustn't be hurt again. *She* suffered the most. More than my mother. Much more.'

He said, 'It's quite unbelievable, but Sadie has somehow —somehow forgiven me. All she's concerned about is my mother and my father and what it will mean to them.'

Maria's voice seemed to be saying words she wasn't thinking first. 'Did you know your mother says good morning to your photograph every morning? That one of you with the shaggy dog. And that every time your father and I go up to the lagoon, he recalls something about you?'

His face was as white as hers. 'I had to see Sadie first. I couldn't just walk in on Mother and Dad. I thought at their age their hearts mightn't be as strong as they were. I'll never forget how I felt when you suddenly mentioned her in the Balcony Tea-rooms. When you said you must leave because you had to see Sadie Gray. The Gray meant nothing to me, but I couldn't help questioning you. But that was all I knew then—that she was a widow with one son. Not that she had borne a son and daughter to me, long ago. You must believe that. I didn't know any more than I knew about you ... till I saw you with my mother, that first time, and you turned round and it was like Janey looking at me. But when you said your name was Willoughby later that day I thought it was just a freak resemblance, yet how strange that you were companion to Aunt Alberta.'

'When did you know I was your daughter?' she asked.

'When you talked about the guesthouse at Osterley, and my aunt staying there. I knew she must have found out something. I took off for London. The rest was comparatively easy. They told me at Willowfield that your stepfather had adopted you. The records gave your name as Maria Louise Smith. That got me, for Janey's sake. When we were first married, before I got restless, I once said if ever we had a daughter I'd like her to be Maria Louise, Aunt Alberta's choice had she had a daughter, and my mother's. To call you that, she must have thought then I might come back some day.

'Jane and I lived next door to a woman called Ruth Stapleton in Dunedin. My aunt showed her some old photos, last year, and she recognised me, then told her that she'd met Mrs Rufus Smith again, next to a guesthouse she stayed at, but that she hadn't long to live, and had asked her to keep quiet about it. Thank God she didn't! Aunt took off immediately, ostensibly to visit Struan, and brought you to the place where you belong.'

Struan. That brought all the misery into the forefront of Maria's mind again. She said, 'But how do you know all this? Sadie couldn't.'

'Sadie knows now, since yesterday, when I learned the last detail for myself. We sent for Aunt Alberta, and she told us. She's been in touch again this morning. She's telling Athol and Johanna now—she wanted them by themselves. I'm not to ring her till she rings me. She said on no account must it get the better of me. That it would be after lunch. She wants to get them composed. That's why I came out here. My hand kept going towards that phone. She's preparing them also for the fact that they have another granddaughter—you.'

The look he gave her had everything of pleading in it. Pleading for understanding, acquiescence. Maria shook her head. 'I—I can't—face it. I've just booked for a flight back to London. I must go back. I can't stay, now less than ever. There's something you—still don't know——'

The world spun round, sea and sky got mixed up and swung into opposite places, she felt the blood leaving her face and her knees buckle. He caught her, lowered her on to the stone stool, forced her head between her knees till the blood came back.

She came round to find her father and a young mother with a toddler bending anxiously over her. She smiled wanly. 'Oh, I'm sorry—it's the first time I've ever fainted in my life. I must have given you a fright.'

The girl said, 'I've got a bottle of orange juice here. Would you have some?' She unscrewed her flask and poured it out. It was icy cold, and Maria drank it thirstily.

Blaise Mandeville said, 'I'm afraid my daughter has overdone things in this heat. We're staying in a motel along the Parade. My car's just over here. I'll get her into it and take her back and she can rest.'

Maria moved as in a dream. The girl, helped by Blaise, assisted her into the car. Maria managed to say, 'Thank you, Father,' thank the girl, wave to the little boy, and they were away.

They turned into a big courtyard, parked, and made their way to his motel. His face was anxious, drawn. He put her into an easy chair.

'What is it, darling? Sadie assured me from the start that Judith wouldn't resent you. Have you feared that? But Judith knows, and only sheer will-power has prevented her from saying anything. Judith said she already loved you as a sister. I'm afraid she's not nearly as reconciled to the thought of me. I can't blame her for that. So what's so dreadful about you being acknowledged as belonging to Heronshaw, Maria?'

She couldn't speak, couldn't put the horrible truth into words, that she'd been looking on Struan as the love of her life, not her half-brother.

He said, 'Alberta has been magnificent. How she's held herself in I don't know. It's quite out of character. She herself knew that she couldn't just announce from England that she'd found a daughter of mine. She knew it could upset Judith and Sadie. So she contrived to get you out here so they would love you for yourself alone. As they have. Judith thinks you've been treated as badly as she has, through your mother. Does that help?'

'No,' said Maria, and shuddered violently. 'It's not Judith's reaction I'm worrying about ... that I could have taken and understood. It ... oh, it's too horrible! It seems all wrong. It seems unnatural now, but we *couldn't* have guessed. But Struan and I ... he proposed to me a night or two ago, and I had to turn him down. He didn't know why then. He soon will. I love him, I love him dearly, I won't diminish that at all. *I do, and I can't help it, but I can't marry my half-brother!*' An audible sob burst from her and she buried her face in her hands.

She thought the silence meant only one thing, that he was as horrified as she was. She was still crying, but she looked up through her hands. He had a strange look on his face, but it wasn't horror. She came to her feet, and he put his arms about her. 'Oh, child, what you've been through! Listen, I can't just blurt it out, you've had one shock on top of another, but ... hush, don't cry. ...' He put a large clean handkerchief into her hands, and she used it, looking up at him dumbly, imploring him to speak, though what——

He said, 'This is something, at last, I can do for my daughter. Listen very carefully, Maria. Sadie, all alone and very ill, had my twins, a son and daughter ... Oh, heavens, what's that? We can't be interrupted *now*!' There had been a thundering knock on the door, and a voice demanding, 'Maria ... are you in there? Maria, answer me!'

The next moment the door was wrenched open and Struan erupted into the scene. He saw Maria enfolded in the embrace of a much older but very handsome man and he saw red. One bound and he'd thrust the man away from her, caught her, demanded, 'What's going on? You're crying—is this man pestering you? What's he to do with you?'

Maria's voice was calm, deliberate, it didn't wobble. 'Struan, this is my father. He's Blaise Mandeville. And he's my father ... and yours. That's why I wouldn't marry you.'

Struan made an indescribable exclamation, spun round, gazed at Blaise Mandeville, then clutched his head, said, 'Not mine ... he couldn't be *mine*.' He looked back at Maria, said her name.

Blaise stepped forward. 'I was just trying to tell her. I'm your father and Judith's, Maria, *but not Struan's. My* son, Stuart, was delicate and died in his third year. That was when they adopted Struan. The little girl Judith fretted and fretted. Twins are very close, I believe. They found a little boy of the same age almost, same colouring, and the names were similar. None of this I knew till two days ago.

I'd got back from London some time before, knowing you were my daughter, not that I had two.'

Struan's face looked as if it were carved in sandstone, then he came to life, took a step towards Maria and said, 'Darling, darling, was it the *only* reason you wouldn't marry me?'

He saw the hazel-green eyes, so like Johanna's, come to radiant life. 'Of course,' she said simply, 'what other reason could there be? Oh, Struan, Struan, Struan!' and she was in his arms.

Presently, aware of their audience, they drew apart. Now her father looked happy, smiling. Maria couldn't imagine how she'd not seen his likeness to Athol before. She put her arms about him and kissed him, said, 'Do we have to hold post-mortems? Your father and mother won't, I'm sure ... and I feel if my mother were here, she'd be glad you and I know each other.'

His face eased back into its sad lines again. 'I think we'll have to go into old wrongdoings. It's the price I must pay for my incredibly unfeeling behaviour of years ago. My worst punishment is guessing at what Sadie went through. It's not much good to say I didn't know. I just wanted to be free. I've been dishonest in some things, weak, above all abominably selfish. I deserted Jane alone in a country not her own ... I've lived hard, jumped ship in half a dozen foreign ports, lived hand to mouth. They told me at Willowfield that Jane had a gem of a husband in Colin Willoughby. Thank God for that!'

Maria said softly, 'Not all her memories could have been hard ones, Father. She kept your Christmas song all those years. Never a Christmas passed without her singing that. She must have thought of you at that time, perhaps prayed for you then.'

It took Blaise a moment to get control of his voice again. 'Fifteen years ago I had a change of heart, through a chaplain at the Seamen's Mission. I owe everything I am to him. It was at an English port. He got me a job with a very fine chap. I managed to help him through an appalling run of bad luck in his business—we pulled it together, and when he died he left it to me. I couldn't have come home a pauper to sponge on my parents, I had to prove I could pull myself up by my own bootlaces. I was nearly ready to come back when—well, I had to pull out a good deal of capital to meet an emergency and decided to make it up before I came back.'

'I know,' said Maria. 'You heard about the disastrous flood at Heronshaw and paid the money into the estate.'

He looked embarrassed. 'But that solicitor said he'd never tell without permission. How did it get out?'

'It didn't.' She was smiling. 'Your mother knew by instinct.'

She was still within the curve of Struan's arm. Her eyes were shining. 'Father, it will be all right. All we have to do now is take you home.'

He said, 'I must take Sadie with me when I go. It was she who gave me the courage to take this final step.'

Maria turned to Struan. 'How did you know I was here? How could you?'

He laughed. 'What a day! I was still thumping mad with you because you wouldn't marry me. Everything in me shouted out that you loved me, that homesickness was no excuse. I was determined I wouldn't let you go, thought I'd live in England if you wouldn't have it any other way. All the time we were moving the sheep I was planning another showdown with you. I told Grandfather, who was as appalled as I was; he said for goodness' sake go and do it now, and if I couldn't manage it, he'd come and lend a hand ... I showered, went across to Amber Knoll and found you'd gone to town.

'I told Aunt Alberta the story. She said in that case perhaps you'd gone to book a flight, but not to worry, things were happening that would probably mean you'd never leave Heronshaw. I thought she'd gone mad, but hadn't time to dally, and shot after you when she said you'd only just gone. By the time you got to Hyderabad Road I wasn't far behind you, but I got held up along Carlisle Street when a lorry dropped a load of cartons all over the road. I cruised all round looking for your car. What a hope!—then I remembered you and Aunt Alberta often parked right along Marine Parade ... but I went to the south end, not the north. Then I had a stroke of luck, and caught sight of you being helped into a car by a man and woman. You were off before I could turn and I only just got a glimpse of you coming into the motel car-park. I had to find parking and was stumped by the fact I'd no idea of the man's name. I cooked up a lame tale at the office of looking for my wife, who'd told me she was going to meet someone here, but had forgotten his name, but he was tall, silver-haired, and wearing a light suit.

'They were most suspicious—no wonder!—and made short work of getting rid of me. I sneaked back in the side entrance, and have been systematically knocking on doors, making up odd stories looking for you. When I got here I heard Maria's voice and thought she was crying. Sorry about that, sir.'

The phone rang. Blaise Mandeville flinched, paled. He said to Maria, 'That'll be Aunt Alberta. I—you speak to her. Tell me if they want to see me.'

It wasn't Alberta, it was Johanna, and she got the shock of her life when she heard Maria's voice. 'What on earth are you doing there, darling?'

Maria gave a low laugh. 'Getting to know my father, Gran. Isn't it wonderful? And Struan's here too. I've just promised to marry him.'

She'd never heard Johanna's voice sound so young, so lilting. 'That just crowns the day! How relieved Athol and Alberta will be! Now, would you tell that stupid son of mine that I can't wait to hear his voice till he gets home. Put him on the line.'

Maria held out the phone to her father, heard him say, 'Mother, oh, Mother,' and she motioned Struan outside. They moved to a railing, stood looking at a little tinkling fountain in the courtyard.

Struan said, 'All will be well, darling. This will be a big day for Heronshaw.' He laughed. 'I was right, wasn't I? Aunt Alberta *was* up to something.'

'She was,' she said, laughing, and suddenly all tension went out of the day. She told him about finding the long-lost heirlooms.

He said, holding her hand, 'And you were just going to

go away, without telling us that indeed two daughters of
the family had found the treasure?'

'It seemed best. I know I was a goose not to suspect ...
Judith would think I knew her little brother died, because when the twins were born, she called the boy
Stuart after her brother. I thought Struan could be the
Gaelic form of that name. And I thought you saying you
didn't know who your mother was, was because you didn't
want Sadie's tragedy of long ago talked about.'

'Never mind, all is told now. What fun it will be getting
that treasure out! And listen, love, how about you and me
and Aunt Alberta having dinner with Judith and Ramsay
tonight, leaving Grandfather and Gran alone with their
son, as it used to be? So much more can be said to bridge
the years if there's not a crowd.'

'That's a lovely idea. When my father's finished on the
phone, would you ring Judith? I imagine they're in a great
state of tension there.'

Presently Blaise came out. Signs of recent emotion were
on his face for all to read. 'I'm to get Sadie and bring her
out. We're to have lunch there. Mother, bless her heart, is
sure that by now we're in the last stages of starvation.' He
hesitated and said, 'We're going to give Judith time to get
used to the idea, but later on Sadie and I are going to
marry. In any case, I must give her time to be really sure.'

Struan went in to ring Judith, leaving Maria alone with
her father. There was a bitter-sweet flavour about this relationship, but time would take care of that. Struan came
out grinning. 'Judith says she'll never get the relationships
in this family straightened out now her adopted brother
is about to become her brother-in-law, or would it be easier
to say her half-sister's husband ... and if your stepsister
and brother come out, what relation will she be to them?'

They came to Heronshaw in the late afternoon. Blaise and
Sadie were in one car, Struan and Maria in the other.
Struan swept on to Hibiscus Hill so the folk at Heronshaw
should have no witnesses to their reunion.

Judith, dear Judith, was starry-eyed. She caught Maria
to her, unshed tears in her eyes. 'Only you will understand

how I feel. It will help me beyond measure to know you too are having to rise above any resentment, any bitterness. We'll be one in this for Mother's sake. I've never seen her like this before, so I can't help being glad for her. And for Gran and Grandfather.'

There was a festive air about the Hibiscus Hill dinner-table, already set. Unlit candles at the ready, low bowls of roses at each end, but in pride of place, most unexpectedly, the épergne Maria had glimpsed in the hidey-hole. Christie had mentioned the old teapots and things at the breakfast-table, and Judith had gone up and asked Aunt Alberta to investigate with her. They'd worked like Trojans to restore them to gleaming order. It had three tiers, and little chains, still bearing faint marks of tarnish, linked exquisitely fashioned silver deer together round the scalloped edges. A coffee-set was polished too, and an excited Christabel, words tumbling out of her, informed them that a lot of stuff was still in the kitchen waiting to be cleaned.

'But there's this ... look ... they just washed this in soap and water. That's all it wanted, Uncle Struan. Mummy said she was sure you'd find a use for it. Why you?'

Struan looked at the small square of black velvet Aunt Alberta had laid upon the white tablecloth. On it lay a pearl ring. Ellaline's ring that Parehuia, Ramsay's forebear, had saved so long ago. 'I'll show you, Christie.' He picked it up, held out his hand for Maria's left hand. 'I can't help it if you longed for diamonds, sweetheart, or if it doesn't fit, because I'll have it altered. But it couldn't be any other ring for you, daughter of the Mandevilles, could it?' He slipped it on, kissed her in front of them all. 'Almost a perfect fit,' he said, 'a good omen.'

A noise from the doorway made them turn. Four people, Athol and Johanna, Blaise and Sadie. Maria took the room at a run. 'Grandmother ... Grandfather!' she cried exultantly, then, 'Let's drink a toast to the one who brought it about ... my Aunt Alberta!'

Later that night, under the moon again, up at Blaise's Eyrie, Maria shut into the hardness and hunger of Struan's arms, all doubts swept away, they were, at last, blessedly alone.

Struan looked down the valley, across the fields of Heronshaw. 'Oh, look, Maria, the light's going on in Blaise's old room. As soon as they knew, they moved the old furniture back. But it won't be for long, because Judith said to me tonight that she wouldn't cast any shadow on his new chance of happiness for her mother. Sadie and Blaise will live in Napier. He'll open a branch of his business here. They'll have frequent trips to Britain, where Sadie'll be able to see her son. She deserves something like that. Gran and Grandfather will move to Amber Knoll with Aunt Alberta, and we'll bring up our family in the safety and security of Heronshaw. What say you to that, sweetheart?'

'Sounds like all this and Heaven too!' said Maria, laughing. She reached up, kissed him.

Struan laughed back at her, the blue eyes glinting between their fair lashes. 'Yes, Heaven and then some!' and gathered her close.

Harlequin Plus

A WORD ABOUT THE AUTHOR

New Zealand-born Essie Summers comes from a long line of storytellers, and she herself began writing verses when she was only eight years old! By the age of ten she was composing short stories; at eighteen, submitting her writing for publication. It wasn't long after that she saw her poems, articles and short stories in print.

Although she says she loves dashing madly around and never walks if she can run, Essie often spends hours bent over a textbook, searching for information that will affect perhaps only two or three paragraphs in her manuscript.

Her husband, Bill, a retired clergyman, is a "kindred spirit" who shares her delight in words and poetry. Today, she and Bill make their home in a picturesque town on New Zealand's North Island. They are the parents of two, and the proud grandparents of seven.

Essie Summers is a Harlequin author of long standing, having debuted in 1961. With more than forty books to her credit, she is also one of our most prolific writers. And, as readers around the world will confirm, she is one of the best loved.

Readers all over the country say Harlequin is the best!

"You're #1."

A.H.*, Hattiesburg, Missouri

"Harlequin is the best in romantic reading."

K.G., Philadelphia, Pennsylvania

"I find Harlequins are the only stories
on the market that give me a satisfying
romance, with sufficient depth without
being maudlin."

C.S., Bangor, Maine

"Keep them coming! They are still
the best books."

R.W., Jersey City, New Jersey

*Names available on request.

FREE!

A hardcover Romance Treasury volume
containing 3 treasured works of romance
by 3 outstanding Harlequin authors...

...as your introduction to Harlequin's
Romance Treasury subscription plan!

Romance Treasury

...almost 600 pages of exciting romance reading
every month at the low cost of $6.97 a volume!

A wonderful way to collect many of Harlequin's most beautiful love
stories, all originally published in the late '60s and early '70s.
Each value-packed volume, bound in a distinctive gold-embossed
leatherette case and wrapped in a colorfully illustrated dust jacket,
contains...
• 3 full-length novels by 3 world-famous authors of romance fiction
• a unique illustration for every novel
• the elegant touch of a delicate bound-in ribbon bookmark...
  and much, much more!

Romance Treasury

...for a library of romance you'll treasure forever!

Complete and mail today the FREE gift certificate and subscription
reservation on the following page.

Romance Treasury

An exciting opportunity to collect treasured works of romance! Almost 600 pages of exciting romance reading in each beautifully bound hardcover volume!

You may cancel your subscription whenever you wish! You don't have to buy any minimum number of volumes. Whenever you decide to stop your subscription just drop us a line and we'll cancel all further shipments.